THE DENES PARK KILLINGS

An absolutely heart-pounding crime thriller

C.J. GRAYSON

DI Max Byrd & DI Orion Tanzy Book 2

Originally published as *Never Came Home*

Revised edition 2023
Joffe Books, London
www.joffebooks.com

First published in Great Britain in 2020
as *Never Came Home*

This paperback edition was first published
in Great Britain in 2023

Cover art by Nebojša Zorić

ISBN: 978-1-83526-009-8

PROLOGUE

Saturday morning, February
Stanhope Park, Darlington

As DI Max Byrd pulled up in his BMW X5 at the side of the park, he noticed DI Orion Tanzy's Golf already there, its white glossy paintwork glistening under the overhanging street lights nearby. Smiling thinly, he accepted another loss in their small battle regarding who arrived at the scene first; they both put great emphasis on the importance of being punctual.

Byrd yawned as he opened the door and stepped out into the bitter cold. The ground was dry, but a thin layer of frost had started to develop. It made a change not being wet with all the unusually heavy rainfall over the previous few days. Rivers had overflowed. Drains had clogged up, not being able to withstand the relentless downpours. But finally, a dry day for Darlington — albeit still freezing.

Byrd, dressed in his long black coat, black jeans, and black shoes, stepped around the back of his car, up onto the path, and through the entrance of Stanhope Park. Up ahead, he saw them in the darkness.

From the small crowd, he could make out Tanzy, standing beside Jacob Tallow, the senior forensic officer. He was accompanied by the other senior forensic officer, Emily Hope. Both of them were dressed in their familiar white disposable overalls and white face masks.

As he got closer, Tanzy glanced his way.

'You made it,' said Tanzy. 'Sorry I woke you.'

Byrd caught the overshoes Tanzy threw at him and tiredly put them on. He bowed under the barrier tape and joined him.

Byrd watched the tall, thin senior forensic, Tallow. 'How long do you think she's been there?'

'A good few hours, Max; she's stone cold,' he replied, crouching down near the body.

Byrd, from a few feet away, looked down on her. The dead woman was positioned on her right side, her left arm down in front of her face. She looked peaceful in a strange way, as if she was sleeping.

'What do you think happened?' Byrd asked, noticing the cloudy saliva around her mouth, under her chin, and around the floor under her face.

'She's clearly vomited. I wouldn't like to say for definite but most likely a drug overdose.'

'Who called it in?'

Tanzy indicated a man standing with PC Weaver, bordering on his early twenties. From what Tanzy and Byrd could see, he couldn't seem to keep still, constantly fidgeting and shivering in the early-morning frost. He didn't look very tall but towered over PC Weaver.

'He called it in, said she'd gone missing from the party,' Tanzy informed him. 'Everyone assumed she was somewhere in the house. After a while, people started to get worried and went out looking for her. And that's when he found her.'

'Where was the party?'

Tanzy pointed south. 'Swinburne Road. She was dead when the ambulance got here. They did what they could but . . .' He fell silent for a moment.

'Do the paramedics think a drug overdose, too?' Byrd asked.

'They think it's very possible but aren't ruling out other possibilities.'

'We're taking the samples we need and will take her to the morgue,' Tallow informed him, overhearing their conversation. 'I've spoken with Dr Hemsley about it.'

'Is he awake?'

'He was when I phoned him,' said Tallow. 'We'll do further tests back at the lab and give you a better picture soon enough.'

'Okay . . .' Byrd drifted off and had a good look around. A red taxi speeding down Stanhope Road caught his attention, no doubt taking a customer home after a wild Friday night in town. Byrd remembered those days, the days of no responsibility and worries. When the biggest choice he had to make was what outfit to wear.

'First impressions, Max?' Tanzy asked him.

Byrd curled his lip but stayed silent in thought. He glanced towards the young, anxious lad who was still with Weaver, then returned his focus to the dead girl. 'It could be anything, Orion, it really could.'

'You know our biggest question, though?'

Byrd smiled thinly. 'Yes, I do . . . where are her clothes?'

Tuesday night, February
The Denes park, Darlington
A year later

He waited patiently in his car, parked by the side of the road, hidden by the darkness of the night. He'd watched the lad who looked somewhere between fifteen and twenty standing on the corner of Salisbury Terrace for the last ten minutes.

His phone rang in his pocket, startling him for a moment. He looked down, plucked it out, pressed ANSWER and put it to his ear.

'Hey,' he said, sheepishly.

'Where are you?' asked his wife.

'I'm going into the shop now. Need anything?'

'No, I'm okay,' she said. 'How's Rob?'

'He's okay. Nice to catch up with him,' he lied. 'I haven't seen him in ages.'

'How's Elaine doing?'

'She's good,' he lied again. Telling her about seeing his friend Jake and his wife was an alibi. 'Are you sure you don't need anything?'

'No, I'm good. See you soon.' She hung up, none the wiser about what he was doing.

He pushed the phone into his pocket and focused through the frost-covered windscreen.

Three people approached the teenager and handed him something in exchange for something else. The man knew what it was. The operation was quick, efficient. If you didn't know what was happening, you'd miss it.

Like a magician's trick.

In the last month, cocaine had been the police's biggest problem — the growth of its use and, consequently, the rise in local crime. It was certainly something they needed to control. But they never would, despite the extra efforts and the new plans they always seemed to be putting in place.

Cocaine. A growing game in Darlington in recent times. There was very little that could be done to prevent it. If one of them was arrested, the gang would send out another desperate soul who'd do anything for a bit of money. It was dangerous, of course, but it beat working nine to five for minimum wage.

The game had its perks. The dealers were powerful, they were *players* around the town. Their friends, when they heard who they were working for, feared them as well as respected them, giving them an air of arrogance and importance in their young naivety.

The man in the car continued to watch, knowing he'd have his chance soon. To him, it was risky. He didn't want to be seen. But it had to be done.

The boy glanced around, constantly keeping his eyes on the street. To his left, just around the corner of the betting shop, a scrawny man appeared, wearing a dark, cheap-looking tracksuit with holes in random places. His eyes scanned the area until he focused on the dealer, then he hurried over, looking desperate. The teenager nodded and said something to him as they met. The man put his hand in his pocket and handed him some cash in exchange for a bag of white powder then quickly disappeared.

A few minutes later, the teenager seemed to decide he'd been there long enough and pulled his hood over his head, then left the corner and crossed the road.

The man watched the teenager walk towards him, stepping up onto the path near his car. After he passed the car, the man watched him in the wing mirror as he sloped alongside the park's metal railings and took a right through the archway entrance into the Denes.

No time like the present; the moment had come. He opened the door, stepped out into the cold and locked the car, the air hitting his skin like a thousand tiny pins. He made his way along the path to the entrance. Through the fence railings, he watched the teenager disappear into the darkness.

It's too risky, the man kept telling himself.

Passing the gates, he peered into the dark, unsure if it was really worth it. He'd been going through a tough time recently; did he really need to buy drugs? Was his life really at that point where drugs would fix his problems?

He sighed, continued deeper into the darkness. Somewhere in front, he heard the teenager's footsteps but couldn't see him. His heart thumped in his chest as he cautiously made his way down the ramp. For a moment, he thought about using the torch on his phone, but he'd risk being seen, which could scare the teenager away, and that was something he didn't want.

The play area to his left was in darkness. He heard a murmur of voices and stopped dead, glaring, but the voices suddenly became silent.

Ahead, he could still hear the footsteps of the teenager, each step getting quieter as he moved away from him. He needed to catch him, otherwise he'd miss his chance.

He moved forward, crossing over the shallow beck, and stopped at the base of the grassy hill, glancing left and right along the path.

Nothing.

'Shit,' he whispered.

He decided to take a right and could hear the slow flow of the shallow stream at the base of the gentle slope, but he couldn't see a thing. Maybe this wasn't such a good—

'Why are you following me?' a voice said from behind him.

He physically jumped and gasped, quickly turning one-eighty, raising his hands up in defence. Under the dim conditions of the park he saw the faintest outline of the teenager standing there, his hood up over his head. He couldn't see his face.

'Why are you following me?' the teenager said again, this time firmer.

'I . . . I was hoping to . . . to . . . erm . . . get some . . .'

'Blow?'

The man bobbed his head. 'Yeah . . . something. Anything.'

'You a cop?' the boy asked.

'No, no cop,' the man explained. 'I need something to . . . to pick me up. Can you help me?'

'You were watching me from the car up there, weren't you?' the teenager asked.

'I . . . was,' he admitted.

'Why?'

In the darkness, the teenager appeared to move closer to him, so he stepped back, now cornered against the base of the grassy hill. There was no one around. The only sounds were the hum of passing cars up on Northcote Terrace and the steady flowing stream in front of him. His heart beat faster, and as each second passed, he wondered why he was doing this.

He glanced around to see if anyone was nearby. 'I . . . I didn't know if I wanted to go through with it,' the man explained, softly.

'Through with what?' the teenager asked.

Very quickly, the man lunged forward and drove the knife he'd been holding behind his back into the teenager's throat. The boy gagged, throwing his hands up to his chin, stumbling back several wobbly paces, gurgling on blood. A moment passed, then he lurched forward, collapsing to his knees, still clutching at his throat.

The man stepped back, watching him struggle, and smiled when he fell back and tumbled down the grassy incline into the stream.

With no one in sight, the man casually placed the knife back into his coat and made his way back across the short bridge, up to Widdowfield Street. He unlocked his car, opened the door, and climbed in.

In the rear-view mirror, he smiled at himself.

It was the first time he'd ever done that.

And he knew it wouldn't be the last.

2

Tuesday night, February
Darlington Town Hall

Mandy Spencer sighed heavily, sitting at the desk in the corner of the spacious office. It had been a long, busy day, leaving her with so little time she'd forgotten to eat. Silence surrounded her, and she was glad of the solitude, the peace allowing her to focus better, but the office felt a little eerie with no one else around.

Her colleagues, Henry Long and Tracy Clarke, had left a few hours ago, with most of the other people in the building and adjoining offices. After the usual 4.30 p.m. finish, a handful of managers and maintenance personnel hung around for a short while before heading home, leaving just the night-shift cleaner, who'd make the place presentable for the following day.

Mandy told Henry and Tracy she'd stay back to look over plans for upcoming applications and would set aside the important ones for tomorrow so they could all study them. The applications, most of the time, were basic, and included typical housing developments, conservatories, single- and double-storey extensions. It would be up to Mandy, Henry, and Tracy to decide whether these plans, based on the current laws and legislations, would be recommended. It wasn't just the laws they needed to adhere to, it was the public too. For example, if an occupier wanted to build a double-storey extension and lived in a semi-detached house, Mandy had to decide if the plans would affect their next-door neighbours. Would the new extension block the sunlight? Would it restrict their view? Everything had to be considered. She always remembered how years ago she dealt with an awkward old lady in Yoredale Avenue who'd complained about a neighbour putting up an extension because she wouldn't be able to see the chimney tops a few streets away. Still made her giggle now, thinking about it.

The biggest planning enquiry recently had come from a wealthy property developer who had purchased the land where the Cactus Jack's nightclub used to be. Located just behind Queen Street, it was a decent plot with a lot of potential, and a prime location. Not only did the buyer now have the small plot and wanted to build flats on it, but he wanted the car parks next to them, to presumably build more developments. This was an issue, as the car parks he desired were owned by the council and the council had, on several occasions, clearly stated that it wasn't up for debate and the car parks would never be sold to him, no doubt the biggest reason being it offered shoppers in Darlington a great place to park. Mandy had had to explain this to the buyer.

She picked up the orange mug that Henry had bought her for her birthday and finished the rest of the lukewarm coffee, placing it back down by her keyboard. She opened another email. Before she read it, the phone to her right started ringing. Frowning, she glanced down at her watch; it was nearly 8 p.m.

'Who's this?' she whispered to herself before answering the call.

'Mrs Spencer?'

Her frown deepened. 'Yes?'

'Have you changed your mind?' the voice asked.

She recognised it. It was the buyer who owned the small plot of land between the two car parks.

'Mr Cairn, we've spoken about this. I'm sorry to inform you but we need to have a meeting with the council and discuss your proposal. We can't just allow buildings to be built anywhere.'

'I need the car parks too.'

She sighed. 'This is something you need to discuss with another department. We're involved with the planning side of things, but before we grant any permission for your apartments, we need to have a meeting with the committee.'

'I need the car parks,' he said sternly.

Mandy sighed, her shoulders dipping. 'You've made that clear, sir. But there's nothing I can do. I really wish there was. I'm so very sorry.'

Mr Cairn didn't answer.

'Are you there?' Mandy asked.

'It must be lonely.'

'I'm sorry?'

'Working in that large office by yourself.'

'I work in a team of three.'

'During the day you do. But not now, sitting at that desk in that black dress you've worn all day. Isn't your husband getting worried about you? He'll be expecting you home soon.'

She quickly scanned the office. It was very quiet. The last time she'd heard the cleaner was almost an hour ago.

'Mrs Spencer?'

'I'm here . . .' she whispered, her eyes still flitting around nervously. The glass windows at the edge of the massive room were black, reflecting the internal office space under the bright lights from the ceiling.

'It's a nice dress you're wearing,' the voice said. 'Does your husband like it?'

Her words got stuck in her throat.

'Does he?' the man said.

'Yeah.'

'I like it too.'

'Can . . . can you see me?' She stood up and looked around the room warily.

'I'm always watching.'

She tried to stay calm and professional. 'Listen, I need to ask you to stop ringing about the planning permission and purchasing the car parks. We have made it abundantly clear you need to speak to a different department regarding the purchase and we have no sway on their decisions. Regarding the permission, we need to assess it fully.'

'I'm very pleased with what you, Henry, and Tracy have done for us in the past. You've been great. If this planning permission doesn't go through, I wouldn't want anything bad to happen to you.'

'Goodbye, Mr Cairn!' she shouted, slamming the phone down into the receiver.

Over the next few minutes, she couldn't concentrate. The comments about her dress were playing over and over in her mind. Had he been in earlier and seen her wearing it? If so, how did he know she was there alone now? She didn't like it one bit and decided to log off her computer and deal with the emails tomorrow with the help of Tracy and Henry. She needed to get out of there. Her son, Damien, and husband, Rick, would be waiting for her to get home. She'd promised them a game of Monopoly tonight.

She stood up, used her fingers to curl her blonde hair behind her ears and grabbed her jacket from the back of the chair. She wasn't looking forward to leaving. It was freezing outside. It had been like that for days. No doubt driving would be dangerous again on the way home; she'd almost skidded off the road yesterday due to some stupid driver who'd braked harshly in front of her for no apparent reason.

At the exit, she hit the switch, and the room behind her plummeted into darkness. She closed the door firmly and locked it, then put the key in her pocket. Each worker had their own key in case they stayed back to work, which was often the case. She made her way along the wide corridor to the lifts, and when she got there, she pressed the button. She was only up two flights, but she always used the lift. It was easier, less strain on the knees. There was a rumbling mechanical sound, then the silver lifts doors opened with a ping.

She glared into the dark lift for a moment, then, bending low enough to see the ceiling of the lift, realised the lights were out.

In two minds whether to take a pitch-black lift down two levels or just use the stairs, she decided to take the stairs instead. When the lift doors pinged closed, she pushed open the stairwell door and started to descend them.

The words of Mr Cairn played heavily on her mind.

The black dress.

Working alone.

She'd dealt with him in the past, but she'd never had the pleasure — if that's what you'd call it — of meeting him. Everything was done over emails and phone calls. But after that phone call, she shivered at the fact he knew she was married and what she was wearing.

She'd almost reached the first floor when it happened.

The lights in the stairwell went off, leaving her in total darkness.

'God, what now?' she muttered, freezing on the spot. Very slowly and cautiously, she descended the remaining three steps with the help of the handrail to her right, edged the doors open onto the first floor, and peered along the pitch-black corridor. To the left, through the floor-to-ceiling glass window, she could see the side of the Dolphin Centre across the road.

'Hello?' she said loudly, more for the benefit of hearing her own voice so she didn't feel alone. 'Is anyone there?' A shadowy silence answered her back.

From her bag, she grabbed her phone quickly, her hands shaking, and scrolled through her contact list until she found the right number, then pressed CALL.

'Hello,' answered the voice.

'Hi, this is Mandy Spencer of Planning Permission. I'm in the office alone, and the lights have gone out. The whole building is in darkness.'

'Hi, Mandy,' said the voice of Tony Mclean, the maintenance man. 'Just hold tight. I'm near the power supply now. Give me two seconds, just stay where you are.'

'Okay, I'm just in the stairwell on the first floor.'

'I'm the opposite end, just going into the utilities room now.'

She heard a click through the phone, then some fiddling around. 'Right, it looks like it's tripped for some reason. Hold on.'

'I'm holding—'

'Oh, by the way, did he come up and see you?' Tony asked.

'Who?' Mandy said, scowling in the darkness.

'The man — don't know his name. Saw him only a few minutes ago. I asked him what he was doing, and he told me he was collecting something from your office on the second floor. Told me he'd checked in with Roger, the security guard.'

She felt the hairs raise on the back of her neck. 'Who . . . who was he?'

'I don't know, he . . . oh, hold on, think I've found the problem,' Tony said, then fell silent. He must be studying the town hall's complicated electrical distribution board.

'Tony?' she said anxiously.

After a long moment of silence, she pulled the phone away from her head, noticing the call had been disconnected. 'Shit.'

She heard quiet footsteps behind her. Then something grabbed her shoulder.

3

Mandy jumped forward, fell to the floor and screamed. With her body twisted, she turned but could barely see the figure standing on the stairs staring down at her.

'What the fuck?' she shouted. 'Who . . . who's there?'

The figure didn't say anything, nor was there any sound in the whole building. She shuffled back towards the double doors on her backside into the corridor of the first floor, almost hyperventilating. In the darkness, she heard footsteps pacing towards her. Her heart rate doubled as she frantically tapped the button on her phone, and when the phone erupted with a bright white light, she shone it into the pitch-black stairwell.

'Jesus, Henry . . . you fucking . . . God . . . you scared me.' She sighed heavily and dropped her face into her trembling hands. 'Never — and I mean never — do that again!'

Henry moved closer, erupting in laughter. 'I . . . I couldn't miss the opportunity. I'm sorry.' He placed a hand on the outside of her arm. 'Are you okay, Mand?'

'I think I've died and come back to life. Honestly, I've never been so scared.'

'What's happened with the electric — why we in darkness?'

'I don't know, it just went off, I was coming down the stairs and it just—'

The staircase filled with light. It took a few seconds for her eyes to adjust and there in front of her was her colleague, Henry, dressed in a dark hoodie and jogging bottoms.

'Why are you here?' she said.

'I left my laptop here. The missus wanted to have a look at holidays for the summer. I was going to Sainsbury's anyway, so thought I'd pop in.' He patted the outside of his hoodie, and there was a ping of keys. 'I'll lock up when I leave. See you in the morning. Watch those roads, by the way, it's icy out there.'

'See you in the morning,' she said with a head bob, then moved around him and descended the stairs.

When she reached the ground floor, she took a right after she went through the doors, making her way along the long corridor to the opposite end. When she reached it, she pushed hard on the exit door and stepped out into the cold car park. Her car was about twenty metres ahead of her. Shivering as she rounded the bonnet of the car, she pulled her keys from her pocket, climbed in and shut the door, the sound echoing around her.

'What a day it's been.' She put her bag onto the passenger seat, turned on the engine, and as she put the car in reverse, she turned to the rear windscreen then stopped, glaring at the piece of paper tucked under her rear wiper.

'What the . . .'

She put the gear back into neutral and got out of the car, frustratedly plucking the paper from the faint grip of the wiper's rubber. There was writing on it.

Something bad is going to happen if I don't get what I want.

4

Six-year-old Ethan had been ill last night. Stomach cramps, his mother thought, but she wasn't sure, so she'd taken him to Moorland's Surgery to be checked. Apparently, he'd eaten something that hadn't agreed with him, according to the doctor's analysis. Calpol and plenty of rest, as usual, was the advised cure.

They took a right onto Hollyhurst Road, walked nearly a minute then went left into the park and made their way down the steady, damp decline.

'How you feeling, Ethan?'

He placed his palm tiredly over his stomach and looked up at her with glassy eyes. 'Tummy hurts, Mummy.' His saddened expression broke her heart.

'Aww baby, we'll give you some medicine when we get home, okay?' She wrapped her arm around him, pulling him close.

He embraced her hug, then turned away and looked back at the path. The park was wet from last night's rain and a smell of damp leaves and moisture hung in the air, reminding them of past camping trips.

As the path levelled out, they saw a man walking a dog heading towards them, a short lead wrapped around his hand. Ethan loved dogs. They used to have a black Lab, but this type was a dog they hadn't seen before.

The man had short, fair hair and a scraggly beard, was somewhere in his sixties, and was dressed in blue denim that was ripped in places and black boots that had seen better days. He glanced up and smiled, showing some missing teeth. 'Good morning.'

Anna smiled courteously. When they were past the man, Ethan turned and watched the dog.

'Ethan, come on,' Anna said, nudging him. 'Stop staring.'

They continued to walk on. The play area was over the other side of the beck and was empty — most children would be in school. Anna couldn't wait to get home and get the kettle on. She'd already informed the school Ethan would be off, as long she provided the doctor's note tomorrow.

'I'm cold,' Ethan said.

'We'll be home soon.'

As they passed the small bridge, Ethan stopped, noticing something down in the beck. 'Mammy . . .'

'Yeah?' She felt his hand tug her back slightly.

'What's that?' He pointed into the beck, a little further up, near the low, narrow tunnel that went under Surtees Street.

She stopped and frowned. 'I . . . I don't know. Probably a pile of clothes, Ethan.'

'I wanna see,' he begged.

Ethan was curious. She'd say to her friends she was sick of him asking every question under the sun but knew one day he'd grow up and shut himself off through the teenage years, which was what her other son, Mark, had done.

They continued along the path towards the object. He was so excited.

'Mammy, what do we do if it's gold? Can we keep it?'

She smiled widely. 'If it's gold, we can keep it. But you have to promise me something?'

He looked up at her with wide eyes.

'That you can't tell anyone. Then we can buy a nice big house and a big car and go on sunny holidays.'

'I promise.'

'Good boy.'

As they approached the shape in the beck, Anna couldn't really figure it out. It looked like fabric but it wasn't clothes piled up. Growing closer, the shape became clearer. She didn't want to believe it.

'Mammy?' Ethan asked, frowning. 'Is that man poorly? Has he fallen over?'

Her heart raised a few notches when she saw the soles of some black Nike Air trainers, then the legs of the body.

'Jesus . . .' she whispered, pulling Ethan back and turning him so he couldn't see.

'Mammy!' he gasped. 'I want to see, I want to see.'

She turned and put her palms on his shoulders, keeping him back. 'Listen, Ethan, you need to stay here, okay? I need to see what it is.'

Reluctantly he waited, watching her approach the beck, carefully making her way down the muddy decline, needing to see if the person was alive.

But she knew the truth.

She knew the person was dead.

And she knew it was a teenage boy. Not because she could see him properly, but because her eldest son, Mark, had been wearing the exact same trainers and tracksuit bottoms yesterday.

And he never came home last night.

5

Wednesday morning
The Denes park

Tanzy was advised by DC Leonard to park up on Willowfield Road. It was easier for access, but it was hectic. People had got wind of what had happened and were there, nosing, desperate for that perfect photo to upload to their social media profiles. Unless they'd come equipped with an optical zoom, they'd have struggled because PC Donny Grearer and PC Eric Timms were watching the gate, only allowing police officers and forensics to get close enough.

Tanzy closed his door, stepped up onto the path and made his way down to Willowfield Road. He'd got a space roughly six houses up Greenbank Road, which gave him time to get ready for what he was about to walk into. He felt them. The butterflies. Flitting around his stomach relentlessly. It never got any easier.

The rusty old metal railings along the side of the park were almost hidden by the plethora of eager people watching, heads raised in wonder. A murmur of excitement and anxiety filled the air. He spotted PC Andrews by the entrance point.

'What is going on here?' Tanzy muttered to himself, shaking his head. He stepped off the path, went around the back of the small crowd, and didn't need to flash his credentials to Grearer and Timms to be allowed through the gate.

'What do you think happened?' PC Andrews asked as they descended the path deeper into the park.

'I have no idea, Josh.'

Andrews must have realised that Tanzy wasn't up for conversation; he said nothing more as they walked over the small bridge. Tanzy noticed DC Leonard and PC Amy Weaver speaking to a woman, and noted she moved with energy and anger, her arms raising and lowering repeatedly, her mouth moving rapidly, but he couldn't hear what she was saying. DC Leonard had mentioned that the body had been found by a woman claiming to be the mother, so Tanzy assumed that was her.

Beyond Leonard and Weaver, a small, blonde boy sat on a bench by himself, no older than the age of seven or eight. His red, puffy eyes indicated he'd been crying.

They grew closer, could now hear the conversation with the mother.

'. . . don't you dare fucking tell me that!' the woman shouted at Leonard. 'How can you stand there while my son is lying in that cold, dirty stream?'

Leonard raised a calming palm, but she moved closer and swatted it out the way. She was wide-eyed and her body trembled.

'Hey, hey!' PC Weaver shouted, stepping forward and grabbing her wrists. She was the same height and build as the mother. 'Mrs Greenwell, that's enough. We need you to calm down, or we will arrest you.'

Anna Greenwell tried to pull away, but Weaver held on tight. 'I wouldn't do that if I was you. Listen, I know you're upset, but we're trying to help you here.'

As a calmness passed over her, she dropped her shoulders an inch and started to cry. Weaver let go of her wrists. 'Why . . . why him? I don't understand!'

'Hey,' Tanzy said softly, just behind Leonard and Weaver. 'What do we have?'

Leonard turned and pointed to the beck. 'Teenager is over there.' He swivelled back. 'This is his mother, Anna, and her son, Ethan.'

Tanzy briefly glanced at Anna, then beyond her to Ethan for a moment longer, seeing the sadness in his small face.

'Hi, Anna, I'm Detective Inspector Orion Tanzy with Durham Constabulary.' He edged forward but didn't invade her personal space. 'I understand you're upset. Our forensic team are doing their best to determine what happened and, from there, we'll gather enough evidence to get to the bottom of this. My only ask is, could you try and be patient and have faith we can do our job?'

Anna sniffed and nodded at Tanzy.

He turned to PC Weaver. 'Would you mind waiting here with Mrs Greenwell while I go speak with forensics?'

'No problem.' Weaver's blue eyes focused on Anna, who bobbed her head implying she'd be no trouble.

Tanzy turned with Andrews and they headed along the path. Although the sun had crept out from behind a cloud, it was freezing and didn't seem to be getting any warmer. In his long grey Parka Tanzy didn't feel it, but the PCs in uniform were visibly shaking.

Underfoot the ground was wet, the grass layered with dew. Up ahead, dressed in their white disposable suits, were Amanda Forrest, Jacob Tallow, and Emily Hope, standing a few metres down the grassy bank. They were staring down at the teenager, whose legs and stomach were on the grass but whose face and shoulders were in the gently flowing stream.

The park entrance at Surtees Street was watched by two officers to prevent any access to the public. Standing at the metal railings behind them were a number of people with phones in their hands, still trying to snap photos of the teenager lying on his front with his face submerged in the water.

'All we need, isn't it . . . those people watching,' Tanzy muttered to Andrews, who turned towards them for a moment.

Amanda noticed them approach, looked away from the display screen of the black camera in her hand. 'Morning.' Not only looking exhausted, she sounded it too, her voice dull and flat, as if all the energy had been drained from her.

'Hey, Amanda,' Tanzy said, noticing her tired appearance. 'What do we have?'

'Male teenager. Aged somewhere between fifteen and eighteen in my opinion. No ID but DC Leonard has spoken to the woman down there who claims to be his mother.'

Tanzy briefly glanced back at the woman who was standing next to Weaver and Leonard. 'He's called Mark, aged seventeen. Has anyone contacted Peter yet?'

'Yeah.'

'Is he coming over?'

'No, he said due to the position of the body, and what Tallow had told him, he's happy to meet us at the hospital later this afternoon,' she replied.

'Okay, good,' Tanzy said, looking past her. Tanzy was aware that when a body was found the police couldn't pronounce the individual as dead, even if the person's head was separated from the body in a sea of blood. Only a paramedic, doctor, or coroner could officially pronounce someone dead. Peter Gibbs, the local coroner, was on his way. His role was office-based, but he liked to do a lot of the fieldwork himself. If there was ever a body found under circumstances which implied something malicious, he usually wanted to see it.

'When's Max back?' Forrest asked.

Tanzy rubbed his cold, bald head. 'Tomorrow, I think. I haven't spoken with him much.'

'How's he doing?' Forrest seemed genuinely concerned.

'He's . . . he's okay. He's coming to terms with things. Would be hard for anyone.'

Forrest replied with a sympathetic close-lipped smile.

'So, what's happened here?' he asked, indicating the riverbank. 'You had a good look?'

She turned. 'We know that Mrs Greenwell found him earlier. She told us she lifted his face up to have a look at him, then dropped him again and started screaming. We've spoken to—' she pointed along the path, then seemed to lose her focus — 'I don't know where he is, but a local man walked past and heard her screaming so ran down to see what was happening. Think DC Leonard spoke with him and took notes.'

'How was he killed? Tripped and fell? Or something more sinister?'

'Knife to the throat,' she said, briefly wincing. 'We lifted his head up to observe the cut. Standard incision. Nothing special about it, really. But after checking his pockets, we found a load of money and a plastic bag filled with a number of smaller bags. A white substance.'

'Cocaine?'

'Probably.'

'So potential dealer. Gang war? Buyer not happy with the product? With the price?'

'Maybe,' Forrest replied, this time shrugging. The why wasn't her concern. 'That's where you come in, Detective.'

'Any other injuries?'

'Not that we can see, not yet. It looks like there's a significant amount of blood on his clothes and hands—' she indicated around her own chest area — 'so whatever happened, he attempted to stop the bleeding quickly.' She shivered for a moment, as if feeling the cold even though she was well padded under her thin white suit.

'Did he have a phone?' Tanzy asked.

'In his left pocket.'

'Good. Bag it up. Take it back for analysis. We need to see his recent calls and text messages. And anything on his social media profiles that could help us.'

'Understood,' she replied.

'I'll come back, I need to speak with his mother,' said Tanzy. They both glanced in her direction. DC Leonard had his palm on her shoulder, attempting to soothe her. 'Get a better idea of the kind of lad he was. It might indicate who did this.'

Forrest turned away and joined Tallow at the side of the stream, who greeted Tanzy with a nod. He too appeared exhausted, his body and posture out of the norm.

DC Leonard seemed to have Anna Greenwell under control. She appeared calmer now, although still upset, occasionally wiping her red eyes. Tanzy went over to Leonard while PC Andrews waited with forensics to take some notes on the teenager's body.

'Hey,' Tanzy said to Leonard, then faced Anna. 'It's an awful time, Mrs Greenwell, I can appreciate that, but remember we're here to help. And we need you to help us. Would you mind answering a few questions?'

She stared vacantly at him, as if she was too tired to stand.

'We'd be ever so grateful,' he added. 'It won't take long.'

'What's going to happen to my son?'

Tanzy kept his voice low, so Ethan, who was sitting on the bench behind, couldn't hear. 'He'll be taken to the hospital for a post-mortem by a pathologist, then we can make arrangements for the rest of the process.'

After absorbing Tanzy's words, more tears came. Tanzy had never lost a child and couldn't understand what she was going through, but if anything ever happened to his own, Eric or Jasmine, the weight of that loss would be devastating.

'It was his birthday last week. Seventeen. God . . . we were planning on going away next weekend with the family. Somewhere in the Lakes.' She paused a beat, lowered her gaze to the floor. 'He . . . he was looking forward to it.'

'Where was he yesterday?'

'He said he was going out with friends. Said he'd be back late.'

'At what time did you get worried that he wasn't home?'

She sighed, glanced back to the floor, as if something was bothering her.

Tanzy waited a few seconds then asked the question again.

'I . . . I fell—' she looked away from the detective towards the stream where her eldest son was — 'asleep.'

'You fell asleep?' Tanzy asked softly, not intending for his words to sound judgemental.

She gave a small, almost unnoticeable nod.

'So, when you woke up this morning, and he wasn't there, what did you do?'

'I rang and rang him. I sent him messages and left a few voicemails, but he never replied. I assumed he stayed at one of his friends but I didn't have any of their numbers. You know what kids are like.'

'Was Mark involved with some bad people?'

She frowned. 'What do you mean . . . bad people?'

'What are his friends like?'

She tilted her head, thinking hard. 'They're . . . nice. Mainly the lads from school. They're no trouble, really.'

Tanzy paused a beat before he said the next part.

'Have you known Mark to ever take any form of drugs?'

Her eyes widened and face straightened as if he'd slapped her. 'Excuse me? Mark, my son?'

'Yes?'

'I absolutely have no idea why you would say that,' she gasped, physically shaking at the accusation. 'How dare you, how dare you think—'

Tanzy elevated a quick palm to try to settle the situation. 'Please listen to me, Mrs Greenwell. The reason I'm asking is because the forensic team found a lot of money and a bag full of drugs in his pockets. It's possible he was involved in something that you weren't aware of. I needed to ask you first in case you knew of anything.'

She opened her mouth but stopped herself, her words falling back down her throat.

Tanzy turned to Weaver. 'Amy, could you and James—' he glanced at Leonard too — 'take Mrs Greenwell and Ethan to their house, and get a witness statement?'

Weaver took a step forward. 'No problem.'

Anna waved Ethan off the bench, who came to her side and tucked himself into her, as if the cold world around him was too much to bear. PC Weaver smiled at them and asked them where they lived. It wasn't far. Other side of the park. Greenbank Road. As Weaver led the way Anna and Ethan slowly trailed behind her, their eyes fixated on Mark down in the stream.

'Hey, Jim,' Tanzy whispered, pulling on DC Leonard's hand. 'Have a look around Mark's bedroom. Tell Anna it's important we get a feel for who he was. You know the drill . . . look for anything. Let me know.'

'Will do,' Leonard said.

'Have you seen DS Stockdale this morning?'

Leonard stopped. 'No, I haven't. Didn't see him at the station.'

'I need to speak to him about a report he did a few days ago, that's all.'

'If I see him, I'll tell him.' With that, Leonard turned and followed Weaver.

Tanzy watched them cross the small bridge and amble tiredly up the path towards the exit. He smiled sadly, wondering what was going through Anna's head. After he took a breath of cold, fresh air, he headed back to where the forensics were.

A loud noise attracted his attention somewhere up the path beyond Tallow and Forrest.

A man walking briskly towards him, face full of thunder.

'For God's sake,' Tanzy whispered, watching him closely.

It was the last person he wanted to see.

6

Wednesday morning
The Denes park

'What the hell is going on, Tanzy?' DCI Fuller shouted.

Tanzy sighed and shrugged, becoming annoyed with the man's attitude. 'What does it look like?'

'It looks like this fucking town is falling apart. And it looks like my DI is doing nothing about it.' Fuller came to a halt in front of him and stared deep into his eyes. A common power tactic that managers often used in situations with lower-ranked individuals. DCI Martin Fuller had taken over the role two months ago.

Tanzy, who never felt threatened or bullied by anyone, held his ground and said nothing. Fuller, although the DCI and usually a scary character to some, realised that Tanzy's stare was unbreakable and consequently was the first one to look away. 'Tanzy, what's happened?'

Tanzy wanted to punch him square in the face. He imagined it in his head for a split second: lunging forward, fist tight, knuckles colliding with Fuller's nose. The sound of knuckle on bone. The way he'd fall back and cry out in pain . . .

'A teenager, aged seventeen. Throat cut, sir. He was found by his mother and younger brother less than an hour ago. Chances are he's been here overnight.'

Fuller tilted his head. 'Why do you suggest that?'

'Suggest what?'

Fuller pulled an *are you thick?* expression. 'That he's been here overnight?'

Tanzy's patience was growing very thin with this new guy. 'Because, according to his mother, he never came home. She assumed he was sleeping at a friend's house. But earlier, she'd gone to the doctor's with her youngest child because he was unwell. They walked back through on their way home and spotted him lying there in the beck. Forensics found a lot of money and multiple bags of a white substance. Possible gang conflict over drugs.' Tanzy pointed past him to where Tallow and Forrest were. Fuller had actually walked past them and not even realised what was going on because he was filled with so much anger, he needed to vent to Tanzy. He'd been warned by Superintendent Barry Eckles it was his job to clean up the streets. Each individual case put more weight on Fuller's shoulders, and he needed to keep a lid on this town.

Tanzy, in general, had a cool head, but when he got sick of someone he wasn't Mr Nice Guy anymore. Hopefully Fuller wouldn't see that side of Tanzy, for everyone's sake.

Fuller glanced away, turned, and stared at Forrest and Tallow, who were standing roughly ten metres from them. 'Seventeen years old, eh?'

'Yeah,' Tanzy said.

'No age, is it?'

Tanzy shook his head. 'Not at all.'

'We need to get this shit figured out, Orion.'

'I couldn't agree more.' He forced a half-smile for Fuller's benefit.

'Why are you smiling?' Fuller asked, frowning.

'I'm smiling because you seem to like blaming everyone else for what's going on in this town.'

Fuller was taken aback by Tanzy's response and narrowed his eyes. 'What do you mean?'

'You seem to blame me and Max for a lot of things. I understand that Barry's on your back about what's going on and what cases we're knee-deep in, but as a DCI, in my opinion, you should recognise that we're valuable members of this force and you need to treat us with more respect. People work more efficiently when they feel appreciated.'

Fuller took a lungful of cold air and expelled it quickly. 'That sounds like a lovely story. And thank you, I'll take your opinions on board, think about them for a few seconds, then forget about them. You need to understand that it isn't my job to make you happy at work. Or are you under the illusion that it is?'

Tanzy stared, holding his gaze, but said nothing, feeling his blood start to warm.

Fuller went on: 'Didn't think so. It's my job to manage everyone under me, including you and Max. So, I guess you'll just have to get used to the way things are from now on.'

Tanzy smiled widely but said nothing. It was either that or lunge forward and headbutt him. The DCI couldn't care less about what anyone thought of him, that much was clear. It was something that Tanzy would have to grin and bear.

'Any other nice little stories you want to share before I go?' Fuller enquired, glancing down at his wristwatch with wide, impatient eyes. 'I have things to do.'

'I'm sure you do, being a DCI is a very responsible position.'

'Yes, it is . . .'

'Then no, that's all the lovely stories for today, boss. I might pop my head in your office tomorrow. I have a few more.'

Fuller gave a sarcastic grin and turned. 'Look forward to it. Now get this fucking shit tidied up. I want your report at the end of the day.'

He turned away, making his way past Tallow and Forrest without saying a word, who, in their defence, were occupied over the body of the teenager so didn't see him go by. They disliked him more than Tanzy did. Just before Fuller reached the gate, a familiar face appeared, who ducked under the temporary tape, making his way down the path.

'Good afternoon, sir.'

Fuller stopped dead. 'You shouldn't be here. You need to go home and come back when you're on duty.'

'Nice to see you too.'

'Go home.'

'But, sir, I—'

'I don't want to hear it. Go home. Come back tomorrow.'

The man stood his ground. 'I've already cleared this with HR, so I'm within my rights to be here. If there's an issue, you can phone Judith at the office.'

Fuller sighed heavily. 'Fine.' He moved around him and left, disappearing through the small crowd of people back to his car.

'Arsehole,' the man whispered to himself.

Tanzy recognised the familiar face coming towards him. He also noticed the unfriendly interaction with DCI. They met near where the forensics were, and both observed the body of the teenager in the beck.

'You haven't chosen the best day to come back,' Tanzy commented.

'I don't want to miss out on the action.'

'That's true, mate.' Tanzy moved closer, placing a hand on the man's shoulder.

'Fuller told me to go home and come back tomorrow.'

'Fuller's a prick who has no respect for anything or anyone,' Tanzy replied.

Tanzy's statement was met with a smile.

'So, have you missed me, Ori?'

'Of course I have, Max, the whole town has. Welcome back, DI Byrd.'

7

Tanzy and Byrd watched Tallow, Hope, and Forrest down at the stream near the body.

'Have I missed much?' Byrd asked.

'Not really, mate. Usual shit.' Tanzy turned his way. 'You look well, by the way.'

Byrd half smiled.

'Seriously,' Tanzy went on, 'the diet you're on is really working. How much weight have you shifted — must be a stone?'

'Nearly two, actually.' A proud smile ran across Byrd's face.

Tanzy patted him on the back. He could see it in his complexion, his cheeks more prominent, less excess fat under his chin. But he didn't know if it was a reaction to losing his parents and hoped Byrd was losing weight the right way. 'Well done. You'll be getting a six pack soon.'

Byrd puffed air from his mouth humorously. 'How's Pip doing?'

'She's better, Max. She's sorting herself out now. Drinking much less. Putting the kids first.' Tanzy turned, meeting his gaze. 'The way it should be, you know.'

Byrd felt a warmth for his friend.

'How are you doing?' Tanzy asked softly.

Byrd smiled sadly. 'I miss them every day.'

Tanzy placed a hand on his shoulder. 'The funeral was a good send-off though. They'd have appreciated all that were there.'

'Most nights I finish my shift, I find myself at their graves, wishing they were still here. I used to pop in and see them sometimes. I'd do anything to see my old man sitting in his chair and listen to him moaning about the world like he did.'

Tanzy wanted to say something useful but couldn't quite find the words.

'It'll be hard if me and Claire ever have kids. I know they'd have been brilliant grandparents.' Byrd mentally gave himself a shake back to the present and turned back to the forensics. 'Story here, then, Ori?'

Tallow looked up at the bank and gave Byrd a wave, who courteously returned it.

'Mark Greenwell. Seventeen. His throat was cut,' Tanzy started. 'Forensics found money and drugs in his pockets. It could be a deal gone wrong or it could be gang wars, hard to say.' Tanzy paused a beat. 'His mother found the body — she was walking through here with her six-year-old, Ethan, on their way back from the doctor's.' Tanzy pointed to their right. 'Moorlands Surgery, just along the road.'

Byrd knew where it was. It was actually his own doctors and had been most of his life. 'Can't have been easy. Especially with his younger brother there.'

'She said he never came home last night and just assumed he'd stopped out. Stayed at a friend's house. You know what seventeen-year-olds are like. At least, I know what I was like at that age.'

Byrd nodded. 'Where is the mother now?'

'Weaver and Leonard have taken her back to her house to get a statement. They just live up the road. Told Leonard to have a quick look in Mark's bedroom to see if he could see anything suspicious.'

'Peter Gibbs been yet?'

'No, he's happy to meet us at the hospital.'

Byrd let out a sigh.

Tanzy studied him. 'You all right? You seem quiet.'

'I'm okay, mate. Nice to get back but at the same time, we're greeted with this.' He pointed down at the beck.

'How was the holiday?'

'Nice to get away, to be honest. We needed it. Think things are on the up. Got that old flame back that I was on about a few weeks ago. Claire's moving in, as it happens. Going to put her house on the market.'

'When she moving in?'

'Today.'

Tanzy smiled. 'Glad to hear it.'

'Hey, what's this anyway?' Byrd raised his fingers to Tanzy's chin.

Tanzy swatted it away playfully.

Tallow slowly made his way up the bank towards the detectives. 'Bloody cold one today.'

'You'll be moaning in the summer when it's too hot,' Tanzy replied, grinning.

'What you make of this?' Byrd asked, although Tanzy had filled him in moments ago. 'Seen anything new in the last ten minutes or so?'

Tallow took a lungful of air and gave a small shake of his head. He was tall and thin, roughly six foot four, almost making Tanzy, who was six foot two, look small. Byrd, although a respectable six foot, looked small in comparison to both.

'Simple knife cut. Seems to be the only wound on him from what I can see. We'll let the pathologists have a closer look at the hospital.'

'You're looking well, Max,' Emily Hope noted, pointing to his gut, smiling, as she sauntered gracefully up the bank in her plastic coveralls.

'Was just saying that before,' Tanzy agreed. 'Nearly two stone.' He patted Byrd's stomach.

'Right, that's enough,' Byrd said, swatting Tanzy's hand away.

'You can tell. Well done,' she said, now level with them. Hope wasn't small but both detectives towered over her. She turned to Tallow. 'We have all the pictures we need, Jacob. The video looks good too, so we can analyse that later. When the pathologists are done I'll request the clothing to see if I can get anything off them.'

Tanzy observed her attractive side profile and short, quirky hairstyle that appeared different to how it was when he last saw her. With her coveralls not fully zipped, Tanzy caught a glimpse of her neck and throat tattoo.

She went on. 'I also see two sets of footprints here. One of them matches with the male's trainers. But the other is different. You see?'

Byrd and Tanzy edged forward, smelling her sweet perfume as they grew a little closer. There was a footprint in a small area of mud at the path's edge.

'Good spot.' Byrd nodded.

'And . . .' Hope added, moving over to the right where she'd placed a couple of yellow counters. They followed. 'See here?'

The detectives focused on where she was pointing.

'Blood droplets. I've taken samples already. Swept the area. Looks like the victim was attacked up here on the path, stumbled forward and fell down into the stream.'

'We okay for the undertakers to come down and handle it?' Byrd enquired.

Tallow looked up at Byrd and gave the thumbs-up.

Byrd backed up a few steps and waved at the PCs at the entrance near Surtees Street.

Grearer waved and headed towards the ambulance, which was parked halfway along the fence.

'Let's see what we find in the post-mortem this afternoon,' Byrd said to Tanzy. 'In the meantime, we'll get Grearer and Timms knocking on doors. Someone might have seen something last night. Slim chance, but you never know.'

8

Wednesday afternoon
Stonedale Crescent, Cleveland Avenue

Alex Richards sat in his office, focusing on the laptop screen in front of him. He studied how local businesses performed compared to last year. As it was February, it was common to see the usual January dip. It happened every year, and this year was no exception. He worked as a business analyst comparing and formulating trends in the local markets. These calculations explained why one company was doing better than another. Companies hired him to provide valuable data and insights to performances.

He'd completed a business management diploma a few years back and decided this was the route he'd like to go down. Before he'd hit the laptop screens, he was in the army. Although he worked from home, upstairs in the small front bedroom that he'd converted into an office, he still wore a shirt, tie, and trousers. He felt it helped him get in the zone and focus better.

His office was a rectangular shape, approximately fifteen feet by ten, housing a desk on the right-hand side, with a shelving unit, packed with files, folders, and paperwork to the right of it. The opposite wall contained photos from his army days with some of the troops. Straight ahead, there was a window and to the left of it, fixed on the wall with a swivel bracket, a twenty-two-inch flatscreen television. ITV News was set on a low volume as the quiet background noise helped him concentrate.

On the screen, a reporter in a grey suit and blue tie, with an overgrown mop of dark hair swept to the side of his plain, serious face, spoke about the latest updates in Darlington.

Alex frowned at hearing the name of his hometown being mentioned and gave the television his full attention.

'We go live now to Greenbank Road,' the news desk reporter said, 'where this tragic event has occurred.' The man gave a short sympathetic nod before the screen switched to a live feed.

In front of a handheld camera was a reporter dressed in a suit looking apprehensive about the news she was about to tell the world, positioned at the entrance of the park.

'Today, in the Denes park behind me—' she angled her body and pointed behind her — 'the police discovered the body of Mark Greenwell, a seventeen-year-old male. According to sources, he'd been violently attacked and, in consequence, unfortunately lost his life. A team of police and forensics have examined the scene to find out exactly what happened. We'll bring you any updates as they come.'

The camera cut back to the studio.

Alex Richards stood up quickly. He was a tall, slim man, standing at six foot one, but underneath his shirt and tie he was lined with a layer of muscle from working out three times a week at the local gym combined with a healthy diet regime. After the army he'd wanted to keep fit. Not for any particular reason but for his own self-fulfilment.

He raced out of his office, dashed down the stairs, along the hall, and into the large kitchen, where his wife, Alice, was preparing food, a black apron wrapped around her waist.

'Alice, you seen the—?'

'Jesus, Alex!' She threw her left hand on her chest. 'You scared me!'

'Sorry . . . You seen the news?' He walked to the table, picked up the remote and turned on the kitchen TV. 'Look at this.'

Frowning, she placed the knife down next to the pile of chopped carrots and shifted over, stopping near him. 'What?'

'Just look.'

As the television flashed to life they focused on the screen but the report had finished, the man in the grey suit and blue tie now talking about something else. Sighing, he pulled his phone from his pocket and unlocked it.

'Shouldn't you be working?' she asked.

'Yeah . . . just have a look at this then I'll go.' He searched for 'Darlington Murder' and pressed GO. He clicked on the first result that came up, quickly scanned the content, and handed his phone to her. 'Read this.'

With furrowed brows, she took the phone and read the article, putting her hand to her mouth in disbelief when she'd finished. 'God, that's awful. One of my mam's friends lives near there.'

She handed the phone back to Alex and went over to the worktop, picked up her own and found a number she needed to ring.

'Who you phoning?'

'Claire,' she replied. 'Max will probably know all about it.'

'Haven't they just got back from their week away?' Alex asked. 'Might be best not bothering her with it just yet.'

'Yeah, but you know what Max is like. He'll have gone straight there. I'll just mention it. Claire might know some gossip.'

Alex sighed. 'Well if she ends up popping over for a coffee, make sure my office door is closed.'

9

DI Byrd had been home and had changed into something more professional. A pair of smart black trousers, a white shirt under a thick black jumper, and his usual long black coat that brushed the side of his knees as he walked.

He was the last one to arrive, and as he closed the door behind him, Tanzy looked in his direction. Already in the dimly lit room with Tanzy was the coroner Peter Gibbs, the senior forensics Tallow and Hope, and the pathologist Arnold Hemsley with a twenty-something black-haired woman Byrd hadn't met before who must be his assistant.

'Welcome, Detective Byrd,' Dr Hemsley said, observing him enter.

'Good afternoon,' Byrd replied, focusing on the paper-work in the pathologist's hands.

'Let's begin,' Hemsley started, then over the next few minutes gave a summary of Mark Greenwell and the cir-cumstances in which he was found. He hadn't seen the body when it was at the park, so when he mentioned cer-tain points, he looked at Tallow and Hope for confirmation.

Because of the nature of the killing, which in Tallow and Hope's opinion was a slice to his neck, there was only need for a visual post-mortem at this stage, instead of a limited or full post-mortem.

During a full post-mortem, the victim's body parts — heart, liver, lungs, blood vessels, intestines, brain — would be carefully removed and samples would be taken for each of these. For a knife cut to the throat there was no need to remove several of the victim's body parts to get samples from.

Usually, a post-mortem happens between two to three days after a person dying and it's common practice for the body itself to be identified by at least two people before the post-mortem takes place. However, under the circumstances where Anna found Mark in the park, it was obvious this was Mark. Because of the nature of his death, Byrd and Tanzy, along with Peter Gibbs, had pushed the post-mortem forward. In similar cases, where foul play has been suspected, the pathology department will prioritise their workloads to aid the police for investigation purposes.

Anna Greenwell had asked to come in and see Mark. She said she wouldn't be able to settle without seeing her son in a peaceful state, and seeing him face down in a stream wasn't the last image she wanted of him. The pathologist, Hemsley, had informed her that because the forensics only needed to carry out a visual inspection, she could come in later. Often, family members requested to see the victim before they were sliced open for a little comfort, to avoid having that one last image of their loved one as a piece of meat with stitches from chest to stomach. Anna had been reassured this wouldn't be the case so had given consent to the forensics and police to carry out the post-mortem.

Once they'd finished speaking, Hemsley led them all into a square-shaped room with a low ceiling and bright white walls. There was a rectangular-shaped metal trolley in the centre of it under a singular bright light where the body of Mark Greenwell lay. To the right, the detectives noticed an array of instruments on a thin, narrow trolley pushed against the wall. The room itself was no doubt the cleanest room they'd been in and smelled so clinical it hit the backs of their throats.

With plenty of room for seven, they circled the table, allowing enough space for Hemsley and his assistant to step forward.

Mark Greenwell was naked. His clothes had been removed and placed neatly in a brown paper evidence bag in a different room. Earlier at the park, Tallow and Hope had taken samples of fibres from Mark's tracksuit, a hair sample, and blood samples from the cut to his throat and were happy for the clothes to be removed for the post-mortem.

After he let out a short sigh, Hemsley focused on the body. Tanzy and Byrd studied him. Hemsley was a slim man with thinning hair that he liked to keep short. He was clean-shaven and the crow's feet around his eyes and mouth indicated he was likely a smoker.

Using the camera hanging around her neck, Hope took a few snaps of Greenwell on the trolley.

While looking at Mark's throat Hemsley said, 'Sorry guys, I never introduced you to Laura, my new assistant.' He glanced in her direction, then back at the body. 'Completed her degree in biomedical science with a focus on haematology. She's doing her training, and I hope, from what I've seen so far, that she'll be with me for as long as I can keep her.'

'Hi, Laura,' Byrd said.

'Hi,' Tanzy added.

The senior forensics, Tallow and Hope, and the coroner Gibbs said nothing, indicating to the detectives that they'd already been introduced at some point recently.

'As we can see, it's a violent knife attack.' Hemsley leaned over the table, observing the cut with the aid of a large magnifying glass. 'The way the skin has separated tells me—' he paused a beat, his eyes in severe concentration — 'the blade used was inserted quickly. It was definitely something malicious.'

Byrd agreed with Hemsley's comment. 'Good enough for me.'

Tanzy said, 'Any other marks on the body, besides the throat?'

The forensics focused on Hemsley, as the last time they'd seen the body, Mark had been fully clothed.

Hemsley looked to his assistant. 'Laura, would you like to tell them?'

Laura nodded several times and coughed quietly, as if readying herself. 'Yeah, I . . . When I removed the clothes I saw something on his back. Something we need to have a good look at.'

Byrd and Tanzy frowned.

'We'll turn him over, let them see,' Hemsley said. 'You take his legs, Laura.' She moved to her right, level with Mark's knees.

'Need a hand?' Tallow asked, standing on the opposite side but willing to move around if needed.

'We're okay, thanks,' Hemsley said.

Hemsley and his assistant carefully turned over the body until Mark was on his front. Hemsley then placed both of the victim's arms down by his side and stepped back, allowing the detectives, the coroner and the forensic investigators to have a look.

Byrd leaned over with wide eyes, focusing on Mark's back. 'What the hell is that?'

10

On the table in front of Jonny Feland there was nearly twenty thousand pounds in cash. Mostly in twenties, the rest in tens and fives. It had been counted by Jamie, who'd worked for him for many, many years. Jamie, now twenty-two, was probably his most loyal servant, his eyes and ears out on the streets, the one he could trust. He'd proved it time and time again.

Feland had picked Jamie up off the streets when he was only twelve years old — Jamie's parents had thrown him out, leaving him with nowhere to stay. Feland could recall the memory, implanted in his mind. He was driving along Neasham Road and saw Jamie sitting inside the bus stop outside the Copper Beach pub.

The following day he went past and saw him again, so decided to pull over to speak to him. Jamie had told Feland that his father relentlessly hit him and that his mother repeatedly spat at him. Feland couldn't believe parents could do that to their own. As the rain pelted down on top of the bus shelter Feland had told Jamie to get in the car and that he could come and live with him. Once Jamie got into the car and explained his situation further, telling him all the bad things his father had done to him, Feland had asked him where his parents lived. They went round and Feland told Jamie to wait in the car.

Feland had kicked the door as hard as he could until it opened. It slammed into the face of a woman, who bawled in pain and stumbled backwards into the hallway. Feland, who was six foot two and nearly as wide as he was tall, stepped inside and punched her six times in the face. From somewhere upstairs, he heard someone shout, 'What the fuck is going on?' Then Jamie's father appeared, roaring down the stairs. He was covered head to toe in tattoos, dressed in his pants and an ill-fitting, grubby white vest.

Jamie's dad swung at Feland but Feland jabbed him in the nose, causing a blood vessel to rupture. He'd fallen back onto the floor near his wife. Before he could get up, Feland straddled the man and beat his face until his knuckles were bloody and his arm had started to tire.

Letting out a sigh, Feland stood up, stepped outside, and casually closed the door, then returned to the car. Jamie had asked him what happened when he saw the blood on his hands but Feland told him not to worry and that everything would be okay from now on. That was ten years ago.

'How much exactly?' Feland said now, needing the details.

Jamie glanced up. 'Nineteen thousand, six hundred.'

Feland frowned, pivoted on his heels, and went over to the huge living room bay window. The grass outside was cut like a golf green and the flowers running down either side to the front wall wouldn't have looked out of place at the Chelsea Flower Show.

He turned back to Jamie, who was looking down at something on his phone.

'It seems we are short, Jamie.'

Jamie glanced up, lowering his phone to give him his full attention. When it came to business and money, Jamie knew Feland was very serious. If he thought his men weren't listening to him and not taking things as seriously as he was, there'd be unpleasant consequences.

Jamie had seen it first-hand two years ago when Feland questioned one of his men about money. The man had been skimming the takings. It didn't take long for a thick glass ashtray to collide with the man's face, taking out three of his front teeth. There was blood all over the carpet. Then Feland had ordered him at gunpoint to clean up his own blood. It had taken him hours to get the stains off the white carpet.

Frowning at Feland, Jamie felt his dark eyes burning holes into his skin. 'We're . . . short?'

'Yes, we are. Why is that?'

'I . . . I think . . . we—'

'Spit it out, Jamie, I haven't got all day.'

Jamie coughed, then forced some saliva down his throat before speaking. 'I think something happened last night with one of the boys.'

'Go on . . .'

'He didn't turn up at meeting time.'

'Which one?'

'Mark Greenwell. He was doing the Denes. I've rung him over and over. When I turned up for the money he wasn't there. None of the other lads have seen him either.'

'Done a runner?' Feland asked, tilting his head to one side.

'No, I highly doubt it.'

'Why?'

'He's loyal to me. He's loyal to you. I know he's been punished in the past but he's a good lad now. I trust him. He knows what would happen if he tried anything. All of the lads do.'

Reluctantly, Feland managed a nod. 'Okay. Do me a favour. Find him. Go to his house if you have to. Ask around. We're a few grand short here and, to be honest, there's more money missing than from just one lad. Did anyone else not turn up?'

'Not that I know of. Only Mark from my crew. I'll ask Andy and Leeroy about their lads.'

'Good. Let me know,' Feland instructed.

Jamie stood there for a moment, his gaze falling to the floor.

'What's the matter, young man?' Feland asked from the window, noticing his hesitation.

'Just thinking. Could it be a local firm cleaning up? Pissed off about us selling in their area?'

Anger flashed in Feland's eyes. 'No one would dare do that, Jamie. You know that. No rival gang has the balls to do that to me. So, go ask around about Mark. He must be somewhere.'

Jamie stood immediately and left the room with urgency.

Feland watched him leave then sat down, staring into the fire crackling under the mantelpiece. The orange flames hissed and spat.

From the other side of the room, there was a knock on the door. Feland turned to see a tall, thin man enter. At nearly six foot six, he had very short dark hair, thick eyebrows, and the darkest eyes Feland had ever seen.

'Thomas,' Feland said. 'Come in.'

Thomas ambled over the dark blue carpet and stopped on the thick white rug in the centre of the room. 'Any news?'

Feland informed him about Mark Greenwell not turning up and being a few grand short.

'That isn't good.'

'Yes . . . I'm aware.' Feland sighed, closed his eyes, and turned back to the bay window again.

Thomas moved over to the leather sofa positioned in front of the bay window and lowered himself into it. 'Is there anything you want me to do about it?'

'Wait till Jamie asks around, then we'll see.'

'Just let me know.' Thomas was his go-to guy and had been by his side for a long time. When things got tricky, instead of sorting it himself, he let Thomas deal with it. That's what he paid him for.

Nearly a decade ago, there was a family that had moved up from Manchester: the Peacocks. They were big players in the drug game back in Manchester, but after a few disagreements with some other dangerous families they'd moved up north, choosing Darlington as their new location for business, meaning it didn't take long for Feland to hear about them. They were a big family consisting of a handful of brothers and cousins and started supplying the town with cocaine at a lower price than Feland did, so users stopped getting in touch with Feland's dealers and started buying from the Peacocks.

Feland had to stop it.

With Thomas, they came up with a plan to remove the family from the town so things could go back to the way they had been. It was a tricky operation, but they targeted them all one by one. Thomas, after speaking with people around town, came up with a hitlist. For weeks he watched them carefully, finding out where they lived and the places they liked to go. Thomas took the list of the unlucky thirteen back to Feland, who gave Thomas permission to do his thing.

With his expertise in martial arts, Thomas took them out over the course of a month. He'd break into their houses at night and deal with it however he saw fit.

Cold-blooded.

Not a care in the world.

He was like that, Thomas. When things returned to normal and Feland's enterprise was back up and running, it hadn't taken long for word to get around that Feland was responsible for the disappearance of the thirteen men, but no one could prove it, and no one would testify. In ten years, no one from outside — and definitely not inside — the town had attempted to cross him. His name was known by everyone but spoken by no one.

In recent times, he'd got into property and planning. With high intelligence and careful studying he saw the potential in developing properties to make money in the markets. Selling drugs and beating people up was getting boring. He wanted to expand. So far he owned several shops on High

Row and three pubs. With money being almost no object he was always looking for ways to expand.

'Did you speak to the council?' Thomas asked.

Feland snapped out of his daydream. 'Yes. They won't budge at all. What happens next is down to them. It's their own fault. I'll tell you the plan later.'

'Very well,' Thomas said, getting to his feet. 'Phone me when you need me.'

After Thomas left the room Feland stood up and went to the window, feeling the cold air seep in. He glared at the passing cars out on the road until his phone rang in his pocket.

For the select few that actually knew him, he was known as Jonny Feland, but for years, he'd carried several different passports and driving licenses with other identities to keep his businesses separate. For the incoming phone call, he was the man in charge of Cairnfield Developments.

He answered the phone. 'Yes, Mr Cairn speaking.'

11

Wednesday, late afternoon
Darlington Memorial Hospital Mortuary

'What is that?' Tanzy whispered, leaning closer to the body of Mark Greenwell. The senior forensics, Tallow, and Hope all squinted, absorbing the marks on his back.

Along the length of his back, from the rear of Mark's right shoulder down to his left hip, there were nine long, thin scars, roughly three to four millimetres thick, varying from twelve to eighteen inches in length. Some of the scars appeared fainter and lighter in colour than the others, as if they'd happened a while ago and had healed.

Hemsley pointed to four of the scars. 'Usually scars like these would be older than two years old.'

Several of the scars looked a darker red colour and slightly raised. Hemsley's finger hovered over them. 'Scars like these are newer, maybe a few months old. Would you agree, Laura?' His gaze fell on his assistant.

'Yes, I'd agree,' she replied, carefully studying them.

'But this one—' he indicated to the longest one, roughly eighteen inches long — 'looks a few weeks old at the most.'

'What has caused this?' Tanzy said with a frown. 'They look like whip marks.'

Hemsley pursed his lips. 'I would have to agree with you, Detective.'

'I'm no whipping expert,' Byrd added, 'but I've seen enough films to agree.'

Hemsley ran his gloved palm over the top of the scars, hovering an inch above them. 'It's like some old ritual punishment. I've seen a lot of strange things over the years, but nothing really like this.'

The room suddenly got cold for the detectives. 'A ritual?' Tanzy asked.

Hemsley half nodded, as if it was merely a thought. 'Whoever has done this has known Mark for a while, at least two years.'

'Why only two years?' Byrd asked.

'As I mentioned before—' Hemsley pointed to the older, flatter scars — 'these are at least two years old. They could be older, I simply can't tell, but I do know a scar like this is a process of the skin healing. That process can take up to two years.'

'So, we need to find out who he's been knocking around with. His friends, his associates. We need to speak to his mother too. She might know something. But often teenagers hide things from their parents and have their own secrets that only their friends know. Some secrets, they keep to themselves. Doctor, could this be self-inflicted?'

'I highly doubt it . . .'

'I would also say no,' Hope chipped in. She stepped back a little, raising her left arm high across her body and clenching her own fist, as if holding the handle of a whip. Then she slowly did the motion as if she was whipping herself on the back over her right shoulder. 'Even if this was possible, he wouldn't generate enough speed or power to cause that damage.'

Tanzy squinted a little. 'The speed of a whip can be surprising, though, Emily. Not saying you're wrong with what you're saying, but the speed of the whip itself can be up to thirty times faster than the speed of the handle.'

Byrd frowned at him curiously.

'Watched a few Westerns with my dad, growing up,' Tanzy explained.

Byrd smiled, then glanced back to the body. 'So, apart from the scars on his back and the mortal wound, there's nothing else?'

Hemsley slowly shook his head, then glanced towards the coroner, Peter Gibbs. 'Peter, as this is only a visual, does anything you see here make you believe we require the need for a limited or full post-mortem to be carried out?'

Gibbs studied the body for a moment. 'No. I think regarding the nature of this crime, it's clear to me how he died. The scars on his back indicate something more sinister, but there'd be no pleasure in cutting him open to search for anything else. Keep the body intact.'

'Orion, let's get going,' Byrd said. 'We have a fun-packed day. No doubt, along with everything else, the media will demand a press conference once they get wind of this.'

Tanzy rubbed his neatly trimmed beard and sighed. 'Yeah, no doubt.'

Byrd looked up at Hemsley and his assistant. 'Thank you for your time.' Then to Tallow and Hope: 'We'll catch up with you later back at the station.'

12

Wednesday, late afternoon
Police station

On their way back to the station, the heavens opened, causing the road drains to fill quickly and overflow. Both of them were saturated and couldn't wait to get out of their coats and hang them in the locker room to dry.

Tanzy stopped at DC Leonard's desk. Leonard glanced up, smiling when he saw Tanzy. 'Look a little damp there, boss.'

Tanzy looked through the window at the pounding rain. 'Tell me about it. What did you find at Mark Greenwell's house?' Tanzy grabbed a chair and took a seat.

'Anna gave us a statement about seeing him yesterday before he went out. He hadn't mentioned about what he was doing or who he was seeing, just that he'd be back later.'

'Did you go to his room?'

Leonard plucked his phone from his pocket and found a photo. 'Have a look.'

Tanzy analysed it. On the screen, in the bottom of a wardrobe, three shoeboxes were stacked on top of each other. The lid of the top box had been removed, and, inside, Tanzy could see a large amount of small white bags stacked closely together.

'What was in the boxes below?' Tanzy said.

'The same. Each box was filled with . . . cocaine, I'd guess.'

'Okay, good work,' Tanzy said. 'Looks like an operation, this one.'

'Find anything at the post-mortem?' Leonard enquired.

'We're going to have a meeting very soon, so you'll find out then. In the meantime I'll contact the magistrate for the warrant. Don't mention to anyone about the drugs. Obviously, Weaver will know, but tell no one else.'

Leonard nodded in understanding.

'Good man.' Tanzy patted his shoulder. 'Right, catch up soon.' Tanzy returned to his desk, where a lukewarm coffee was waiting for him on the desk.

'Where've you been?' Byrd said, watching him approach. 'Your coffee's there.'

'Thanks, Max.' After pulling the chair out, he took a seat. 'Talking with Leonard. I need to get a search warrant issued to search the Greenwell's house.'

Byrd knew exactly why. He focused his attention on his computer screen. Behind them, the door to DCI Fuller's office opened.

'You two. In here. I need an update pronto.'

As Tanzy let out a tired sigh, he found Byrd squinting at him. He didn't need to say anything as they both stood up and pushed their chairs in. 'This'll be fun,' said Tanzy.

* * *

'Close the door, please,' Fuller said.

Byrd and Tanzy each took a seat in front of the large, wide desk in front of DCI Fuller. Nothing about the room had changed since DCI Thornton was in charge. The position of the desk, the drawers to the left corner, the shelving to the right. The window on the left still possessed the ageing grey pull-down blind that had seen better days. The only noticeable change was that the certificates Thornton used to have hanging on the wall behind her had gone. Fuller had not put any credentials up yet. Neither Tanzy nor Byrd knew a lot about him, so didn't really know what credentials he had.

Fuller was not tall, not short, but a respectable six foot, a similar height to Byrd. Fuller had wide shoulders and a strong accent. He'd transferred from the West Midlands to replace DCI Thornton. According to rumour, he'd spent a lot of time with the martial arts instructors in his previous role of DCI at West Midlands.

Since taking over two months ago, Fuller had rattled a few cages and hadn't been bothered about upsetting his colleagues along the way. He was old school. Tanzy had discussed his management style with Byrd in the first few days but Byrd told him it is what it is. 'He's our boss, it's his way or no way,' Byrd had said.

'So, what's the score?' said Fuller now. 'I had to shoot off for a meeting with Eckles. He asked me every question under the sun.'

Tanzy told him about what happened at the hospital, about the scars on Mark Greenwell's back.

Fuller raised his chin. 'Interesting. Some kind of punishment?'

'It's possible,' Tanzy replied.

Then Fuller looked at Byrd. 'I want to apologise for earlier, Max. I was harsh with you when you turned up. I didn't expect you until tomorrow. After you told me that you'd cleared it with Judith in HR, that should have been that. Eckles is really on my case at the moment. I think what happened to DCI Thornton has put him under some extreme pressure and he needs me to pull through and keep this town safe. So, I apologise to you, Max.'

Byrd held up a palm and gave a small accepting smile.

'So, what's next?' Fuller asked.

'We need to get a search warrant for Mark Greenwell's house,' Byrd said. 'Finding the drugs and money in his pocket and the possibility this was gang-related gives us enough ammunition to search his bedroom as a minimum. We need to speak with his mother too. It's important we find out about the scars on his back. There's a possibility that she's aware of them, and also a possibility that she isn't. We won't know until we ask her.'

'Also, we need to find out who he's been knocking around with,' Tanzy added. 'For at least two years. The scars that we saw, in the pathologist's opinion, could go back that far. The person responsible for the scars might be the person responsible for his murder.'

Fuller leaned back a few inches. 'Good. Get on it. I've just had word that the media are wanting a press release and Barry Eckles has agreed that for tonight.'

'Tonight?' Byrd frowned.

'He's putting us under as much pressure as possible. He wants to see me crumble. Seven o'clock at Darlington Business Centre on Yarm Road.'

When Fuller said no more, Byrd and Tanzy stood and made their way to the door.

'Oh, by the way . . .'

The detectives turned back.

'Which one of you likes public speaking? Whichever is the best can do the press conference.'

Byrd craned his neck towards Tanzy. 'I did the last one, pal. It's your turn.'

'Great . . .'

13

Wednesday, late afternoon
Police station, conference room

Byrd and Tanzy stood at the front of the large rectangular conference room on the first floor of the station. Seated on the chairs in the centre of the room were DC James Leonard, DC Anne Tiffin, DC Phil Cornty, DS Phil Stockdale, PC Amy Weaver, PC Josh Andrews, PC Donny Grearer, and PC Eric Timms, all positioned in a semicircle. Through the window, they could see it had finally stopped raining but the roads and pathways on St Cuthbert's Way were saturated.

'The boss not sitting in for this one?' PC Cornty asked.

'Not this time . . . unfortunately,' Tanzy replied. 'Fuller is tied up with other cases.'

Everyone smiled for a moment. It appeared DCI Fuller's old-school management techniques had annoyed more people than just Byrd and Tanzy.

'Right,' Byrd said, 'let's make a start.' He used the small black remote in his hand to open up the presentation he'd spent the last twenty minutes putting together about the events of the day so far. The first slide came up, telling everyone the day and date. 'This morning,' he began,

'Anna Greenwell was walking through the park when she came across the body of a teenage male lying in the beck. She knew without a shadow of a doubt that it was her son, Mark. She said he went out last night and never came home. Tallow and Hope found a stash of money and what looked to be cocaine, a Class A drug that many in this town seem to be a little partial to.'

'Not me, sir, I'm a good boy,' PC Cornty chipped in, grinning.

Tanzy briefly smiled but didn't comment on it.

Byrd ignored it and carried on: 'We've sent a number of samples off to the lab to determine what it actually is.' He paused a beat, turned back to the screen and pressed the button on the remote to reveal a photo. 'At the scene Hope found a footprint on the grass which she believes doesn't belong to Mark. She also found several blood droplets too, which she's taken samples of. Chances are that the print could belong to the person who did this.'

'How did the post-mortem go?' asked PC Andrews from the right.

Byrd clicked the remote again. An image of the knife wound came up. 'When Orion and I went to the hospital for the visual,' Byrd went on, 'the pathologist was confident this was a deliberately vicious attack, judging by the way the knife had torn the skin on Mark's throat. Looking at the items found in his pocket, we'd say it could be gang-related. Maybe some pissed-off local dealers not happy. We don't know for sure yet.'

'Has anyone been to his house?' DS Stockdale asked.

Tanzy exchanged a very brief glance with DC Leonard, then focused on Stockdale. 'Leonard and Weaver went to speak with his mother, Anna, to obtain a statement. Due to the items found in his pocket I've requested a warrant to search the house.'

'When will we get it?' Weaver asked.

'Spoken with the magistrates just before this meeting, so I'm hoping quite soon,' Tanzy said.

'Okay.'

Byrd nodded after the question had been answered and pressed the button for the next slide.

'What the hell is that?' Cornty blurted, pointing.

'I'm about to tell you. When Orion and I were at the hospital the pathologist wanted to show us something else, something unusual. These marks were on his back.' Byrd indicated several diagonal lines through the air with his finger. 'They seem to have come from a whip.'

Byrd looked unamused. 'Strange thing is, they all happened at different times. Some, according to the pathologist, are over two years old. Some are fresh, could have happened last week.' His focus fell on PC Cornty. 'Phil, I need you to do some digging on Mark Greenwell. Go back a minimum of two years. Previous jobs, colleges, even his school. Check all of his social media profiles. We need to know who he's been knocking around with.'

Cornty accepted the challenge. 'I'll make a start straight away.'

'Good. Thanks, Phil. Whoever caused this damage to his back could be the person responsible for this.'

'Okay, that's all folk—'

The door opened suddenly. It was Tallow, the senior forensic, with a serious look on his face.

'Jacob?' Byrd said. 'What is it?'

'Results are back from the blood found on the grass at the park. Max, you need to see this.'

14

Byrd exchanged worried glances with Tanzy on their way down the corridor towards the lab. It was clear to see that Tallow was distressed about something. They stepped through the door into the cool room.

'Come and see,' Tallow said, pointing towards Hope, who was sitting at her desk, her focus on the computer in front of her. Tallow pulled the chair out next to her and sat.

'Hey, guys,' she said, a little urgency in her voice.

'Hey, Emily.' Tanzy stopped beside her. 'What do we have?'

She ignored Tanzy and focused on Byrd. 'Max, the results have come back. Have a seat.'

Frowning, Byrd grabbed a chair, dragged it towards the computer, and dropped into it, wondering why she'd addressed him specifically. 'What is it, Emily?'

'DNA from the blood droplets found at the park. We have two sets. Obviously, one is Mark Greenwell's.'

'The other?' Byrd enquired.

'Lyle Wilson,' she said quietly.

Byrd took a lungful of cool air, sighed heavily, and brought his palms up to his face. 'Jesus.'

'Who's Lyle Wilson?' Tanzy asked, not familiar with the name.

Byrd tilted his head back in Tanzy's direction. 'You know my friend Keith?'

'Guy you've known since school?'

Byrd nodded. 'Lyle is his son. About a year ago, Cornty and Weaver caught him shoplifting in town, attempting to walk out of Binns with a handful of T-shirts. Cornty had been notified by the security guard that there was someone acting suspiciously in the store. Cornty and Weaver followed him around the shop, until Lyle walked out with the stuff. Nearly three hundred pounds' worth. Anyway, they searched him and found cocaine on him, along with a load of money. They brought him in. He actually requested to see me to explain himself. He told me that he was sorry for taking the clothes, but the drugs weren't his. He was looking after them for a "friend".'

'Never heard that one before . . .' Tanzy humoured him.

'I did my best for him, but he got four months inside for it.'

'Lucky,' Tanzy said, 'could have got longer.'

'Yeah, I know. Since that happened I haven't spoken with Keith about it. He said I should have done better and got him off. I tried to explain I was the reason he only got four months and not a day more. But like the stubborn old fool he is, he was having none of it.'

'So, Lyle has been out around eight months?'

'Yeah, roughly.'

'Keith not been in touch during that time?'

Byrd shrugged. 'The odd text here and there but nothing more,' Byrd explained, rubbing his chin. 'I haven't seen him in over a year.'

'Just thought I'd let you know first, Max,' Tallow said. 'I've taken it no further. I wasn't sure how you wanted to handle this one.'

'Appreciate that,' Byrd said. 'I'll go speak with Keith. See if Lyle is at home, because at the moment, and it's an awful thought, Lyle Wilson is our prime suspect.' Byrd glanced down at his watch. 'Orion, you better be making a move for the conference. Go do your thing.'

'I'll give you a ring later,' Tanzy replied. 'You taking one of the PCs with you?'

Byrd considered it. 'No, I'll be okay. I need to hear what Keith has to say first and, of course, what Lyle has to say. I need to know why he was at the park last night.'

With that Byrd stood up, thanked Tallow and Hope for their discretion, and left the room.

15

Byrd got out of his car, locked it, and stepped onto the pavement. He looked at Keith Wilson's house, realising it had been a while since he was last there, but even in the dark he could see it still needed some TLC. The paintwork and condition of the windows looked older than Byrd did. The garden was still full of weeds and the grass was nearly a foot tall.

Keith had always been the same. Ever since his wife died three years ago he'd neglected things at home. As a self-employed plumber Keith spent the majority of his time working, often out of town, which meant he needed to set off early and often returned home late. For three years, his son Lyle had, to an extent, been on his own. He'd make his own tea and sort himself out. At nineteen you would expect no less but, since Janice had been diagnosed with breast cancer and died soon after, things between Keith and Lyle had been different. It was clear to most, especially to Byrd, they'd grown apart.

Taking a lungful of cold winter air, Byrd knocked three times on the door, the sound echoing around the silent street. After waiting a minute he tried again.

Although there was a dim light coming from the living room, it was possible Keith could be in the kitchen or upstairs. Byrd pulled his phone out and rang his friend. The automated voice told Byrd that the number was no longer in use.

Byrd tried the handle but it was locked.

From his jacket pocket he grabbed his mini torch and moved away from the door to the side of the house. At the end of the torch's light, along the narrow space between the house and the fence, he could see the gate.

Very quietly, Byrd pressed the latch down and applied a little pressure against the gate, edging it open.

He took a right, slowly cornering the brickwork of the utility extension, his torch sweeping across the area behind the house, briefly highlighting a chair and table set which looked old and stained.

Trying the handle of the back door, Byrd was shocked when it opened. As quietly as possible, he stepped up into the dark utility room and closed the door behind him. He felt the warmth of the central heating and could smell curry coming from the kitchen. He peered around the doorframe but no one was there. The under-cupboard lights were on, shining down on the clustered items on the black worktops. Through the long kitchen he could see the light in the dining room shining on the table underneath it. A mug was positioned next to some paperwork. He turned his torch off.

Before he reached the door he paused, turning his head to the side to listen carefully. Not a sound from anywhere, not even a television or a whispered murmur of conversation from the dining room, living room, or upstairs.

The gurgle of the washing machine draining coming from the utility behind him made him tense, but he recognised the sound and composed himself, then carefully padded forward into the dining room where—

By the time he saw the object coming towards his head it was too late. His legs buckled from under him and he blacked out.

16

Before he got out of the car Tanzy picked up his phone from the passenger seat and found his wife's number.

'Hey, Ori,' she answered softly.

'Hey, Pip. You okay?'

He nonchalantly scanned the car park, eyeing up the handful of people making their way towards the doors of the building's entrance in idle conversation. Several of them had cameras hanging from their necks and a few had notepads in their hands. Bloody reporters.

'Yeah, just sorting the kids,' she said. 'Mam's just left. She bathed them while I made tea. Just finishing the dishes now. Saves you a job for when you get in.'

'Thank you, that's kind.'

'Everything okay, Ori?' she asked, picking up on something in his voice.

'I'm about to stand in front of the press.'

'Oh my God. What happened?'

'Found a seventeen-year-old this morning at the Denes park.'

'How old did you say? Seventeen?'

'Yeah . . .'

'My God.' She fell silent for a few seconds. 'Are you coming home straight after?'

'Yeah, my stomach is rumbling. What's for tea?' He took his eyes off the building's entrance and checked the time on the dashboard: 6.48 p.m.

'Your favourite.'

'Say no more. Hey, listen Pip, I need to go. I'll see you soon.'

He hung up the phone before she replied and looked forward to the spaghetti bolognese that would be waiting when he got home. He unclipped his seat belt, opened the car door, and stepped out into the cold. It wasn't raining but there was moisture in the air that certainly threatened it. As he passed through the sliding entrance doors a man appeared from his right wearing a bland, faded blue uniform and black shoes, raising a hand.

'Can I see some identification please, sir?' His voice was deep, as if he smoked forty a day.

'Sure.' Tanzy reached into the inside pocket of his long grey Parka and pulled out his credentials. The security guard, if that's what he was meant to be, eyed it for a while, as if making the most of the power he possessed. Finally, he moved aside to allow him through.

'Thanks.' Tanzy placed his badge back into his pocket and stepped around him.

'Just go through there, it's starting soon,' the man in blue told him.

Tanzy passed a couple of people scattered in the lobby area, overhearing a young-looking woman speaking with an older man about Mark's murder as he approached the door, where he was stopped by Barbara, a forty-something classy blonde dressed in a tight-fitting blue suit, who recognised him and told him to go straight in.

Things got underway and Tanzy was called up to the podium. His heart was thumping through his chest as he heard the clicking of the cameras. He took a long breath, absorbing it all, trying to remain calm. A conference about a murder was different to a missing person's appeal. He remembered standing in the same position with Ray and Jane Jones when their daughter, Evelyn, went missing over two months ago. Luckily, they'd found her, thank God. But when it was about a murder the damage was done; the hurt had already been caused. And now it was down to the police to not only find out why, but to catch and arrest the person responsible for it.

'Welcome, everyone,' Tanzy started, his voice a little shaky. 'My name is Detective Inspector Orion Tanzy of Durham Constabulary. This morning—'

'Not Detective Inspector Onion, then?' a voice from near the back heckles, to the murmured amusement of others in the crowd.

Ignoring the stupid comment, Tanzy continued: 'This morning the body of a seventeen-year-old, Mark Greenwell, was found in the Denes park, near the Greenbank Road area of Darlington.' He paused for breath. 'The cause of his death was a violent knife attack. His body was found in the beck.'

'Any idea who did this?' The question came from a woman in the second row.

'At this moment, we don't know. We have our suspicions, but we can't comment until we have the evidence to back those suspicions up. With the help of our forensic team we're hoping to come up with some new findings very soon and are currently running DNA tests on some samples of blood we obtained. Once we know more we'll move forward with this investigation.'

'What about cameras? CCTV?' another reporter asked. Tanzy shifted his focus over to the left, where a grey-haired man sat in a black suit, a pen in his hand and a notepad resting on his lap.

'After checking the cameras in the nearby area, it appears they are of no use, unfortunately.'

'Isn't it your job to keep us safe?' A different voice this time. Tanzy scowled over to the familiar face of an eager reporter from the *Northern Echo*.

Tanzy smiled. 'Yes, it certainly is.'

'So, what're the police going to do, then, Detective Inspector?'

'We have made enquiries in the local area, asking people if they saw anything between last night and this morning. We need to speak to his mother again as there's a few issues we need to clear up before moving forward.'

'What issues?' a voice asked near the back. 'Do you think his mother has something to do with this?'

'Come on, Onion, tell us!' a different voice clamoured.

Tanzy felt his face getting warm. 'Issues that won't be discussed at present.'

'What's the mother done to him?'

Tanzy took a deep breath before speaking, knowing he was close to snapping. He hated these things, dealing with these types of people.

'Detective Onion, what's going on in this town?' someone asked, followed by a few laughs that raised smiles on people's face.

Tanzy stood abruptly. 'Our biggest lead is the blood we found near Mark's body. As soon as we know who it belongs to, we can move forward. Thanks for coming.' He'd had enough and walked out of the room.

17

Wednesday, early evening
Willow Road, the Denes

Byrd's eyes flickered open. Attempting to move, he realised he was unable to, as if his muscles didn't work.

'Max . . . en tee . . .' a voice said near his ear then faded out.

A sudden severe pain erupted at side of his head, pounding throbs coming in waves.

'Max?' the voice said, this time clearer. 'Max, is that you?'

Byrd grunted a few times and lifted his left hand to the side of his head, tenderly touching the bruise that was swelling rapidly.

'Jesus . . .' Byrd whispered.

'Max, is that you? God, Max, what are you doing here?'

'Keith?' Byrd asked, his eyes still closed.

'Yeah mate, it's me. Let . . . let me help you.' Byrd felt firm hands grab his left arm and slowly pull him up to a sitting position.

'Jesus, my head . . .' Byrd sighed heavily, the throbs worsening.

'I wouldn't have done that if I'd known it was you.' Keith kept hold of his arm to steady him.

Finally opening his eyes, he saw Keith standing in front of him, wearing a black T-shirt and red shorts. He had no socks on. 'What did you hit me with, a bloody baseball bat?'

'A cricket bat actually.'

'Thanks . . .'

'Listen, I'm sorry about that. I noticed someone's outline through the blinds here—' he pointed to his right at the window — 'and instinct took over. I didn't recognise you.'

Byrd smiled briefly, still touching the side of his head.

'Just a bruise, Max, nothing a tough copper like you can't shake off.' Keith looked at him up and down. 'You've lost a few pounds haven't you?'

Byrd peered up at him, his face wincing in pain. 'Two stone. Well, almost two stone.'

'You look great, you really do.' Keith stood up and went to the sink, poured a glass of water, then brought it over to Byrd. 'Drink this, might help.'

'Thanks,' he said, taking a sip.

'How come you're here?' Keith asked.

'I think we better sit down.'

'Let me help you.' Keith guided Byrd up and aided him to the kitchen table.

'I need to speak with Lyle. Is he in?'

The frown on Keith's face deepened. 'Lyle? No, he isn't, I haven't seen him all day. Why do you need to speak with him?'

Byrd waited a few seconds, managed to lower his hand from his head and turned towards his friend. 'You hear about the murder down in the Denes this morning?'

Keith nodded several times, leaning back on his chair. 'I . . . did.'

'Well, there were traces of Lyle's blood at the scene, Keith. My forensic team came to me first with it. No one else knows about it. Out of respect to you and him, I needed to speak with him first before reporting it. I need to know why his blood is there.'

Keith let out a long sigh.

'What is it?'

'He didn't come home last night,' Keith explained. 'We had an argument about something stupid and he stormed out around eight o'clock. It was eleven before I went to bed, but I figured he'd get home later than that anyway, so I didn't wait up for him. I sent him a text telling him I loved him. When I woke up this morning, he wasn't here. He's probably pissed off at me.'

Byrd hesitated for a moment. 'What was the argument about?'

'About his mother. Well, not really. It ended with me telling him he needed to clean up his act, start doing his bit around the house. We started swearing at each other and he left, slamming the door on his way out. My fault really, it started over his dirty underwear on the stairs. Then, as things normally do, they escalated.'

'And he hasn't been back today?'

Shaking his head, Keith said, 'No.'

'Is he still working for that builder?'

'Yeah, yeah, he's still on with him. Nearly qualified, so looking forward to the pay increase.'

'I bet.' Byrd paused a brief moment. 'Listen, Keith, I think Lyle could be in some serious trouble here. I really need to talk to him.'

'I could ring him?'

'Please.'

Keith grabbed his phone from his pocket, unlocked it, and found his son's number.

'It just rings then goes to voicemail. I'll try again.' Silence passed, then: 'Voicemail again.'

'Who does he knock around with?'

'There's a lad called Simmo . . . or Simon. Don't know how he says it. Lives somewhere on Greenbank Road. Another lad is called Liam H. Don't know his second name, or where he lives. They often hang around the park. Drinking, smoking, that kinda thing.'

'Okay. Does Lyle use any drugs, Keith?'

Keith shrugged. 'Not under this roof he doesn't, Max. But what he does when he's out, I can't say for certain.'

'You don't seem too concerned.'

He shrugged again. 'I have enough to deal with keeping this house going, Max. He's big boy, he can make his own decisions.'

'Is there anything that could help me find him?'

It was a difficult situation, but Keith obviously realised that all Byrd was doing was his job, so he tried again, but his son's phone rang until it reached voicemail. Keith shook his head.

'If you wouldn't mind, could I have his number? It's so important I speak to him. Forensics will have to report it tomorrow at the latest and he'll be our prime suspect in this murder enquiry if I can't rule him out before that.'

Keith sighed slowly and reluctantly provided Byrd the number.

Byrd stood wearily, feeling the effects from the blow to his head. 'I'll look for him. He can't be far. Let me know when he comes home or if he contacts you. He doesn't have long, Keith, until the whole of the station knows.'

Keith smiled sadly.

Byrd turned, made his way through the kitchen towards the back door.

'Max?'

Byrd backed up a little. 'Yeah?'

'Sorry about the head,' Keith said, sincerely.

Byrd stepped into the cold night and closed the door. Once he was back inside the car, he mentally calculated where in the park Keith was referring to, then put his gear in first and edged out into the road.

Almost a minute later, Byrd stopped his car on Surtees Street, close to where the body of Mark Greenwell had been found earlier that morning. He opened the door, got out, and briefly looked through the metal railings down into the pitch-black park. He couldn't see anyone or hear anything, but there was a faint smell of cannabis coming from somewhere.

From inside his coat, he grabbed his phone and his mini Maglite, then dialled the number Keith had given him. It rang and rang and rang until it reached voicemail. He dialled again in frustration and let it ring. He was approaching the part of the stream where Mark Greenwell had been found face down earlier.

Somewhere up ahead he heard quiet footsteps and near-inaudible whispers he couldn't make out. Knowing the park, he knew teenagers hung around at the play area where the swings and climbing apparatus were on the other side of the stream, so assumed they were coming from over there.

Gingerly, he made his way down the path.

He stopped dead when he heard it.

'What . . . ?' he said, turning round.

The sound of a song was coming from somewhere. To the left, the direction of the beck. He pulled the phone away from his head and listened carefully. Some kind of pop song. Something familiar.

The call went to voicemail. He disconnected and phoned again. Reaching where he'd stood earlier in the day with Tanzy, he focused on the stream, hearing the tranquil, gently flowing water moving along. Slowly padding down the bank he dug the soles of his shoes hard into the grass to reduce the chance of slipping and searched the area. The music grew louder the closer he got to the water.

'Where is it coming from?' he whispered, feeling like he was on to something.

He reached the water's edge and shone his powerful light into the stream, the brilliant beam highlighting a handful of tiny fish swimming in multiple directions. Moving the light across the water, he pointed it at the lengthy tufts of grass on the opposite side. When he saw movement he stiffened a little, hearing something scurry off into the grass. His heart was racing. The music was very close, the song now something he recognised. A remix of 'Dancing in the

Moonlight'. Hated the original but didn't mind this version. He moved to the left—

Crack. The sound of something under his foot. He bent down, picked up the ringing phone, saw his number on the screen with an option to answer or end the call.

'Shit,' he said. It was good he'd found the phone but not good that Lyle wasn't with it.

He ended the call and put his own phone away, then noticed there'd been umpteen missed calls and countless messages. On the lock screen, he saw a text message from Keith. It read: *I'm sorry Lyle. I love you man x*

The text message hadn't been opened, meaning Lyle had probably been without his phone since sometime last night. Byrd thought hard, wondering how forensics hadn't discovered it earlier. Or was the phone placed here between sometime this morning and now to make it appear Lyle was involved? Either way, it worried Byrd, discovering the phone right here where they'd found Mark Greenwell earlier that morning. In Byrd's mind, Lyle could have murdered Mark Greenwell for whatever reason and fled the scene, accidently losing his phone in the process, making him the prime suspect of this investigation. It certainly was believable Lyle mixed in these circles. Or perhaps it was something else — what if Lyle had done no wrong and was another innocent victim? After all, his blood had been found here.

Either way, something very bad had happened.

'Where the hell are you, Lyle?' he asked, looking out into the empty darkness.

18

Wednesday night
Edward Street, Albert Hill Industrial Estate, Darlington

Sitting in the car alone, the man checked the time on the dashboard: 8.46 p.m. His wife wouldn't be getting worried because he'd told her he was going round a friend's house for a catch-up, so he had a few hours before she'd expect him home.

The video playing on his phone had just finished. It was the sixth time he'd watched it on the *Northern Echo* website and he was satisfied he was safe. The detective standing at the podium, Orion Tanzy, didn't seem to know much about what was happening. So far, the police had nothing on him. The only worry was he'd cut his lip when he'd attacked Mark Greenwell, and feared he'd left traces of blood at the scene. Earlier that morning, his wife had asked him what happened to his lip but he said he couldn't remember, unable to explain the blood on his pillow

He sighed, locked the phone, threw it down on the passenger seat, and stared out across the small road, eagerly watching an old-looking man at unit 17 tinkering with something inside. The unit itself never had a sign on, so he didn't know if it was a business, but the man was dressed in red overalls covered in black oil. The harsh, cold light inside shone down on an array of car parts and boxes.

Minutes later, the man in the overalls pulled down the shutters, the clattering sound disturbing the silence, and the area became dark. After securing the padlock, the old man padded over to a brown truck that looked like it should have been scrapped in the eighties. The truck took three attempts to start before the rear lights finally stayed on and the ancient engine rumbled. The truck reversed then painfully crept away from unit 17 towards Cleveland Street, leaving the space to plummet into darkness.

This was a good place.

It was out of the way. No streetlights or cameras.

'At last,' the man whispered. He tipped his head back, thinking about his daughter. He wasn't a mean person. He was a kind, gentle individual who'd do anything for anyone. It was hard to accept what had happened to her and he'd almost moved on. But knowing now who was responsible, no one was going to stand in his way.

After weeks of research he'd come up with a list. It wasn't random. The individuals on the list were there because they deserved to be, and he'd feel not one ounce of regret until he finally got the man responsible for what had happened.

Smiling, he turned his head to look at the teenager on the back seat, lying down with duct tape over his mouth, his hands and legs both tied behind his back. He glared up at him with fear, not knowing what was to come. It was time to play.

'Let's have some fun, shall we, Lyle?' the man whispered.

19

Tanzy pulled up outside his semi-detached house. The front of the house was covered in a thin film of frost which glistened under a nearby streetlight, making it look almost magical. A castle from one of Jasmine's reading books. The living room curtains were closed but a light was on. Upstairs, he noticed both Eric's and Jasmine's bedroom lights were on, meaning they were still awake.

Grabbing his phone, he found Byrd's number and pressed CALL.

'Ori,' Byrd answered.

'Hey, Max.'

'How'd it go?'

'Not the best,' Tanzy noted. 'Got hounded by the press. Some awkward people out there, you know.' He sounded tired.

'You know what people are like, just doing their job. Hopefully, someone comes forward with something.' Byrd fell silent for a moment, then: 'Went to see Keith about Lyle . . .'

'Speak with Lyle?'

'I wish I had, would've made up for the cricket bat to the side of the head.'

'What?'

Byrd filled him in, telling Tanzy that Keith had knocked him out and then told him he hadn't seen Lyle since the night before.

'After I left Keith's, I headed to the Denes. According to Keith, Lyle likes to hang around there drinking with his mates.'

'Same place Mark was found?'

'Yeah,' Byrd replied. 'Keith gave me Lyle's number. When I got close to the stream where Mark's body was found, I phoned it and heard it ringing. It's strange because I don't know how Tallow or Hope missed it, to be honest. So, what I'm assuming here is one of two things. One: Lyle was involved in Mark's murder. Maybe they had a fight, and he dropped his phone when he fled.

'Second thing?'

'Mark was with Lyle at the time and someone attacked them both. The suspect killed Mark, leaving him in the stream, and took Lyle.'

Tanzy thought for a moment. 'Interesting theory. Would have been the work of two people, I'd guess. Have you got the phone? Lyle's phone?'

'Yeah, I'm back in the car now. I picked it up with gloves and bagged it. The phone is locked. I've tried a few combinations — I'll get digital forensics to have a crack.'

'Take it to Keith. He might know it.'

'I don't want to panic him just yet,' Byrd confessed. 'It's early stages.'

'Teenagers don't just leave their phones anywhere,' Tanzy said.

Byrd had to agree with him.

'What pin combinations have you tried?'

'A few.'

'Try one one one one,' Tanzy suggested.

Byrd removed the phone from the bag. 'Ori, I don't think . . .' Byrd keyed in the number. 'What . . . ? How did—'

'You in?'

'Yeah, I'm in. How did you . . . never mind.'

'See if there's a Mark Greenwell in his contacts.'

Byrd went quiet for a moment. 'Hold on . . . There's a Mark G.'

'Good start. Now click on that number and it should show the recent communications between them. Phone calls and text messages. Usually.'

'Both,' Byrd said. 'Last phone call was 7 p.m. last night, Ori.'

'What did the last text say?'

'Hold on . . . I can barely work this thing.'

'Old people and technology . . .'

After a long moment, Byrd told him the last message had been sent yesterday just before 6 p.m.

'What did it say?'

'It says, *On the green tonight?*'

'The green,' Tanzy repeated, deep in thought. 'By the green, he could mean the park. Is he selling on the green. Sounds like they could be a part of a little operation here. Did Lyle reply to that?'

'He texted back saying, *Yeah.*'

Silence grew between them and Tanzy knew Byrd well enough to know what he was thinking. 'I know you don't want to hear this, Max, but I think he was a part of something big.'

'I'll ring DFU,' Byrd said abruptly.

'You think digital forensics will be open this late?'

'I overheard Mac say he was staying late tonight, so I'll see if he's looked at Mark's phone. What if Mark G isn't Mark Greenwell?'

'Only one way to find out, Max.'

'Let you know what I find,' Byrd said, then hung up.

20

Wednesday night
Low Coniscliffe, outskirts of Darlington

Byrd hung his long black coat on the bottom of the stairs and took off his shoes, placing them in the new shoe rack that Claire had bought last week. Usually, Byrd left his shoes wherever he liked but things had changed now. The place needed a woman's touch and that's exactly what Claire was going to give it.

'Hey, you!' she said as he entered the kitchen.

Smiling, he made his way over and kissed her. 'Missed you today.'

'You too,' she replied, hugging him. 'Thanks for abandoning me and letting me unpack the clothes and do all the washing.'

Byrd picked up on the humour in her tone, gave her a smile, and moved over to the right to grab one of his favourite mugs — the one that Tanzy bought him last year that said, *I'm never wrong . . .*

'You want one?'

She nodded. 'How was your day? Happy to be back?'

'Phenomenal to be back . . .'

They shared a laugh. Then Byrd told her briefly what had happened at the park earlier that morning after the body of Mark Greenwell had been found.

'Yeah, Alice rang me asking if I knew anything about it.'

Byrd smiled. 'Women and gossip, eh?'

Claire shrugged and noticed the mark on the side of his head.

'What on earth is that?' She placed the basket of damp clothes on the side and went over. He then explained about the blood results coming back from the murder scene. How it matched up with his friend's son, Lyle Wilson, and that he'd gone to his house and his father, Keith, had used his head as a cricket ball.

'Your own fault for sneaking around in other people's houses,' she mused, then frowned at it. 'It does look bad.'

'It's throbbing, but I'll live.'

'How come you're so late, anyway?'

After explaining he'd gone to the park where the body of the teenager was found this morning, he told her he'd found Lyle's phone.

'Have you spoken to Keith about what you've found?'

Byrd moved over to the table and dropped into a chair. 'It's too soon. I don't want to panic him just yet.'

'Maybe he has a right to know. It's his son.' She curled her lip in thought. 'Where's Lyle's phone?'

'At the station,' he said. 'I dropped it off for digital forensics to have a good look at it. There's loads of messages and phone calls on it. There's communication between Lyle and the teenager who was found dead too. Could have been friends.'

She gave a sad smile and padded over to him. He leaned in and held her for a few moments, saying nothing. In her pocket, her phone vibrated.

'Oh, that'll be Alice.' She unlocked it and read the message. 'What's she wanting?'

'To come over tomorrow for a few glasses of wine.' Claire's eyes fell on Byrd's stare. 'That is okay, isn't it? Jesus, sorry, I never asked you—'

'Hey, you live here now. This is your house too,' he reassured her.

'We'll stay in the living room, out the way,' she said, leaning over and kissing him. 'Thanks.'

Claire had met Alice at her Zumba classes which she'd gone to for nearly a year now. Having much in common, Claire had been out with her a few times around the town in the last six months and they'd been to each other's houses for coffee. Alice worked in town at Barclays Bank as a customer support assistant.

Although Byrd had seen the pictures of them both on social media, he'd not met Alice yet. Most of his time was spent working and occasionally playing football, and he didn't do much else. Over two months had passed since Byrd, Claire, Tanzy, and Pip had been out for a meal, but it had felt longer for Byrd.

'Your tea is on there,' she said, knowing he'd be hungry. As she reached the door with the basket of washing, she turned back. 'Max, we should all do something together. Me, you, Alice, and Alex. She says he gets bored on a night and doesn't really do a lot. In fact, I think he plays football.'

Byrd raised his eyebrows. 'Does he?'

'Think so. Apart from that, though, he doesn't get out a lot. It'll be good for us to do something. Alice tells me he wants to meet you. They went walking in the Lakes last year, so I suggested maybe us four going together at some point. What you think?'

Byrd had seen pictures of Alex on social media too. Claire said he was nice but that he seemed a little lonely. She'd said his life had changed since he left the army last year, and working from home doing his business analysis stuff was okay, but it wasn't fulfilling him like the army days did. According to Alice, anyway.

'What do you think?' Claire asked again, tilting her head to one side, her straight black hair falling over her right shoulder.

Byrd grinned. 'Sounds good. We'll sort something.'

'I've planned to do something this weekend,' she said, smiling as she left the kitchen. 'Saturday night at Uno Momento in town.'

He went over to the plate of cheesy pasta and put it in the microwave, closed the door, set a timer, and stood waiting while it whirred. Staring at nothing, he realised he was focusing on the photograph on the opposite wall, just next to the door. He edged away from the worktop and went to it. It was A4-sized, the colours vivid and bright. The two people on it were both smiling, their teeth perfectly white and bright, even if he knew they were false.

Ignoring the microwave ping behind him, he looked into their eyes as they stared back with happiness into the lens of the camera. 'I miss you guys so much. Love you, Mam and Dad.'

21

Wednesday night
Brougham Street

Mandy Spencer stood at her nine-year-old's bedroom door watching him drift off to sleep. Everything about tonight had been great and, most importantly, Damien had really enjoyed himself. During his parents' evening, his teacher at school, Mrs Everitt, had told her that Damien was doing very well, topping the class in most of his subjects. For a treat he had chosen ham-and-pineapple pizza, which wasn't Mandy's favourite, but that didn't matter.

Once he was asleep, she pulled the door to, leaving it open an inch to allow the light on the landing to get in. She paused just outside his room when a worrying thought returned. Deciding she needed to tell someone, she took out her phone and dialled the number.

After four rings, Tracy Clarke picked up. 'Mand, you all right?'

'Hey, Tracy,' she said, slowly descending the stairs. 'I'm okay. Listen, I forgot to tell you something earlier, but when I came back to my desk, you'd gone home.'

'What?'

'Mr Cairn rang again today.'

'I don't see why he keeps ringing.'

'I know,' Mandy said, 'I've told him we've done all we can to persuade the council to sell him the car parks, but he won't have it. I think because we've helped him out in the past, he's expecting us to do it again.'

'We can only do what we can do, Mandy . . .'

'I know.' Mandy paused a beat, reaching the kitchen. 'I just think things are getting . . . out of control.'

'Why?'

'When I got back to my car there was another note on the back window. Same as the one from yesterday. It said if he doesn't get what he wants, something bad will happen.'

Tracy sighed heavily. 'Did you check the cameras when you found the first note yesterday?'

'I spoke with Roger, the security guard. He checked the cameras, but I was parked in a blind spot. We saw no one. Same again tonight.'

'Think we should ring the police?'

'I don't know. That's two notes within two days now. I'm assuming it's coming directly from Mr Cairn but there's no way of proving it. I suppose if we told the police and explained what was going on, then they could go and speak with him.'

Tracy mulled over her words. 'I suppose.'

'Henry seemed a little off today, I thought.'

'How do you mean?'

'Seemed quiet, not quite himself, as if there was something on his mind. He's usually talkative and smiley but today was the first time in however long I've known him that he's been a little . . . strangely subdued. And he left a few hours early too.'

'Told me he was taking his son to the doctor's. Thinks he has a problem with his heart. Says when he sleeps at night, he watches him, and sometimes Eddy doesn't breathe for up to a minute.'

'God, I hope he doesn't have what Damien has, it's awful,' Mandy admitted.

'Remind me of Damien's condition, Mandy?'

'Congenital heart disease. He takes tablets twice a day to thin his blood so it can reach his heart properly. Even with them, running around can be a struggle. It'll be like that for ever. But hey, that's life.'

'Bless him,' Tracy said, softly. 'Melissa loves Damien. They sit next to each other in class, don't they? Mel says he's very clever. She's even admitted to copying some of his work, the cheeky little thing.'

'I bet Damien lets her too — think he has a crush on her.'

They shared a laugh, then Tracy said, 'Think Eddy and Damien will have to fight it out. Henry says Eddy follows her around all day.'

'The three of them are cute together, aren't they?'

'They are,' Tracy replied. 'So, what are you going to do about Cairn?'

'If he rings again tomorrow, I'll explain that the next stage is contacting the police about the letters. Maybe he'll leave it at that.'

'Remember the trouble last year with that property developer? Sending emails and calling us all the time? He left notes on our cars too, didn't he?'

'I remember.'

'So it wouldn't be the first time we've been threatened.'

'And he turned up at the office with a spade! As if he was going to start the work himself without any approval.'

'Let's hope that doesn't happen again. Oh, hold on . . .' said Tracy.

'What is it, Trace?'

'I've just heard the letterbox. Weird.' Tracy pulled the phone away from her ear. 'Melissa, is that you?'

'What's happening?' Mandy asked.

Tracy brought the phone closer. 'I've just heard the letterbox go. Melissa's upstairs in bed. Murphy's working. Why would someone be at the door at this time?' She went to the door. 'It's a note.'

'A note?'

'Yeah — hold on.' Tracy unfolded it and gasped when she read the words.

'What does it say?' Mandy asked.

'*You're too late. Time to face the consequences.*'

22

Wednesday night
Darlington

Thomas stepped into Jonny Feland's living room, feeling the heat from the open fire to the left. Feland sat comfortably on the three-seater sofa in the centre of the room, his focus on the huge flatscreen television in the corner resting on an expensive-looking wooden cabinet, close to the fire. To his right, through the large bay window, he could see the long garden and the quiet road at the end of it, well-lit from the bright street lamps scattered along it.

On the screen there was a news report about the death of Mark Greenwell. A local detective, Detective Inspector Orion Tanzy, was being hounded by reporters, asking him what the police were going to do. For once Feland felt like he was on the same side as the police, as he too needed to know what happened to Mark.

Thomas stopped at the sofa, dropped down near Feland, and focused on the screen. 'He's not a bad-looking bloke,' Thomas said, pointing to DI Tanzy.

'He's your type, isn't he?'

Thomas nodded sombrely. Rarely a smile found his lips, and Feland could probably count on one hand how many times he'd heard Thomas laugh in the years he'd employed him.

'Have you finalised the plan?' Thomas asked, eagerly.

'Ah, straight to business, Thomas, I like that,' Feland said, standing and going over to a large, wide dark oak unit in the corner. From one of the higher shelves Feland pulled out a file, then went back to the sofa and dropped it on Thomas's lap.

For a few minutes, Thomas, with focused eyes, studied the three separate pages.

'Who are these people?'

'These, my friend, are people that haven't done their job properly, and will now be punished. These people will learn from their mistakes and will face the consequences of their actions, or in this case, their inaction.'

Thomas nodded silently.

'Can you do it?'

'Of course.' Thomas's eyes narrowed for a moment. 'Have you spoken with Jamie or Andy about what happened with Mark yet?'

Just as Feland was about to reply, Jamie entered the room carrying three shoeboxes.

'Speak of the devil!' Feland shouted.

Jamie came over to the sofa and placed the shoeboxes next to Feland. 'Mark Greenwell's stash. I've been over to his place to get it.'

Feland's eyes narrowed. 'You didn't go hurting anyone, did you?'

'I put something in his mam's wine, waited a while till it knocked her out. Then went in, got the gear.'

'Impressive.' He glanced down at the boxes. 'All full?'

Jamie nodded towards him, in a *see for yourself* kind of way. Feland lifted the lid from the top box and saw the small bags of white powder. 'Good lad.'

'I spoke with Andy earlier. He said that Lyle Wilson never turned up last night either. Said he didn't go to the house on Craig Street.'

'He didn't?' Feland frowned again.

Jamie shook his head. 'No, he didn't. I'll go to his place and—'

Feland held up a palm. 'Leave it for now, we have bigger things going on.' He indicated the file on Thomas's lap and, immediately, Jamie understood.

'Need any help with it?' Jamie asked Thomas.

Thomas shook his head. 'I'll be just fine.' With that, he stood up and walked out of the room with the file in his hand.

* * *

It had been over twenty-four hours since Lyle Wilson had been seen by his father, Keith, or by any of his friends.

A rope hung from a securely fixed hook in the ceiling of the small unit in Albert Hill, holding him up by his wrists. Although he still had the ability to stand on his tiptoes, his legs were tired, causing him to bend every so often, putting massive pressure on the rope gouging into his wrists, causing them to bleed.

'What the fuck do you want with me?' he cried.

'Isn't it strange,' the man said, almost as quiet as a whisper, 'that when you put people in vulnerable positions, they see things differently?'

Lyle frowned at him, distracted by the pain coming from his bloody wrists.

'You see these people strutting around so confidently, like they own everything, like they possess some magical invincibility?'

Lyle didn't answer him.

The man prodded Lyle's chest so hard his fingernail nearly pierced the skin. 'You are one of them.'

Lyle cried out in agony.

'You, Lyle fucking Wilson,' the man went on, his voice stern and filled with a calm, frightening anger, 'walk around that park like you own it. You pick on young, vulnerable teenagers, almost forcing them to buy your drugs.'

Lyle didn't say a word. Instead, he looked away.

'Hey!' the man shouted. 'Look at me when I'm speaking. You're not dealing with kids at the park tonight. You're here with me, hung up from a rope. And your answer to my next question will determine if you leave here alive or dead. It's your choice.'

Lyle felt more focused than he had since he'd first been strung up. 'I don't understand.'

The man came within an inch of Lyle's face, his warm breath on his skin. Lyle stared into the man's serious eyes.

'You want to know what the question is?'

'Yes . . .'

'Okay,' the man said, turning away from Lyle. From the shelving unit over to the right he picked up a pair of scissors, opened and closed them a few times, so Lyle could hear and see clearly what they were. When he saw the blades reflect the light on the ceiling, his eyes widened and his heart rate multiplied.

'What are you—'

'Shh, Lyle, it's not time to answer the question just yet.'

The man brought the scissors up to his face, then he opened the blade and snapped them shut quickly. Lyle edged back, causing the man to burst out in laughter.

'It's warm in here, isn't it?'

Lyle frowned. It was freezing. The man brought the scissors close to his face again. Lyle watched the small, sharp blades carefully, not knowing what the man intended to do with them. Lyle edged back and quickly brought his tied feet up in an attempt to kick the man, but he saw it coming and moved out of the way. The pain in his wrists made him cry out. He couldn't try that again.

'Oooo, that's it. A little fight in you. Good.' The man placed the scissors in his left hand and punched him hard in the gut with his right, causing Lyle's body to bend in agony. 'Try that kick again, I dare you.'

Winded, Lyle took quick, tight breaths to deal with the blow.

The man took hold of the bottom of the hoodie. Then, using the scissors, he started slicing into the material, cutting upwards until he reached his throat. The hoodie fell open.

'Are you a little cooler now?'

Lyle was too afraid to answer, not knowing where this was going. He thought about trying to kick him again, but his wrists were pouring with blood now. The man used the scissors to cut all of his clothes off, leaving him naked.

Lyle started to cry. He'd never felt so defenceless in his whole life.

'Aw, what's the matter, little Lyle?' The man leaned closer, whispering in his ear, 'It isn't nice, is it? Can you imagine taking so many drugs you end up taking off all your clothes and going outside at two in the morning? Then, when your friends are looking for you, they find you in a park, dead?'

Lyle wasn't following the man's words.

'Lyle! Focus! You know what makes it worse?' the man said. 'It's that you don't even know what I'm talking about, do you?'

Quivering, Lyle shook his head a few times, then his eyes rolled back into his head for a moment. The thin slugs of blood had reached his armpits. He was losing blood quicker now, the cuts on his wrists becoming deeper and wider.

'Stay with me, young man,' the man told him firmly.

For a short intense moment, his attention returned after the man slapped his face a few times. Then he gave him one final slap and asked him a very particular question.

'If you had the choice to start again, which one would you choose? Option A or Option B. Option A, you get into drug dealing and realise it isn't for you. You walk away from it and lead a hard-working innocent life. Or Option B, you get drawn into the life of drugs and selling it and think, hey, I'm making so much money here, I'm going to continue to do it, not caring if you hurt others along the way, as long as you have the fancy watches and the nice cars.'

Lyle's eyes narrowed. 'Option A . . . A. I choose A.'

The man tilted his head and smiled. 'Good answer. Because of your answer, Lyle, I'm going to let you go. '

Sighing with relief, Lyle closed his eyes for a few seconds, exhausted.

The man went over to the shutters and flicked the light off, the cold garage becoming pitch black. Lyle, unable to see a thing, grunted in fear.

'Calm down. Hold on,' the man said softly.

Then a loud continuous mechanical sound erupted to Lyle's left. A sliver of moonlight entered, allowing the teenager to see his feet. The garage door opened fully and he felt exposed, standing with his hands tied above his head, naked.

'I'm going to release your wrists, Lyle. If you try anything I'll stab you in the throat. Do you understand?'

Lyle nodded.

The man cut the rope and Lyle tumbled to the damp icy ground in a heap. The freezing ground hit his skin, but he didn't care. He was happy to be free, and not hung up like some helpless pig.

'Okay, young man,' the man said. 'You can go.'

Without even looking for his clothes he dashed out of the unit, took a right towards Cleveland Street. Somewhere behind him he heard the mechanical hum of the garage door chatter away but he couldn't see anything.

Then he heard another sound.

A car door closing.

Naked and desperate to get away he took a left, his bare feet slapping off the concrete, in the hope he'd soon see a passing car.

Nearly fifty metres down the road, he heard a car somewhere behind him.

Fast, sharp breaths left his lungs as he turned, waving his hands in the air, beyond caring he was naked and covered in blood.

The car coming from the direction of the railway bridge approached fast, then slowed, the driver spotting him from a distance. Seconds later, with his hands waving in the air, a relieved smile grew on Lyle's face as he observed the vehicle slowing. It looked to be a four-by-four, quite high and wide. He wasn't sure of the make, but the colour could have been blue.

'Thank God,' he panted. His body trembled so much, even breathing was difficult.

The four-by-four slowed. Then very suddenly the engine roared and the vehicle surged forward, picking up speed as the driver manoeuvred onto the path towards him.

With wide, terrified eyes, Lyle watched the vehicle speed towards him. Then, with a thud, he bounced off the fast-moving bonnet, high into the air. He landed on the road a few metres beyond the car with a sickening crunch.

The driver stopped the car, casually got out, and closed his door. Glancing around, he walked briskly to the front of the car and observed the quivering, bloody figure on the ground. Lyle's body was mangled, distorted. There was a new pool of blood appearing between his head and the road. The man grinned widely.

'You chose the right option, but I don't believe you meant it, Lyle,' the man whispered, his cold words fading in the gentle winds. He leaned over, picked up Lyle, and put him in the boot of his car, then drove away.

23

Parked up at the side of the road, Thomas sat patiently in his car. For the twenty-six minutes he'd been there, he'd focused on the red door of the house about a third of the way up the street. He'd checked over the file that Feland had given him last night and been through it so many times, he'd memorised every word.

It would only be a matter of time. The boy was running later than usual today. Probably getting his school bag ready.

The road was covered in a fine coating of ice from the sub-zero temperatures that Darlington had endured overnight. Although the sun was trying its best to rise, a cluster of thick black clouds covered it, leaving the street in a chilly grey mist.

The time on the dashboard was 8.23 a.m.

The red door opened. A small boy walked out and turned to his short, blonde-haired mother, who leaned over and kissed him. Once he pulled the rucksack higher onto his shoulder, he stepped down onto the path.

It was a shame the mother didn't know that would be the last time she'd get to do that. The boy casually started trotting up the street in the direction of North Park, the small keyrings attached to his zip clinking with each small stride he took.

The man put the car into first gear and edged out slowly, then crawled along at a steady 7 mph.

Through the windscreen he saw the boy take a left down the alley between Brougham Street and Zetland Street.

Thomas increased the speed of the car until he reached the alley, then slowed, taking the left. The boy was dawdling ahead, halfway down the alley between Brougham street and Zetland Street, and turned when he heard the car's tyres on the cobbles behind him. Seeing the car, he kept to the left so it could pass safely.

But the car never passed.

Thomas lowered the passenger side window. 'Hey, Damien.'

The boy frowned at him, his young brain trying to work out where he'd seen the man before.

'Mrs Everitt has asked me to pick you up.'

'My teacher?' A heavy scowl ran across the top of the boy's eyes.

'Yeah. You want to jump in, and I'll take you from here? It's freezing out there.'

'I . . . it's just up there, I'm okay walking,' he replied, pointing towards the school.

'It's no trouble, honestly. I'm going that way anyway. We have a lot of fun things planned for the class today.'

A puzzled look came on the boy's face. He studied Thomas with caution. Damien was highly intelligent for his age and observed everything about the man. Short black hair. Skin which looked like it had been bronzed by a few days in the sun. Thick, black eyebrows over the top of dark brown eyes.

'Who . . . who are you? I've never seen you before,' Damien said.

'I'm the assistant teacher today. My name is Mr Simms. I've just actually knocked on your door, but your mother said you'd started walking and that it would be okay to catch you up.'

'You spoke to my mum?'

'Yeah.'

'What does my mum look like?' he asked.

'She has blonde hair and today she's wearing a white blouse and black skirt,' Thomas replied, hoping that would be enough. It wasn't.

'What accent does she speak with?'

Thomas sighed, feeling anger growing inside. 'I don't know, I couldn't quite place it. Now come on, get in, we're just around the corner.'

'I don't know,' Damien said sheepishly, almost folding into himself. 'I don't really know you. I shouldn't really be getting into a stranger's car.' He took a few steps back until his rucksack hit the brick wall behind him.

'Hey, don't be afraid.' Thomas leaned over, opening the passenger door for him. 'I'm the assistant teacher today. Like I said, my name is Mr Simms. I'll be helping you with your maths and English. Come on, get in.'

Damien kept his focus on the man's large hands, how his fingers looked abnormally big for a human's.

'Come on, Damien, nothing to be scared of. Get in,' he pressured, keeping his big brown eyes on him.

Damien didn't move and slowly shook his head. 'I . . . I don't thin—'

'Damien, get in!' Thomas shouted through gritted teeth, his face drastically changing.

After witnessing his anger, Damien edged back a little and shuffled to the right, his bag scraping off the wall until he rounded the corner and stepped back into the alley that ran parallel with Brougham Street and Zetland Street.

'Damien, get in the fucking car now!'

Damien's body started to shake, and he turned and ran as fast as his little legs could carry him.

Thomas jumped out of the car, and with surging anger in his face, bolted after him down the alley.

24

Thursday morning
Brougham Street, North Road

Damien's legs burned as he galloped down the cold alley away from the car. His heart pounded so hard, he could feel it coming through his chest, like a continuous drumroll of frantic panic radiating from him. The weight of the bag collided with his spine every stride he took. His back ached and the straps of the bag rubbed against his bony shoulders.

Over the frantic echo of his small school shoes pounding on the frosty cobbles he could hear large, heavy, quicker strides behind him, growing louder.

Suddenly there was a metallic ping behind him, but he didn't turn to see what it was.

Keeping his focus ahead he knew he had a choice to make once he hit the end of the alley. He could go left, or he could go right. If he went left he could run back into Brougham Street and try make it home and shout for help. Alternatively, turning right would take him onto Zetland Street, away from his home but closer to his school.

'Damien! Stop!' the man shouted, sounding so close now.

As he approached the T-junction of the alley he slowed a fraction and angled his body, deciding to take the left. The blood pounding in his ears was the only thing he heard, the absolute desperation of getting away from this stranger setting his nerves on fire. He took the left, but his heavy bag kept going forward and the momentum of the external weight pulled him around further than he needed to go, swinging him around one hundred and eighty degrees.

In a split second he felt himself flying through the air and landing hard on the cobbles with a sickening thud. Luckily, his bag took most of the impact but he'd fallen awkwardly, trapping his arm underneath him and scraping his right knee off the icy cobbles.

'Ahhhh . . .' he cried out, feeling a sudden wave of white heat in his wrist, and a general pain all over his body.

Near him, the heavy footsteps slowed then eventually stopped. The air around him was silent, except for the sound of the morning traffic tinkering along North Road past the row of houses behind him.

'Damien . . . why didn't you just get in the car?' Thomas said, panting from running the length of the alley.

Damien warily glanced up at him. He looked like a giant and seemed taller because he was so thin.

'What do you want from me?' Damien asked, wincing in pain from his sore wrist.

'It doesn't matt—'

'Is he okay?' they both heard a concerned voice say from the opening of the alley at Brougham Street.

Thomas looked to the left, seeing an elderly lady standing there with a walking stick. She was wearing a long red coat, and glasses that resembled jam jar bottoms. She was short and hunched over.

'He's fine, don't worry about him.'

'Is that . . . is that you, Damien?' she said, squinting.

Damien looked up. It was Sheena from three doors down. She lived at the house with the black door and spoke with his mother often. She occasionally baked them cakes, which Damien wasn't too fussed about but ate to be kind.

'Sheena,' Damien begged, 'you nee—'

'Damien is fine,' Thomas said, cutting him off, holding a soft palm out towards her. She didn't seem convinced. 'Isn't that right, Damien?' he asked him.

Damien didn't say a word. Instead, he glared at the cobbles below her.

'Damien, what's wrong?' Sheena asked, waddling into the alley with the aid of her stick. She'd had a hip replacement the previous year and needed the other hip doing soon.

'The boy is fine!' Thomas claimed, agitation creeping into his voice.

'Well, from where I'm standing, mister, he doesn't look fine to me.' She stopped near him. 'Have you fallen, Damien?'

Damien bowed his head and never looked up. He liked Sheena. She used to look after him when his parents went out for meals. She was almost like another grandmother to him.

'Come on, let's get you up,' she said, bending down slightly, extending her arm.

'The boy is coming with me,' Thomas said, coldly.

Sheena paused and frowned, angling her focus up at him. 'I'm sorry — hey, aren't you the guy who was in the red Mondeo? You were parked across the road earlier?'

Thomas frowned, surprised at her perceptiveness.

'Yes, you are,' she said without a reply. 'I knew you looked familiar.' She turned away from him and lowered again to Damien.

Thomas leaned forward and grabbed her wrist, then pulled her close to him with so much ease it frightened her.

'I really wish you had minded your own business,' he whispered in her ear.

'Hey, let go of me, you can't—'

She stopped talking and gasped loudly when the knife pierced her frail, wrinkly throat, just above the collar of her red coat. Blood fell over the blade and soaked the front of her clothes. She dropped her silver walking stick and threw both hands up to her face in an attempt to stop it, but she gurgled uncontrollably. Thomas let go of her and watched her wobble a couple of steps before she collapsed to the cold cobbles below.

Damien, with wide terrified eyes, watched his lifelong neighbour wriggling in agony, clutching at her throat with frantic hands. When her eyes and body became still, the reality of what he'd just witnessed hit him hard.

The man pushed the knife back inside his jacket and zipped it up. Then he looked down at Damien and smiled.

'If you don't get in the car, the same will happen to you. Understand?'

Damien quickly nodded at him, then glared back down at the pooling blood as it glistened in the morning frost.

'Come on, let's go,' Thomas said, turning and walking back up the alley towards his car.

Damien, his body trembling, slowly found his feet, and followed Thomas back to the red Mondeo.

25

'Morning, Ori,' Byrd said, approaching his desk with a coffee in his hand.

Tanzy looked up, smiling. 'Morning.' He'd already been in the office nearly half an hour due to an early judo class, now on Thursday mornings.

'You've lost more weight, haven't you?'

Byrd was wearing a different coat today. It was shorter than his usual black one but it was woven with a similar material and looked similar. It seemed to narrow his shoulder width and pull in his stomach. He took a seat next to him and told Tanzy it was probably only the jacket that made him appear that way. He took it off and hung it on the back of his chair.

Tanzy noticed the paper in his hand and enquired about it.

'Numbers and texts from Lyle's phone,' Byrd informed him. 'Mac printed it out and left it for me.'

Tanzy slid over on his desk chair and studied them. 'What's that at the bottom?'

Byrd ran a hand through his hair. 'These are the places the phone has been the most over the last two weeks. He mentioned something about the location settings and being able to see them. See here—' Byrd placed his finger on the largest dot — 'Mac explained this was his most frequently visited spot.'

Tanzy frowned. 'Is that somewhere in the Denes?'

Byrd nodded twice. 'Craig Street. See here, there's Hollyhurst Road and along there is Greenbank Road.'

Tanzy followed his finger. 'And he lives . . . on Willow Road?'

'He does, but from this it seems he's spent more time at Craig Street than his own home.'

'Could be a friend of his,' Tanzy said. 'That's probably why Keith wasn't too worried about his whereabouts. He probably comes and goes when he pleases. If Keith's busy working all the time, sometimes out of town, he probably just lets Lyle get on with it.' Tanzy looked for a few moments. 'Do we know what number on Craig Street?'

Shaking his head, Byrd said they needed to find that out for themselves. 'We'll set up surveillance soon, see if there's any activity.'

Tanzy agreed.

'You two!' blurted DCI Fuller.

Frowning, Byrd and Tanzy both turned.

'Get to Brougham Street off North Road. A woman's been stabbed.'

Byrd and Tanzy turned, logged off their computers, and put their chairs under their desks with urgency. Within minutes, they were inside Tanzy's Golf, heading for Brougham Street.

26

DI Tanzy pulled up to the side of the road and switched off the engine.

Tanzy and Byrd got out of the car and had a quick look around. Several residents stood on their doorsteps peeking along the street to see what all the commotion was about. Down the road, a number of PCs manned a temporary barrier to prevent access. DC Leonard was speaking to a woman on her doorstep, dressed in a pink dressing gown, the expression on her face showing she was both upset and appalled at what had happened in the alley behind. Leonard held a notepad in his hand and intently nodded as she answered his questions.

Byrd and Tanzy started walking down the street towards the tape.

'Morning, sir,' DC Leonard said, as the woman he was speaking to backed into her house and closed the door. He folded his small notepad and placed it back into the inside pocket of his coat. He said the same to Byrd and gave him a thin smile.

'Good morning,' Tanzy replied. 'What's the score?'

'Forensics are in the alley. Cornty and Weaver are minding this tape—' he waved at the cordon twenty-five metres away from them — 'and Grearer and Timms are on the opposite side.'

'Okay, what are you doing?'

'Knocking on doors, seeing if anyone had seen anything that could be useful. So far, nothing at all—'

'Wait, sir, you can't be in here!' cried a voice down the street.

Tanzy, Byrd, and Leonard turned to the voice. An elderly gentleman had stepped under the tape and was charging up the alley as PC Cornty trailed behind him.

'Wait, sir, you can't—'

'Get the fuck off me!' the man shouted, flaying his arms at Cornty. Weaver watched the minor commotion from the tape, looking as if she was wondering whether to assist him.

'Never a dull moment in this town,' Tanzy said as they approached the temporary cordon. Weaver lifted up the tape to allow the three of them under and, as they rounded the brickwork of the last house, they saw Cornty restraining the old man, preventing him going any further.

'Please, sir,' Cornty said, 'you need to calm down. You can't be in here. This is a crime scene.'

'I know, I . . . it's my wife,' he pleaded. 'Please, I need to see if it's my wife. She hasn't come home yet.'

A sick feeling grew in the pit of Tanzy's stomach. He joined Cornty and placed a soft hand on the man's back. Byrd and Leonard were a few steps behind. 'Excuse me, sir.' He felt the man trembling through the thick, feather-filled coat he wore. 'Listen, what's your name, sir?'

'Malcolm Edwards.' His long nose propped up a pair of heavy-framed glasses which magnified his brown eyes almost to the point of it becoming comical. His skin was a little blotchy and his hair was so thin Tanzy could see his scalp through the fine strands that remained.

'I understand your concern, Mr Edwards. But for the moment, could I ask my colleague—' he looked at PC

Cornty — 'to take you to one side and speak with you. We can't risk contaminating any evidence that could help us with this investigation. I'll personally come and speak with you very, very soon. You have my word, Mr Edwards.' He turned to Cornty. 'Phil, can you speak with Malcolm on the other side of the tape, please?'

Leonard walked with Byrd and Tanzy until they reached DS Stockdale, who was standing at the corner of the cobbled T-junction. So far, the body wasn't visible to them. They assumed it would be up the alley.

'Morning,' Stockdale said, glancing up. There was a notepad and a pen in his hand. He was first responder, signing people in and out of the area.

Tanzy peered up the alley, seeing Tallow and Hope leaning down to the floor over a body, both wearing their white overalls.

Amanda Forrest stood a few metres back with a camera in her hand, also wearing the compulsory whites, taking pictures of the blood spatter on the faded brick wall behind the body of the old lady. With no wind in the alley the air was cold and still. A faint mist hung around them, adding to the terrifying effect of another crime scene.

'Who found her?' asked Tanzy.

'Two boys on their way to school,' said Stockdale. 'They phoned it in. I was on North Road when dispatch put it out.'

'Where are they now?'

'On Zetland Street. We've contacted their parents to come and collect them. They're still speaking with PC Andrews.'

'You going in?' Stockdale asked, ready with his notepad and pen.

'I'd like to speak with the boys first,' Tanzy replied, angling his focus towards Zetland Street. 'Just round there?'

'Yeah to the right,' Stockdale confirmed.

'Let's go see.'

Tanzy and Leonard approached the tape fixed across the Zetland Street alley entrance secured by PC Donny Grearer and PC Eric Timms. They both smiled and stepped back, leaving enough room for them to bend down under the tape.

On Zetland Street, to the right, PC Josh Andrews was kneeling, speaking with a small group of people. Two of them were young boys, who were standing but at the same level as Andrews kneeling. The tactic was never to speak down to a frightened child because they'd never open up.

If Tanzy had to guess he'd say the two boys were around the age of ten or eleven. The others in the group, judging by the positions, were the children's parents. Hard to question children who had seen something so terrible. Hard to do it in front of protective parents. But he had to talk to them now, while everything was still fresh in their minds — had they seen the murder itself? He took a breath and moved towards them.

* * *

While Tanzy was talking to the witnesses, Byrd and Leonard made their way to the heart of the scene.

The elderly lady was up on the right, close to the wall. She lay on her right side, her arms tucked into herself, with her feet pointing towards them. From this position Byrd could see a trail of blood from under her body to where DS Stockdale stood.

'Morning,' he said to Tallow and Hope. Leonard hung back a stride, allowing Byrd to lead the conversation.

Tallow, in his white disposable overalls, stood back from the body, his eyes and fingers fixed on his tablet. Forrest was on the other side of him showing him the photos which she'd taken so far. He nodded his approval, stepped away, and glanced at Byrd.

Byrd said, 'What's happened?'

Tallow lowered his tablet. 'Knife wound to her throat. Judging by the cut, and the skin around the cut, there wasn't much force to it, which means it was a very sharp knife. Probably not one you could get from any local DIY supplier.'

'Hunting knife?'

'Maybe. It was very finely sharpened. From the blood spatter—' he moved a few steps down towards the direction of the tape and pointed further down the alley where the trail of blood was thinner — 'it looks like she was attacked there, then judging by the colour of her hands, she'd tried to stop the blood and only managed a few steps before her body couldn't stand any longer.'

'She did well to make it that far, considering she had a walking stick.'

'I had a quick look at the rest of her neck and throat, and even her wrists. There's no immediate bruising. Whoever did this must have grabbed her by the coat.'

Byrd spent a moment looking at the blood around her. 'So much blood. Have you checked her pockets for ID, or do we know who she is?'

'The only items in her pockets were a packet of cigarettes, a lighter, and a handful of change. She was more than likely coming back from the shop.'

'How long has she been dead?'

'Not long at all, Max,' Tallow replied. 'Maybe two hours. She's cold but that's because it's February.'

Byrd nodded. Apart from the blood, the elderly lady could appear to be sleeping peacefully.

Footsteps came from their left. It was Emily Hope with an unusual look on her face. 'I've found something. It could be nothing, but . . .'

In her gloved hand she was holding two items. One was a small yellow smiley face keyring. The other was a rectangular metal pencil case with something written on it.

'Where'd you find them?' Byrd asked, looking down at them.

'Just up there, about halfway up. Against the wall.'

'What does it say on the pencil case?'

'It's looks like a name — Damien.'

'Who's Damien?'

27

Tanzy sipped his coffee at his desk. It had been an eventful day so far and, little did he know, it would get busier. He hadn't got much from the kids who'd found the body — they hadn't seen the murder itself — but the police had been able to identify the victim, at least. Poor Malcolm Edwards had been right in his suspicions — it was his wife who had been killed.

He had confirmed her identity from her red coat and her shoes, which he could see from the end of the alley. He had collapsed to the cold ground in helpless sobs, filling the hearts of nearby people with sadness and sympathy.

Peter Gibbs had turned up to see the body of Sheena Edwards before she was taken to Darlington Memorial, where he'd take part in the post-mortem.

Tallow, Hope, and Forrest had wrapped everything up before they left. Tallow had taken a video, which he normally did, so they could watch that during further analysis. The original assumption of Sheena being stabbed then stumbling a few steps before she fell seemed the likely sequence of events, but the blood spatter analysis would later settle that.

As Tanzy looked at his computer screen with intense concentration, the door behind him opened.

'Orion — in here, please.' DCI Fuller's tone was stern, a tinge of apprehension about it.

Tanzy stood up.

'What happened with the woman? Fill me in,' Fuller asked as Tanzy dropped into the seat on the opposite side of his desk. Tanzy explained.

'Did anyone see anything?'

'We've knocked on most of the houses on Zetland Street and Brougham Street. No one saw a thing.'

Superintendent Barry Eckles had been on the phone to Fuller earlier, telling him to get shit under control as soon as possible, or Fuller wouldn't like the consequences. He'd promised the chief superintendent, Garry Best, and the assistant chief constable, Edward Johnson, that he would get things sorted, that Darlington would be a safe place for the people living in it.

Of course, it was inevitable that crime would happen. It's only a natural process for some people. Some don't know any different.

'Okay, Orion, good work. Have forensics found anything unusual?'

'Tallow claims there wasn't much of a struggle, that the wound implied she was taken by surprise — oh, we found something else down the alley too.'

Fuller raised his eyebrows.

'We found a small keyring and a pencil case with a name on it. It could be something innocent like a kid dropping it in the alley.'

'What was the name on the pencil case?'

'Damien,' Tanzy said.

'Okay, could have been left with the—'

There were several sharp knocks at the door.

Tanzy turned. Fuller shouted, 'Come in!'

PC Cornty opened the door, panting a little, a look of worry in his eye. 'Orion, I need to speak with you.'

'Go on.'

'There's been a call from a woman who lives on Brougham Street. She says her son didn't arrive at school this morning — a nine-year-old.'

'What's her son's name?'

'Damien Spencer.'

28

Thursday afternoon
Brougham Street

PC Amy Weaver knocked on the white door and took a step back, level with Tanzy. It wasn't long before the latch turned and the door opened. Standing there was a woman in her forties, dressed in a white blouse and black trousers, with short blonde hair and bright green eyes. The smell of smoke lingered from inside the house.

'Mrs Spencer?' Tanzy asked.

She stepped back. 'Yes. Please come in.' It was warm in the hallway, heat blasting from a radiator to their left. The faint smell of lavender coming from a plug-in near the small table at the base of the stairs was an admirable effort but came second place to the stale lingering smoke.

Tanzy hated it.

'The living room, we'll sit in there,' she said, indicating with her hand towards the right. 'Sorry the house is a mess, I really—'

'Don't worry about a thing, Mrs Spencer,' Weaver reassured her, stepping into the small room. It was nicely decorated; colours of creams and browns combined, giving it a modern feel. The room was occupied by two large white leather sofas, a large flatscreen television fixed above the fireplace, and a coffee table in the centre of the room.

Mandy Spencer sat on the opposite sofa, her eyes falling on the carrier bag that Tanzy had brought in with him.

'Mrs Spencer, let—'

'Please, call me Mandy,' she said, smiling nervously.

'Mandy, let me start by asking about the phone call from the school earlier.'

She took a breath, as if readying herself for the explanation she was about to give. 'The receptionist phoned me, but I was at work. When I checked my phone, I listened to the message and rang straight back. She said that Damien wasn't in class, and that after looking around the school, no one could find him . . .' She trailed off, tears forming. 'They said he hadn't turned up. I told my supervisor I had to leave and came home.'

Weaver gave a heartfelt smile. 'Where do you work, Mandy?'

'At the town hall. In the planning office. I think it might have something to do with one of our clients.'

'Your clients? Please explain,' encouraged Tanzy.

'We've been receiving threats from a client who we knocked back for the purchase of a piece of land in the town centre. He seemed very angry about it all. There's been notes left on my car saying something bad will happen if the planning permission doesn't go through.'

PC Weaver frowned and grabbed a notepad. 'Who's the client?'

Mandy remained silent, as if scared to say.

'Mrs Spencer, we need to know.'

'He's called Andrew Cairn. Owner of Cairnfield Developments. I don't know if it has anything to do with it but it seems funny, you know.'

PC Weaver noted it.

'We'll immediately enquire about that, but first,' Tanzy said, lowering his hand into the carrier bag, bringing out the pencil case and broken keyring, 'we found these in the alley between this road and Zetland Street.'

She studied them but it didn't take long to realise they belonged to her son. She began to cry.

'Can you confirm these belong to your son, Damien?'

She bobbed her head several times, tears streaming down her face. 'Where were they?'

Before he could answer, there were loud, quick knocks at the front door, frantic bursts of energy colliding against the wood, echoing through the terraced house.

They all frowned, angling their focus to the hallway.

'I'm sorry, I better answer that.' Mandy rose to her feet and opened the front door, finding Jackie, a neighbour from just up the street, standing there with wide eyes.

'Jackie? What's the matter?'

Jackie seemed alert and upset. 'Mandy, Mandy, I've just spoken to Jerry up the street — you know his house is opposite the alley to Zetland Street?' She continued quickly, 'I heard you were looking for Damien, that he's missing?'

'Yeah, he is . . .' Mandy said, sadly.

'Jerry said he saw a red car parked down the alley. He said he was unsure what to do.'

Tanzy and Weaver came to the door after hearing the conversation.

'Jerry said a tall man, maybe six foot, came back to the car with Damien following him. Damien then got into the passenger seat and the car left.'

'Why has he just told you now?' Tanzy asked.

'He's on tablets, he doesn't know what day it is half the time. I clean for him. I was dusting the skirting boards when I heard him say to himself that he hopes the boy is okay, so I looked up asking him, what boy? I assumed he was seeing or imagining things but he was standing at the window looking out. He told me what he'd seen earlier, but then he said he thought it might have been a dream.'

Weaver sighed, unconvinced.

Mandy raised her hands to her mouth, her eyes growing with fear about who this man could be. 'A man has taken my boy?'

'According to Jerry, yes. He said Damien just got in the car and off they went.'

'We need to speak with Jerry, immediately,' Tanzy said. 'Can you take us to him?'

Jackie nodded quickly.

29

Thursday afternoon
Brougham Street

Jerry cautiously opened his old white front door, and Jackie asked if it would be okay for Tanzy and Weaver to speak about what he'd seen in the alley earlier that morning.

Instead of allowing them in, he stood there, his face blank, as if he didn't know who Jackie was. There was a slight recognition in his face when his eyes fell on Mandy Spencer.

'Jerry, can we come in?' Jackie asked again, dragging his fading attention back to her.

He pointed at Tanzy. 'Who is that bald man?'

'He's from the police,' she explained slowly. 'Can they come in and ask you a few questions?'

He didn't reply, still weighing up the strangers standing on his doorstep.

'She's a pretty one,' he said, indicating Weaver, who blushed. Then his face became serious. 'I've paid my taxes, you know. I pay them every time I receive my money. You don't have to worry ab—'

'Sir,' Tanzy said, cutting him off, not wanting to waste any unnecessary time. 'My name is Orion Tanzy. I'm with the police. If it's okay with you, could we ask you a few questions about what you saw earlier? It's very important.'

'Orion? I used to have an Orion. A Ford Orion. It was red. Fast. The girls loved it.'

Tanzy let out a small, frustrated sigh, doing his best not to let it show. In one way, Jerry reminded Tanzy of his grandad. Awkward. 'I bet they did. They were nice cars. Can we come in?'

Jerry, surprisingly, nodded and shuffled back.

Jackie half smiled at Tanzy, rolling her eyes. 'Come on, this'll be fun.'

The four of them stepped up into the house. The central heating had been on all day and it gently slapped them in the face as they padded down the hallway. The creaking floor beneath them was carpeted with a hideous, ancient flower design that was only popular before Tanzy was alive. The walls were lined with a thick, padded cream pattern, and the ceiling was covered with nauseating swirling patterns.

They took a left into the living room, where a fire was burning. Dancing orange flames wavered in the brass surround. Jerry went to the window, stared out onto the street.

Tanzy and Weaver stopped side by side in the centre of the room, watching him, waiting for him to turn. Jackie, in her stained blue apron, moved around them and went to the window. 'Jerry?' She placed a hand on his back. 'Can the police ask you a few questions? It's very important.'

'Oh . . . yeah, of course.' He slowly turned, looked down at his watch, then lifted his head and stared at Tanzy. 'Ask away.'

Tanzy smiled. 'Jackie tells me that you saw a red car parked over there in the alley. And you saw a tall man, walking back to it with a young boy?'

For a moment, Jerry looked puzzled, his eyebrows furrowing to the centre of his forehead. He then turned to the window, gazed out for a few seconds. 'A red car?'

Tanzy sighed, knowing valuable time was being wasted here.

But if the story that Jackie had told him was true, and the information was correct, it could be vital. They knew patience would be the winner here.

'Yes, a red car. You told Jackie—' he pointed back to her — 'that you saw a red car parked in the alley. Do you remember? It happened this morning.'

Jerry suddenly seemed alert, as if a switch had been flicked. 'Of course, it happened this morning, I was sitting on the chair over there and saw it.'

Finally getting somewhere.

'What did you see?' Tanzy probed.

'The red car was parked there for a while. I thought it was a strange place to park, so I stood up and waited to see if the driver came back, otherwise I would have reported it. I don't drive myself, but I know you're not allowed to park in an alley, in case of emergency vehicle access.'

'That's right,' Tanzy agreed, trying to hurry the story along. 'Then what happened?'

'A man appeared. He was tall. Very thin. He had a brown jacket on, the zip high up to his pointy chin. He walked in a strange way. Huge strides. Weird. He came around the car and got in the driver's door. Then Damien got into the passenger seat.'

It was a long shot. 'Can you remember what model of car it was?'

'Yes. A Mondeo Titanium.'

Tanzy found himself frowning, surprised at how confident Jerry seemed. 'You sure?'

'Yes. It was a newer model, ST Line. I've always liked my cars.'

Tanzy felt like this was going somewhere, but was unsure if he believed him. 'By any chance, you don't happen to remember the registration plate?'

'NA66 CFD.'

Tanzy was taken aback for a moment, tilting his head. 'Are you sure?'

'Absolutely.'

'Did you write it down?'

'No, I memorised it. I only have to look at something once. Numbers and letters. My son calls it a photographic memory. I used to be better than I am now, but I'm sure.'

Without being obvious, Tanzy gazed over towards Jackie, who agreed that chances are he would be right. He returned to Jerry.

'Thank you, Jerry.' Tanzy turned to Weaver. 'You got that?'

Weaver finished typing the registration plate of the Mondeo into her phone, then peered up. 'Got it.'

'We'll run the plate, see who it belongs to.' Tanzy turned back to Jerry. 'Thank you again, you've been a very big help.'

'Please find my boy,' pleaded Mandy, standing near the door. 'He has a medical condition.'

'Which condition does he have?' Tanzy asked her.

'Congenital heart disease. If he doesn't take his tablets twice a day, he'll get very sick. I gave him one before he left this morning. He gets his second dose when he comes in from school. They thin his blood, so his heart can pump it properly.'

'What happens if he doesn't take the second dose?' Tanzy asked, becoming more worried than he already was.

'His heart will eventually fail, sooner or later.'

Tanzy and Weaver understood the magnitude of her words. They both headed for the hallway, passing Jackie.

'What about the other children?' Jerry asked, still standing at the window.

Tanzy paused and swivelled before he reached the door. 'I'm sorry?'

'What about the other children?'

'I don't understand.' Tanzy appeared puzzled. 'Which other children?'

'The boy and girl sitting in the back of the red Mondeo.'

30

Before Tanzy managed to reach his desk he was stopped half-way down the office by DC Leonard, who informed him that a call had come in from a worried mother who lived on Westmoreland Street, saying her nine-year-old daughter hadn't turned up at school and that she didn't know where she was.

'Okay,' Tanzy said, his head swimming with this new information. 'Did you go to the house?'

'Cornty and I went round to speak with her. Kid's name is Melissa Clarke. We took a witness statement and a recent photograph of Melissa. She goes to the same school as Damien Spencer, sir.'

'Right.' Tanzy gulped. 'Thanks for letting me know. File the report. I need to speak to Fuller.' Tanzy turned away from Leonard.

'Orion?' he heard a voice coming from the right this time. It was DS Stockdale.

'Hey,' Tanzy said, padding towards him. Stockdale remained seated, looking up to his superior.

'Thought you should know. Just after you left, a call came in from a woman who lives on Zetland Street about her missing—'

'Son?' Tanzy said, finishing the sentence, remembering what Jerry had said about the children in the back seat of the Mondeo.

Stockdale's eyebrows furrowed. 'Yeah, Eddy Long. Nine years old. How did you know?'

'Did you go to the house?'

'Yeah, took Andrews with me. We haven't been back long.'

'Did you get a photo of him?'

'Yes.'

'Good,' Tanzy said. 'File the report, I'll speak to Fuller. We need a meeting as soon as possible about what's happened this morning. Never a dull day in this town.'

Tanzy rapped his knuckles on Fuller's door and waited.

'Come in,' a drowned-out voice said. Tanzy entered the warm office. The DCI was on a phone call but it wasn't too long before he ended the call and told Tanzy to take a seat.

'We have a witness who said he saw Damien Spencer get into a car. He also claimed he saw a boy and a girl in the back.'

Fuller nodded. 'Hence the two calls while you were out?'

'Yeah. All the kids are nine years old, all of them attend the same school.'

'What about the car, did the witness . . .'

'We have a registration plate. But, unfortunately, the plates are fake. They don't exist.'

Fuller sighed, picked up his half-drunk cup of coffee and took a swig, then placed it back down on the desk.

'So, we have three children missing. Likely the same man responsible for taking them?'

'We need to find this guy ASAP,' confirmed Tanzy.

'If it's true what the witness said, I find it strange that Damien just went with him so easily,' Fuller noted.

'You do know it was the same alley Sheena Edwards was killed in, don't you? Maybe he was threatened with a weapon? God, maybe he actually saw it happen.'

'What about the other children?'

'Could have had the knife and used that to scare them too. Perhaps when he tried to get Damien, Sheena was in the wrong place at the wrong time.'

'Do we have a list of the children?' Fuller took another long sip of coffee.

Tanzy nodded. 'Damien Spencer, Melissa Clarke, and Eddy Long.'

'Photos?'

'Should be on the system by now. According to Mandy Spencer, Damien's mother, she's been having some bother at work. One of the clients, a Mr Andrew Cairn of Cairnfield Developments, has been threatening her and leaving notes on her car because they're not granting permission for a plot of land. The latest one was left on her car, saying something bad will happen if they don't get what they want.'

'Well, we need to speak to Andrew Cairn immediately. Did you speak to other people in the street about Damien?'

'Yeah, we knocked on most of the doors on Brougham Street. No one had seen anything. We have nothing to go on, especially with the plate being fake.'

'So . . . say his story is true, it would be wise to assume the other missing children reported by the school and parents were in the same car. Next step is checking the CCTV camera in that area. You have a contact at the control room, don't you?'

'I do. Jennifer Lucas.'

'Speak with her, see if she can pick up the red Mondeo. It's a long shot, but we know the time and we know the place and, although the reg is fake, we can hopefully track its movements.'

'I'll get straight on it,' Tanzy said, standing. 'I'll go to the school as well. I need to speak to their headteacher. I need to know why these specific three children have been taken.'

'Good. Take one of the PCs or DCs. Let me know if there's any developments regarding the forensics report on Sheena Edwards. I know the basics, but if they find anything else or the pathologist finds anything unusual, please let me know as soon as possible. Eckles has been on my case all day. You know what he's like.'

'Will do.'

Back at his desk Tanzy picked up the phone but, before he made the phone call, he noticed there was a text from his wife, Pip, who was at home cooking another one of his favourite meals. Lasagne. He replied, thanking her, then found Jennifer Lucas's number and pressed CALL.

31

Thursday afternoon
Duke Street, Darlington town centre

'Where is it?' Weaver asked, scanning the different business names and logos on the buildings on either side of the road.

'There!' DC Leonard pointed to the right.

Weaver slowed the Astra, flicked her indicator on, and pulled in. Once she'd turned the engine off, they looked to the building on the right. A sign was fixed on the wall next to a large blue door containing three business names.

One was Peter Main Graphic Design. The next name down was Helen's Flowers. The last one was the one they were looking for.

Cairnfield Developments.

After Mandy Spencer had told Tanzy about the notes left on her car and the numerous phone calls from Mr Cairn, Tanzy had run a check on him and informed Leonard of his findings.

'Anything come up on the database?' Weaver asked.

Leonard shook his head. 'No, nothing at all. Judging by what Mandy had told Tanzy, I'm surprised. Squeaky clean, apparently.'

They got out and shut their doors. Considering the time, Duke Street was busy, people walking into town dressed smartly, presumably on their breaks, others in casual clothes, probably finishing college.

The air was cold as they stepped up onto the path. Leonard wore black trousers and a white shirt, covered by a dark blue padded fleece, and took the lead, pushing open the main door and stepping inside, followed by Weaver, who was wearing her usual uniform.

The hallway was like any other hallway. There were three doors. Leonard stopped at the first door on the left, seeing a bright, colourful, funky sign fixed to it: Peter Main Graphic Design.

They checked the next door. It had no sign on, so he continued towards the door at the end of the hallway, where he saw Cairnfield Developments.

He knocked on the door several times, then tried the handle, but it was locked.

'Did DI Tanzy give you a number to call?' Weaver asked him.

Leonard nodded. 'Yeah. He said the planning office passed on the number they use to contact Mr Cairn. Apparently Cairn's had a lot of involvement with them over the past few years in relation to various building work and property developments.' Leonard pulled out a small slip of paper that Tanzy had given him and punched the number into his phone. After pressing CALL, he put it to his ear. Weaver waited behind him.

'No answer,' he told her, then tried again. 'Hey, we'll ask in the graphic design place. See if they know anything about them.'

Leonard knocked at the door with the jazzy sign and went inside. He was greeted by a modernised rectangular space, although it wasn't great in size. In the bay window looking out onto the street, there was a built-in desk with a computer on it, the screen facing into the room so the person using it could look out onto the street.

To their left was a seating area with a plethora of samples of design work that the company had done. Behind the desk, on the opposite wall, there was a flatscreen television against lime-green wallpaper with architectural shapes.

In the centre of the room there was a circular table, which had an array of business cards and leaflets, most of them offering the customers who walked in samples of their ideas and a taster of what type of work they dealt with.

Over to the right of the room, an area they couldn't quite see, they heard a sound. An almost inaudible humming which Leonard thought sounded familiar. A moment later, a teenager with a large mop of hair walked into view and noticed him.

'Jesus,' he gasped, raising a palm to his chest and taking a few steps back. 'I . . . Wow, Jesus. I never heard you come in.'

'Sorry to startle you,' Leonard said. 'Could I ask you a few questions?'

The lad nodded enthusiastically. 'Sure. Please sit down at the table.' As Leonard moved, the young man noticed Weaver in her uniform behind and paused suddenly. 'Wait — what's this about?'

'No cause for concern,' Leonard assured him, pulling out a seat. 'Just need to ask you about Cairnfield Developments.'

The teenager sat down and placed his coffee on the table.

'What's your name, sir?' Weaver asked him as she took a seat.

'Danny. Danny Ledge.'

'Is this your business?' she said, glancing around briefly.

He shook his head and made a face, as if it would be a dream of his to own something like this. 'No, I'm an apprentice. In my second year. Peter owns it. He's out for the morning up in Newcastle. He'll be back after lunch. Yeah, after lunch,' he confirmed with himself.

'Do you know the owner of Cairnfield Developments, just down the hall?'

Danny shook his head. 'I've never seen him since I've been here. That's just over a year. I did a year full-time at college then they found me a placement with an employer. I was lucky to be put with Peter. Some of the work we do are these business cards and flyers here.' He pointed to the various objects on the table in front of Leonard and Weaver.

'That's good work,' Leonard commented.

'This is my design,' he said, pointing to a red-and-black business card.

'Very good,' Weaver agreed, then smiled. 'So, you've never seen the owner, or anyone, go into that office?'

'No, sorry. Peter has been here a while, so he might know, but I'm not sure.'

'Okay. We'll pop back a little later this afternoon, hopefully speak to him then.'

'I'd say go and ask Helen who had the flower shop upstairs, but she moved to Spain a few months ago. I kind of miss her. She made these amazing hot chocolates with marshmallows.'

Weaver stood up, as did Leonard, and they both stepped out into the hallway. 'Thanks for your time,' Weaver said to him.

The geeky-looking young man waved at her and carried his coffee over towards the computer at the window.

'Who are you calling?' Weaver asked Leonard as he took his phone from his pocket.

'Tanzy. To let him know.' A few seconds of silence passed. 'Boss, it's James. We've just spoken to a lad who works at the office in the front of the building. He said he's never seen anyone go into the Cairnfield Developments office in the year or so that he's been here. The office upstairs used to belong to a woman called Helen, but she moved away a few months ago.'

'Is the door to Cairnfield Developments locked?' Tanzy asked.

'Yeah. We've knocked a few times without any response.'

'Have you got your tools with you?' Tanzy asked.

'In the car,' Leonard said. 'You want me to . . .'

'Yeah. If there's a slim chance no one will turn up, do it. We need a lead on this. Eckles is on Fuller's case, which means he's on ours, which means—'

'You're on ours?' said Leonard, finishing his train of thought.

'You're getting good at this detective thing, Jim.'

'Give me a few minutes. I'll ring you back.' Leonard ended the call, put his phone away, and went outside.

'Jim, we aren't doing what I think we are?'

He turned back, smiling.

She sighed, knowing what he was getting from the car and what he was planning to do.

A moment later, he returned with a small rectangular box in his hand. Weaver moved out of the way and watched Leonard lower to his knees, so the lock of the door to Cairnfield Developments was at eye level. It took him around two minutes to get in — it had been a while since he'd done it.

'Bingo,' he said, standing. He pushed the door open to see the long rectangular room was empty, not a single piece of furniture inside it. Disheartened, he plucked the phone from his pocket and phoned Tanzy to tell him the office was empty.

Tanzy thanked him and asked them to return to the station.

Leonard and Weaver were very competent individuals, but they had missed something. Above the door to Cairnfield Developments, a small video camera was recording twenty-four/seven. They were being watched.

32

Thursday afternoon
Darlington

The red Mondeo slowly came to a halt at the end of the long driveway, just in front of the white double garage behind the back of the house. Thomas applied the handbrake and turned off the engine. He studied Damien, who met his stare with wide, terrified eyes, then looked into the back of the car towards Melissa and Eddy, who were both physically shaking.

Thomas saw a wet patch on the seat next to the little girl.

'You haven't wet yourself, have you?'

Melissa didn't answer and started to cry.

The man sighed, looking forward towards the double garage, then started humming a tune that suddenly silenced Melissa.

When Damien had got into the car earlier, he'd noticed his classmates in the back, but before he'd had the chance to speak, the tall man had told them all to be silent and not to make a sound. He'd told them that if they wanted to cry, they could, but if it was louder than the classical music he was playing on his car CD, the consequences would be severe.

Thomas opened the door, stepped out into the cold air, then closed it, the sound echoing around the quiet grounds of the house. Standing at the back door of the mansion, he saw Jonny Feland watching them.

Thomas turned back to the car, leaning into the open driver's door.

'You three wait here, I'll be back soon.' He closed the door, pressed the button on the fob to lock them in, and made his way across the gravel towards his boss.

* * *

'Damien,' Melissa whispered from the back of the car. He turned around. 'Why are we here? What is this place?'

'I don't know,' he replied. He lifted his head, watched the tall man walking towards the house through the rear windscreen. 'He has a knife. I watched him kill someone. A woman. Sheena. My mum's friend.'

Melissa threw her hands to her mouth as her eyes filled with more tears. 'Really?'

'He . . . he killed someone?' Eddy asked, his voice almost sticking in his throat.

Damien told them what had happened.

'Oh, God,' Eddy said, pure terror on his face.

'We need to do what he says,' Damien said. 'He's very dangerous.'

'But why has he taken us?'

Damien shrugged. 'I don't know, but we need to do something soon.'

* * *

'How was it?' Feland asked Thomas. 'Everything go to plan?'

'We ran into a problem.'

Feland tilted his head, narrowing his eyes. 'A problem?'

'Yes. When I grabbed Damien, a neighbour saw us in the alley.'

Thomas smiled.

'You didn't kill her, did you?'

He smiled wider.

'Fuck sakes, Thomas.' Feland looked away, shaking his head. 'Did anyone see you?'

'No one was around.'

'You sure?'

Thomas's words were convincing. 'I'm sure.'

'Okay, well, the room is ready for them. Take them up there. The others are waiting.'

'Understood.' He turned, heading back to the car.

Feland's phone rang in his pocket. He didn't recognise the number but he knew, in this game, you didn't have many numbers saved. He answered it.

'Is this Feland?'

'Speaking.'

'I was told you're the man to supply me with what I'm after,' the voice said.

'And what is it you're after?'

The man on the other end explained his needs.

'Yes . . . we have something which I think you'll like,' Feland said. 'Funny enough, one of them has just arrived here.'

33

Thursday afternoon
Darlington Town Hall

Tanzy and PC Josh Andrews entered through the sliding glass doors of the town hall and made their way to the reception desk, where a small, plump woman was focused on the computer screen in front of her.

'Can I help?' she said, peeling her attention away from it.

'Here to see Jennifer Lucas. She knows we're coming.'

'Hold on a second,' the woman said, picking up the phone to her right.

Tanzy smiled, turned a full one-eighty, and glanced outside through the glass doors. 'Miserable day, eh?'

Andrews turned, watched the dark, grey clouds above, and agreed. 'Meant to be like this for a few days, boss. You never know, though. Might brighten up. They're known to be wrong sometimes.'

'*Only* sometimes?' Tanzy joked.

The receptionist put the phone down. 'Just go right up. Lift or stairs, take your pick.'

'Thanks.'

They took the stairs and stepped out onto the first floor, then took a right. The carpet still smelled new, the white paint on the walls still giving off a faint smell, but Tanzy knew it had been over two months since they were last painted, unless they'd been done again.

He knocked three times on the door labelled 'Control Room' and waited for a response.

'Come in,' a muffled voice said from behind the closed door.

Sitting at the table in the centre of the dark room, facing the computer screens to the left, was Jennifer Lucas. Tanzy almost paused for a second when he laid eyes on her. Wearing a tight black shirt, a red-chequered pencil skirt, and black tights with black ankle boots, she looked beautiful. Her black, shiny hair was tightly tied up into a ponytail, then trailed halfway down her back. The gentle glow from the screens in front of her did what they always did when she was sitting there: highlighted her beauty.

'Hello, Orion,' she said softly, her accent indicating she was born somewhere between Durham and Newcastle. Her voice alone made him go weak at the knees.

'Hi, Jennifer,' he said, sauntering in towards her.

Andrews trailed Tanzy, glancing around the room, absorbing the screens to the left, the desks in the middle and some on the right. It was the first time he'd been here. On the ceiling, there were roughly ten spotlights scattered around the room, making sure it was adequately lit but dark enough so the computer screens could be easily monitored without having to strain your eyes.

'How you doing?' Tanzy asked her, pulling out the chair next to her and dropping into it, able to smell her sweet perfume. It was so nice, he could have leaned forward and sniffed her neck, then—

Focus, he told himself. 'Did you find it?' he then asked, referring to the red Mondeo.

'Eventually. But then . . .' She winced. 'I kind of lost it again. The cameras around there are not very good at all.'

'I know,' Tanzy replied.

'You say the car left Brougham Street and headed in the direction of town, according to the witness, the elderly gent who was watching through the window.' Tanzy nodded. She went on. 'I checked North Road. North and south. Nothing. I then looked at the map and drew out several alternate routes to where, if I was driving, I would be heading. It took a while.'

Tanzy kept still, watching her, inhaling the sweet scent of her perfume, her—

'What did you find?' Andrews asked behind him.

Tanzy had almost forgotten he was there. He needed to get a grip. He'd just started sorting things out with Pip; they were falling back in love. The kids were happy. But despite this, there was something about Jennifer. She seemed perfect in every way.

'I mapped out the route that would take me down Whessoe Road, up Brinkburn Road, through Cockerton. The first camera that picked me up was in Cockerton.'

'There's no cameras from Zetland Street to Cockerton?' Tanzy frowned, not believing what he was hearing.

'There is, except two of them don't work. And that's an issue.'

'Typical.' Andrews sighed.

Jennifer glanced up at him and smiled. 'Don't worry, I've told maintenance about them. I've even put repair tickets in for them, but the council seem to want to spend money on flowerbeds. Unfortunately, I'm not in charge of how we spend the money, I can only advise and point out what works and what doesn't. It used to aggravate me in the past, but I just accept it now,' she said with a heavy shrug.

Andrews nodded.

'Yeah, definitely,' Tanzy agreed, stealing a look.

She fiddled with the mouse on the desk. 'Look at this.'

The red Mondeo turned left on West Auckland Road and headed down past the Co-op into Cockerton. The camera then lost it, but the car was picked up by the next camera further down. It was clear to them that the car then took a left, towards the small roundabout at the end of Woodland Road, passing the Cockerton Club on the left-hand side.

'Where is he going?' Andrews asked no one in particular.

As the Mondeo reached the roundabout, it took a right, towards the next mini-roundabout, then disappeared.

'Where's he gone?' Tanzy said, flicking his concentration to the other screens, hoping to pick up the Mondeo without success.

'This is where I lose him,' Jennifer explained. She clicked the mouse a few times. 'There should be, last time I checked, a camera somewhere up here.' She paused the frame and used the cursor to point to the right top corner.

'Is it not working?' Tanzy asked, turning to her.

'I don't know. It's the first time I've noticed it hasn't been. I'll need to contact maintenance about that one too.' She rolled her eyes.

'So . . .' Tanzy tilted his head. 'We have him going left up Carmel Road or right onto . . .'

'Staindrop Road,' Jennifer said, finishing his train of thought.

'So, they either went left or right?'

'That's true, but there's a camera roughly two hundred metres further up on Carmel Road. Maybe a little more. And there's a camera near the Mowden Pub along Staindrop Road. Neither camera sees the Mondeo.'

'Which means the car didn't make it that far in either direction,' Tanzy replied. 'Meaning the car is somewhere in that area.'

Jennifer looked up. 'I'd say so, yeah.'

'Okay. Do you have a map handy? I mean a paper one? It's easier to get a sense of an area on paper than on screen.'

'Yeah, sure, hold on.' She pushed her chair out, stood up, and made her way over to the shelving units behind them. He did his best but Tanzy couldn't help watching her move in that red patterned skirt. She pulled out a large, folded piece of paper from one of the units and returned to the desk.

Jennifer placed it down and located the area with her thin, manicured finger. The map itself didn't show the whole of Darlington. It was the west end of Darlington.

'Here,' she said, her finger stopping at the small round-about they last saw the Mondeo on the camera.

'Round the corner from the Denes park,' Andrews said. 'We seem to be spending a lot of time there at the moment.'

'So, where roughly do you think the other cameras are?' Tanzy asked Jennifer. 'The ones that didn't pick it up?'

She studied the map for a moment, her eyes concentrating on the array of roads, streets, and cul-de-sacs. 'The camera on Carmel Road is here.' She pointed to a spot close to Nunnery Lane. 'And . . . the other is . . . here.' She indicated the position of the Mowden Pub.

'Leaves a lot of choices for a driver to make,' Tanzy commented. 'Quite a few turn-offs before you get to those spots.'

'All those houses too,' Andrews added with a beaten look on his face.

'I'll ring the station, get a search going around that area for the red Mondeo. We might spot something.' He stood and glanced down at Jennifer. 'Thanks. Let me know if you find anything else.'

'Anything for you, Orion.'

Tanzy and Andrews left the large, dark room and stepped into the brightly lit, white painted hallway. As they waited for the lift, Andrews angled his gaze on Tanzy for a moment.

'What?' Tanzy said, noticing his sudden interest in him.

'Nothing, sir.' Andrews had picked up on the way they'd exchanged looks, could physically feel the tension between Tanzy and Jennifer, but decided not to mention it. Whatever it was, harmless or not, it wasn't his business.

34

Thursday afternoon
HSS Hire, Cleveland Street

Cleveland Street was a quiet part of town, full of builders'
yards, storage units and tile shops. HHS Hire, the tool hire
unit, faced onto the street, with a large garage-style door
that looked perpetually open, and a smaller door that DC
Leonard and PC Weaver opted to use.

It was warm and stuffy inside the reception area but beat
the cold outside. A smell of coffee lingered in the air.

Standing behind the counter was a tall thin man, watching them over the top of narrow glasses. 'You guys from the
police?' he asked unnecessarily, his eyes on Weaver's uniform.

'We are,' Leonard said. 'I'm DC Leonard, and this is PC
Weaver. We're here to speak to Mr Liddle.'

Just as the words left his mouth, a man rushed through
an open door behind the desk. 'That's me.' He was almost
panting. 'Please, please, come through, you need to see this,'
he told them, lifting up the hatch. 'This way.'

Liddle showed them into a cramped little office filled
with overflowing boxes of paperwork. Perched on a desk

between piles of paper was a new-looking computer, which Liddle made for. He clicked several times on the mouse and opened a video. 'This is from last night. Filming's set off by motion sensors — it's not busy round here at night.'

'Okay.' Leonard focused on the screen.

'I'll skip to the right part.' All of them watched the time speed up rapidly. 'It was almost midnight when this happened.'

He pressed play. A figure ran into the shot, naked, then seemed to hear something. He waved as if flagging down a car. Then—

'Jesus,' Weaver gasped. 'They ran him down. Didn't they see him there?'

'They've stopped to help,' Leonard said. 'Hard to make out . . .'

The officers gasped as the driver opened the car's boot and pushed the — dead? dying? — man inside.

Weaver frowned as they watched the driver get back into the car and drive off. 'So, whoever did this just picked him up and put him in the boot?'

'It looks like.'

Weaver agreed.

They all watched the dark blue four-by-four pass the screen and disappear to the left.

Liddle turned to Leonard, who was peering over his shoulder. 'Who is he? There must be someone missing, or someone must've filed a missing person's report?'

Leonard frowned. 'Play it again, please.'

The manager did as he was told and the three of them watched it again.

Weaver pulled a memory stick from her pocket and held it up. 'We need to copy that video file onto here, then take it back to the station to analyse it.'

'Of course, of course,' Liddle replied, happy to help.

* * *

Back out in the car, Leonard sighed heavily.

'What's up, Jim?' Weaver asked, settling into the driver's seat and putting on her seatbelt. She looked over at him, noticing his defeated posture.

'It never ends, does it?'

She frowned. 'What doesn't?'

'This . . .' He opened his palms, indicating either the situation they were in or something else. Weaver wasn't really sure. 'It's non-stop all the time.' He glanced away, focused out the window, watching a green Renault Clio drive past.

Silence filled the car for a few moments. 'It's relentless, I know, with everything that's gone on in the past few days, then this. But that's what we signed up for, Jim, you know that.'

'I know . . .' He turned his head towards her and held her gaze a second too long. In the time he'd been working with her, he'd never really noticed how attractive she was. Was it the angle of her face, or the perfect fall of her straight blonde hair, or the faint afternoon light that had slipped through a crack in the clouds above? He wasn't sure. He also didn't know why she and PC Cornty had stopped seeing each other, but he'd heard them argue in the office over the past few weeks, so hadn't been surprised to hear Weaver had broken it off. Cornty hadn't really spoken much about it, but Leonard could see how she might be the argumentative type.

'Come on, chin up,' she said, smiling. 'This isn't like you.' She patted him on the thigh twice then pulled her hand back slowly, taking hold of the gear stick.

He angled her way.

'We'll have to hurry or we'll be late for the meeting,' she said quickly. 'Byrd and Tanzy have enough on their plates without reminding us about being punctual.'

35

The time was ticking on. Nearly 6 p.m.

Byrd was standing at the front of the meeting room, a small black remote in his hand, waiting for the others to sit down.

During the time he waited, he thought about his life. How twelve years ago he had his sister and both parents, until his sister, Emma had been brutally murdered. Byrd knew he used to be a bubbly, outgoing character, but the night when Emma was stabbed four times in the stomach by a drug addict in an alley in town was the night that everything changed for DI Max Byrd. The new version of Byrd was more determined, more hard-working. For some it may have killed their ambitions and morals as an officer of the law, taught them the harsh lesson that this life is nothing short of cruel. But his father always used to say to them both: 'Things will happen to you that don't seem fair. You want to know why? Because life just isn't fair. You have to play the cards that you've been dealt to the best of your ability.' His words would stay in his head for ever. Byrd was always looking to improve and mend this so-called broken system. He would do his very best to prevent these things happening again. But life would be life, and as his father said, 'Life just isn't fair.'

DS Stockdale entered through the door, giving him a small apologetic wave for his lateness.

'We're missing a couple, but we'd better make a start,' said Tanzy.

'Okay,' Byrd started, 'we'll run a brief re-cap of yesterday before we move onto the events of today.' Everyone nodded. 'Mark Greenwell was found at the Denes park yesterday morning, his throat cut. Time of death, the pathologist tells me, was Tuesday night between ten and midnight. Forensics—' he pointed over to Tallow and Hope, who were sitting towards the back of the room — 'found drugs on his person — results have just come back positive for cocaine. After Mark was taken to the pathology department and underwent an examination, we found whip marks on his back. Some of the marks were dated two years prior to his death and some of them were new. I assume he suffered in the past at the hands of, probably, the same person. I'll update you guys later with any further findings. I spoke with Mac in DFU about his phone, which gave us his location over the past few weeks, showing a hotspot on Craig Street where I want to set up surveillance over the next few nights.' He looked around the room. 'Any thoughts?'

Byrd took the silence as agreement. 'We think he was a part of something bigger and we need to find out what.' He sighed. 'There was a drop of blood found near Mark Greenwell. The blood belongs to Lyle Wilson.'

The name was familiar to some of them. Byrd could see the cogs turning.

PC Cornty said, 'Is that the son of your friend Keith?'

Byrd nodded sadly.

'Have you spoken with Lyle? Brought him in yet?'

'I've been to his house, but Lyle wasn't there. His father, Keith, said he hasn't seen him since Tuesday night.'

'The same night Mark Greenwell was murdered?'

'Correct,' Byrd said. 'At the moment, he's our prime suspect.'

Byrd paused for breath and clamped his eyes shut for a moment, bringing his left hand up to his temple in reaction to a sharp pain that ran across it.

Silence filled the room as everyone stared at him, wondering what the issue was. He squinted for a few seconds, and eventually it seemed to pass. Then he opened his eyes. 'Sorry about that . . .' He leaned to his left, handing Tanzy the remote. 'Can you do the next slide?'

'No problem,' Tanzy said, moving forward, eyeing him with concern.

Worried stares lingered on Byrd as he padded a few steps over to the nearest chair and sat down into it.

'You okay, Max?' Tanzy asked him.

Byrd waved it away. 'I'll be fine, Ori, thanks. Go on.'

Tanzy moved on, pressing the button on the small remote, bringing up an image of Sheena Edwards lying dead in the alley between Brougham Street and Zetland Street. 'This morning,' he said, turning back to the room, 'the body of this elderly lady, Sheena Edwards, was found by two young boys on their way to school. Death occurred somewhere between eight thirty, when she left the local corner shop, and eight fifty, when the boys arrived.'

Tanzy clicked the button and a closer shot of Sheena Edwards flashed onto the screen. She was on her front, her arms awkwardly bent, a pool of blood surrounding her. 'Max, could you tell the team anything that was found at the post-mortem?'

Byrd coughed and slowly stood back up. 'Yeah, the lead pathologist didn't find anything other than the cut to her throat. They told me she was attacked with a very sharp blade. One he thinks couldn't be purchased from an ordinary shop, indicating a specialist kind of knife.'

PC Cornty raised his hand.

'Yes, Phil?' Byrd said.

'Are there similarities between the knife attack on Sheena Edwards and the knife attack on Mark Greenwell?'

'Well, it's the same MO, but from what Arnold says, the knives were of different sharpness. Hard to say more than that, other than: different victims, different surroundings. I'd say these probably aren't linked.'

Cornty smiled thinly.

'Good point though, Phil,' Tanzy said. The next slide came up, showing an image of a nine-year-old boy, standing in a small kitchen, wearing a smile on his face and a school uniform, with a book bag gripped in his hand.

'Who's that, sir?' DC Anne Tiffin asked.

'This is Damien Spencer, nine years old. His keyring and pencil case were found at the site of Sheena Edwards' stabbing. The school receptionist phoned his mother, Mandy, around nine thirty this morning to inform her that Damien hadn't turned up for school. Damien had, like any other morning, set off to school in the direction he'd normally walk, at about eight thirty. Regarding the pencil case and keyring, we spoke to Mandy Spencer and she confirmed they belonged to her son, but she couldn't understand why he would walk that way to school.'

'They must be linked,' Cornty said confidently, leaning forward.

'That's what we are assuming.' Tanzy looked to Byrd, holding the remote out to him.

Byrd took it with a smile and clicked the button. The screen showed a picture of a girl. 'This is Melissa Clarke, again nine years old — in fact, she sits next to Damien at school. She also didn't arrive at school today.' Byrd angled his body again to the screen as another image flashed up. 'And this is Eddy Long. Nine years old. Any guesses what happened to him this morning?'

'He didn't turn up at school?' Tiffin asked. 'Same class as the others?'

Byrd and Tanzy both nodded in unison, and Byrd clicked the button again, the screen showing the same three pictures but much smaller, so they could all fit on one slide.

'We have a witness who saw Damien getting into a car near the alley where Sheena Edwards was killed. Driver was a tall man, about six foot. Red Mondeo. Apparently the other two children were already in the car.'

'Getting in willingly?'

'My theory is the driver was chasing him, Sheena intervened and was killed — and that frightened Damien enough to get into the car without putting up any more of a fight.'

'Do we have a reg plate?' Cornty asked.

'Yes. We ran it through. Plates are fake, but PC Andrews and I went to the town hall to speak to Jennifer Lucas about the CCTV in the surrounding area. We narrowed down an area where the Mondeo may have gone but the area is vast.'

'Why haven't cameras picked it up?' Stockdale asked, frowning.

'Some don't work, some are waiting on maintenance,' Tanzy replied with the slightest of shrugs. 'And I found something else out today. The parents of these children work together—'

The door opened quickly.

Byrd and Tanzy and everyone else started as DC Leonard and PC Weaver stepped through the door.

'Sorry we're late,' DC Leonard said.

Tanzy looked disappointed in them.

'There's something you need to see,' Leonard said, handing over the USB memory stick to Byrd. 'We need to watch this now.'

'What's on it?' Byrd asked, taking it from him, plugging it into the laptop nearby.

He opened the file and clicked play. They watched the footage that was taken from the camera above HSS Hire.

Byrd sighed heavily.

'What is it, Max?' Tanzy said.

'I know who the naked man is.'

'Who?'

'Lyle Wilson. Our missing suspect.'

'Maybe he's not a suspect anymore, Max. He's another victim,' Tanzy said.

36

After Damien, Melissa, and Eddy had been taken up to the large room on the first floor of the house earlier that morning, they had looked around the high-ceilinged room in both awe and fear. They'd never seen a room like it. The ceiling looked as high as the sky. The walls were painted white, and the carpet was black. There were six single beds in the room, three on the right, three on the left, the foot of each bed pointing to the centre of the room, leaving a space in the middle. Each bed was spaced apart and had a small bedside unit with a lamp on and a glass of water. Beyond the beds was a wide bay window giving a fantastic view of the long rear garden. In the window there were toys, board games, remote-control cars and trucks. A hint of lavender lingered in the air and the room was hot.

When Thomas left them and locked the door, the children moved further into the room and, at the far end, below the bay window, they saw three other children down on their knees playing with toys.

'Hello,' Damien had said to the children. There was a young girl and two boys, all similar in age to Damien, Eddy, and Melissa.

'Have you come to hurt us?' one of the boys said in a Scottish accent.

'No,' Damien said softly, shaking his head.

'You won't hurt us?' the girl asked them with fear in her face.

'No, we won't hurt anyone.'

Damien, Melissa, and Eddy shuffled gingerly towards them.

'My name is Damien, what's yours?'

'I'm Joseph. This is Tess—' he motioned to the girl, then pointed to the other boy — 'this is John. He's my twin. When did you get here?'

'Just now. The tall man brought us straight up. Why are you here?'

'We were walking to school, all of us, and the red car pulled up and the tall man told us he was our new teacher, and he would drive us to school,' Joseph went on. 'Then he brought us here. We were driving for a few hours.'

'Where are you from?'

'Just near Glasgow,' Joseph had said.

'In Scotland?' Damien didn't understand.

'Yeah. Then they made us wear these clothes.' They were all dressed in grey pyjamas, two-piece sets made from cotton. 'Where are you from?'

'We live in Darlington,' Damien had told him.

'Where is Darlington?' Joseph asked. 'I've never heard of it.'

'That's where we are now. I don't know what the road is called but we're still in Darlington.' Damien had a worried look on his face, wondering why three children from Scotland were in the same room as them. 'Do your parents know you're here?'

They all shrugged. 'We don't know.'

As the sun gradually dipped below the horizon they heard footsteps outside the bedroom door. The Scottish children went quiet suddenly and jumped into bed. Damien, Eddy, and Melissa froze, not really knowing what to do, their little hearts beating so quickly in their chests it hurt.

The door opened and in walked Thomas with a tray of food to hand out.

'This is your dinner. Make it last until later,' he said, placing it down on a small table near the door. Then another man walked in who was much smaller than the tall man and much rounder. In his hands he had some grey pyjamas, which he handed to Thomas and left. 'And when you've finished you three need to put these on. Remember, if you need the toilet, just press this buzzer and someone will come up and take you.' He pointed to the button on the wall near the door.

'I need the toilet,' Melissa had said, still damp from her incident in the Mondeo.

'Come with me.' Thomas took Melissa out of the room for a little while before returning with her. She was now wearing her pyjamas. The children had watched her when she returned, fearing what had happened while she'd been away from them.

As Thomas turned to leave, Damien had said, 'When do we get to go home?'

He stopped and turned to the young boy. 'Very soon, Damien, very soon. Just eat your food and put these on.'

Once they had eaten and put their pyjamas on, they played with the toys for a while. Time seemed to slip by, the moon now moving across the window.

Then Damien asked the question which both Eddy and Melissa also wanted to know.

'Why do you all have no hair? Are you all poorly?'

'They shaved it off,' Joseph explained, sadly. He looked to his left at his twin, who was quietly playing with some small racing cars. 'How many times has it been, John?'

'Six times now,' John confirmed, not taking his eyes from the racetrack imprinted on the square mat below him. 'They cut it when it gets too long.'

At one point, the children attempted to open the door, which proved pointless. It was secured externally. Eventually, an alarm went off somewhere in the room. Joseph, John, and Tess stood up, leaving the toys where they were, and got into their individual beds.

'What's going on?' Damien asked.

'It's bedtime. Put your pyjamas on.'

Damien climbed into one of the beds, pulling the covers up over him. In the next few moments the lights went out, leaving it in total darkness, causing Eddy and Melissa to gasp in panic.

'It goes off the same time every night,' Joseph informed them.

Damien didn't understand, staring into the darkness. 'How long . . . how long have you been here?'

'I've counted fifty-nine days,' Joseph said, slowly. 'We haven't left this house since we got here.'

37

Thursday evening
Brougham Street, North Road

After a knock at her front door, Mandy Spencer opened it to find Melissa Clarke's mother, Tracy, with an anxious look on her face.

Tracy stepped up and they hugged each other tightly.

'How you holding up, Trace?' Mandy asked, closing the door.

'I don't know what to do with myself, Mand. I'm climbing the walls,' she confessed quietly, trailing Mandy down the hallway into the dining room. The house was hot. Tracy took off her light-blue Berghaus jacket, which she placed on the back of one of the dining room chairs.

'You want a coffee?' Mandy asked.

'I could do with a vodka . . .' she joked, fidgeting with her fingers.

Mandy stopped and turned. 'I do have vodka if you want one?'

'I need it, Mand. Don't judge me, I—'

'Believe me, there's no one judging you here. Come through to the kitchen. Henry's here too.'

At the far end of the narrow kitchen, sitting on a high stool, was Eddy's dad, Henry. They waved at each other before sharing a long hug.

'How you doing, Tracy?' he asked softly, rubbing her back.

Tracy pulled away, dabbing the tears from her eyes. 'I can't cope. I don't know what to do with myself.'

'Start by drinking this,' Mandy said, offering her a half-pint glass of vodka and coke. She'd only asked for vodka but Mandy, after working with her for several years, knew her favourite drink was vodka and coke.

Tracy took it and had a big gulp, draining nearly half of it, before sitting on the other free stool.

'It's just awful,' Tracy struggled to say, the words clogging in her throat. She raised her hand to her eyes, where more tears had formed. 'Why has someone taken our babies?'

When DI Tanzy had returned to the station he'd phoned Mandy, telling her that there'd been missing reports about Eddy Long and Melissa Clarke. Mandy explained all three of them were in the same class and that Eddy was Henry's son and Melissa was Tracy's daughter, and that she found it very strange as she worked with both Henry and Tracy in the Planning Permission department at the town hall.

'Has it been on yet?' Henry asked, glancing down at his watch.

Mandy checked the time and shook her head. 'It'll start soon. Come on, we'll sit in the living room.'

Minutes later, they were sitting in front of the television. The lamp in the corner was on and the curtains were closed. After a car advert had finished on the screen, the local news started. A news reporter, sitting behind a low desk, dressed in a dark blue suit and blue tie with his hair gelled up to one side, told viewers today was a day that would be remembered in Darlington for all the wrong reasons.

'Let's go to one of our reporters, who spoke to a local detective earlier at the crime scene,' the man said.

As the screen changed, a woman standing at the bottom of Brougham Street earlier that day introduced herself as Wendy Lynn, the local reporter for ITV News. 'The body of an elderly lady was found just behind me earlier this morning. Two young boys making their way to school came across the body, lying in a pool of blood. Local police were at the scene within minutes. The elderly female, now identified as Mrs Sheena Edwards, was pronounced dead at the scene, the apparent victim of a violent crime. It's a shock to everyone in the town. We have few details on what occurred or why, but as soon as we know, further information will be given. Forensic officers have attended the scene and are currently in the process of gathering the evidence they feel is necessary to take back for analysis. This is Wendy Lynn, ITV News.'

'Bloody awful,' Mandy said, wiping her eyes, 'Sheena was lovely. Used to look after Damien when he was younger.'

The TV presenter offered his heartfelt feelings to the public and to the family of Sheena Edwards before moving onto the next story.

'In the same street, earlier today, a further incident occurred. We go back to Brougham Street and once again speak to our reporter Wendy Lynn.'

Wendy Lynn stood further up the street outside Jerry's house. Next to Wendy stood Jerry's cleaner, Jackie, who looked both sad and nervous about being on camera.

'It's a very sad day in this street,' Wendy said. 'After the brutal murder just along this road, we learned that three children appear to have been kidnapped around the same time. I'm standing here with Jackie, who lives in the area, who'll give us more information.' The lighting of the street was a little darker, clearly showing it was later in the afternoon. Jackie had changed out of her blue apron and was wearing a black jumper and had a little make-up on her face.

'I'm friends with Mandy Spencer,' Jackie started, 'I've known her for years. I was cleaning in the house behind me when Jerry, my client, had said that he hoped the little boy was okay. I asked him what he meant. He explained that Mandy's son, Damien, had been taken on his way to school earlier. Then he'd mentioned about the children in the back

151

of the car. He said there was a little boy and a little girl too. It's just awful. I just hope they find them soon.'

'Thank you, Jackie, for your time,' Wendy said, facing the camera again. 'If anyone knows anything that can help with this investigation, please don't hesitate to get in touch by contacting the police on the numbers below.'

Numbers for Missing Persons and the ITV News desk appeared at the bottom of the screen.

'This is Wendy Lynn, on this very sad, dark day in Darlington. Back to the studio.'

Tracy leaned forward, bubbling with tears, her wet face soaked in the palms of her hands. Mandy, who was on her left, placed a trembling hand on her back to soothe her while she wept. Henry leaned over to comfort them both.

'They'll find them. They have their photographs. It's only a matter of time,' he told them, his eyes too filling up.

'I just want to know why!' Tracy bawled. 'Why our children?'

Henry pulled her close and held her for a few minutes. 'We'll find . . . them, I . . . promise,' he whispered, the words clogging in his throat.

38

Tanzy opened the email Jennifer Lucas had sent last night, with a different camera angle giving a better view of what had happened to the naked man outside the tool hire shop.

Tanzy opened the video file and the image filled the screen. The camera seemed to be positioned near the railway bridge, quite high up, with a great view of the road.

The quality of the video could've been better, but it was better than nothing. The time in the screen's corner told Tanzy it was 11.43 p.m. He focused hard until something caught his eye on the left. The naked man ran onto Cleveland Street, then sprinted as quickly as he could away from the camera.

A few moments later a four-by-four crept out and went left, accelerating down the road towards the running man.

Tanzy paused the video and rewound it back, then paused it when the car was at the end of Edward Street just before it turned left. He used the 'zoom in' button to see if he could get a better, clearer image of the driver, but the nearby streetlights reflected off the driver's window too brightly.

He pressed play, then paused it again when he could see the rear of the car. Zooming in once again, he couldn't determine the colour but he recognised the shape of it. He wasn't one hundred per cent sure but it looked like a Kia Sportage. Not the newest model. Perhaps the one before, dating back a couple of years. He tapped on the 'down' arrow and looked at the registration plate.

'Shit,' he said in frustration, seeing the plate had been removed. 'Brilliant.'

He pressed play, and the Kia Sportage sped away from the camera. In the distance Tanzy watched the naked man stop and turn, then start waving towards the oncoming car. Seconds later the Sportage drifted over to the left and knocked the man down. He disappeared from Tanzy's view somewhere in front of the car. Tanzy watched in awe as the brake lights came on, and the driver casually stepped out of the car and went around the front of it.

'What are you watching?' a voice said from his left, startling him.

'Morning, Max. The video from the CCTV that Jennifer sent me.' He leaned back and pointed to the screen. 'The naked man, who you believe could be Lyle Wilson, being run down on Cleveland Street late on Wednesday night.'

Byrd's eyes widened as he placed his coffee down on his desk, grabbed his chair and sat down to watch it. 'I'll take it back to the beginning,' Tanzy told him.

They watched it again. Byrd commented straight away about the car having no plates and agreed with Tanzy that it was a Kia Sportage. 'Is it blue? Black?'

'It's hard to tell,' Tanzy said.

The man disappeared from view at the front of the car then returned with the naked man over his shoulder. He opened the boot of the car, threw the man inside, then shut it quickly. The camera was some distance from the car but they could make out what was happening. After the man climbed inside the Sportage, he drove away in the direction of North Road.

'And just like that, gone,' Byrd said, a hint of anger in his tone.

'I'll speak to Jennifer, see if any other cameras pick it up on North Road.'

'Yeah, good shout,' Byrd agreed.

'How'd you sleep last night? You look terrible, Max.'

Byrd raised his eyebrows. 'You do have a way with words, Mr Tanzy, I'll give you that.' He half smiled towards him. 'I slept pretty shit, to be honest. Had three whiskeys and still hardly slept. Claire had her friend Alice round for a takeaway and a few drinks. She left around ten when her boyfriend, Alex, picked her up.'

'That the one who plays football?'

'Yeah, that's him. Plays seven-a-side over Longfield a few nights a week. Might see if I can get a game with him. I'm feeling fit at the moment.'

'Still old and slow though, eh?' Tanzy said.

Byrd gently jabbed his arm. 'Speak with Jennifer, see what she can find. We need to find that Kia Sportage.'

39

Friday morning
Claxton Avenue, Mowden

A dark blue Kia Sportage pulled up against the frosty curb and came to a gradual halt, the tyres quietly crunching on the wafer-thin layer of ice on the damp road. The man inside smiled to himself and leaned to the left, picking up the thin pile of paperwork from the front passenger seat. He put it inside his fleece pocket and zipped it up. From the footwell of the passenger seat, he picked up a square box, roughly a foot by a foot in size.

Before he got out of the car, he reached over and took a photo from the glovebox. A reminder of why he was doing this. The photo was of him, his wife, and his two children, taken when they were at Disneyland Paris three years ago. As he stared into the eyes of his children, his heart felt heavy as the memories flooded back to him in sharp waves, as if he'd been stabbed in the chest multiple times. What an amazing holiday it was — probably one of the best ever. Their infectious smiles made him grin, as if nothing in the world mattered and everything was good again. Just like it had been in that perfect moment. If only he could have stopped time then.

But those days were long gone.

He carefully placed the photograph back into the glove-box, opened the driver's door, and stepped down onto the path with the box in his hand. He padded down the slightly inclined driveway and knocked on the front door. He was just over six foot with narrow but muscular shoulders. On top of the dark-coloured fleece and jeans he wore a high-vis vest.

It was all a part of the image.

The disguise.

After he knocked, it wasn't long before a man opened the door, wearing a curious smile, the kind people used for a stranger at their door.

The man with the box held up his badge, which hung from a green lanyard around his neck. 'Got a delivery for you.'

The man standing inside the house frowned. 'You have?'

'Yup.'

'I haven't ordered anything.' He frowned.

'For Mrs Everitt,' the man said, turning the box and showing him the label.

'That's my wife. Let me ring her first. I've told her about ordering things without telling me.' He plucked his phone from his pocket and put it to his ear. 'Ahh, she isn't answering,' he said in frustration. 'What's inside?'

The man in the vest shrugged. 'Not sure, Mr Everitt. I'm just the driver.'

'Okay, I'll take it.'

'Don't suppose I could be cheeky and ask to use your toilet?' the man asked. 'I didn't have time this morning and I don't know if I'll get a chance soon. I feel bad for asking but—'

Everitt waved him in. 'Yeah, no worries. Just down the hall and on the left.' He went back into the dining room and placed the package on the table next to his open laptop while the delivery man closed the small toilet door under the stairs.

As Brian Everitt looked at the reports for the last quarter of the year, he sensed someone behind him. He could feel the carpet near his chair dip slightly. The way the still air had changed around him. He was sure—

By then it was too late.

He gasped when something very, very tight wrapped around his throat. Whatever it was, it dug into his skin fiercely and only got tighter. He pushed up off the chair backwards and stumbled, grabbing at his throat, trying to free whatever it was. It felt like a very thin wire. It was so tight he couldn't get his fingertips between his skin and the wire to free it.

The oxygen supply being cut off to his brain made him delirious as he was dragged back onto the floor, his heart pounding in his chest. A moment later, he dropped his arms beside him, and his world went black.

When Brian Everitt's body went still, the man holding the wire loosened his grip and let Brian fall onto his side, then climbed to his feet. He knew he wouldn't have long before Brian gained consciousness but there'd be enough time to do what he needed to do.

Enough time to make him suffer.

40

After Byrd knocked on the door, he took a few steps back. The window curtains moved a little, then became still.

A car passed behind them and someone shouted something inaudible, but neither Byrd nor DC Tiffin could decipher what it was, nor did they really care.

The faded-white front door opened and standing there was Mark Greenwell's mother, Anna.

'Hi, Anna,' Byrd said, smiling thinly.

'Hi,' she said, her eyes widening. Was it news about her son, Mark? Had they found the person responsible for his murder?

'Is it okay if we come in?'

She moved aside to allow them room to enter. The house was small and compact, the hallway narrow but decorated pleasantly. The living room was the first door on the right, then the stairs, then another doorway straight ahead led to the dining room and kitchen.

'How you holding up, Mrs Greenwell?' Byrd asked softly, trailing her into the dining room. She appeared slimmer than she did a few days ago, her shoulders narrow, her movements frail as if she ached. Tiffin slowly followed them, glancing right into the living room as she passed the doorway, noticing two bed covers on the floor with pillows and empty sweet wrappers strewn around them.

Before she answered him, she offered coffees. They both declined and stopped in the dining room.

'It's a terrible mess in here,' she confessed. 'I really need to get things cleaned up. Ethan stayed up late last night and we watched a film.'

Byrd eyed the bowls half filled with sweets on the small table against the wall to the left. 'Don't worry about a thing, Mrs Greenwell.'

She let out a small smile and glanced to the floor.

'How you holding up?'

'I'm not, to be honest.' She raised her hand to her forehead, as if preventing an oncoming headache. 'I . . . I just don't know what to do anymore.'

Both detectives absorbed her words with sympathy. Tiffin had never felt a loss close to hers but Byrd had. Losing his sister in a similar kind of way, and his parents very recently, he could relate to how Anna was feeling.

'I know you don't think it will, Anna, but it'll get easier in time. Trust me, I've been through a similar thing in my life.'

Her eyebrows furrowed. 'Your own child?'

Byrd shook his head. 'No, sorry, I don't have children. My sister was stabbed to death, twelve years ago. And . . . my parents died two months ago.'

'Sorry for your loss,' she said quietly.

'The pain doesn't go away but you learn to cope with it,' Byrd assured her. 'It may feel like you won't be able to, but you will. You're a strong woman, I can see that.'

She looked back at the floor, unsure how to respond to the compliment.

'We were wondering,' Byrd said, 'would it be okay to have a quick look in Mark's room? See if there's anything that may be able to help us with our enquiry?' Byrd pulled the search warrant from his pocket. He didn't want to use it but once it had been signed he knew he had to act and leave the paperwork with Anna.

She managed a nod but didn't say anything.

'Thank you.' Byrd and Tiffin made their way up the stairs. They recalled DC Leonard seeing the shoeboxes in Mark's wardrobe full of drugs on Wednesday morning and would collect them for evidence.

'It's just up on the left,' Anna said, appearing at the bottom of the stairs.

'Thanks,' Tiffin said, concentrating on the steep incline.

Byrd grabbed the handle, wondering if Anna had been in there since she'd found Mark's body. Often, he found, when a family suffered the loss of a child, they didn't touch the room or didn't clean it. They left it exactly how it was when the child was there. That way they could feel them, could smell their scent. It often brought comfort to the parents. He pushed down the handle and edged the door open. The faintest smell of aftershave hung in the still, cold air. The bed to the left wasn't made. There was a small pile of folded clean clothes at the base of the radiator under the window. They were mainly interested in the contents of the wardrobe, so they headed over to it. Byrd pulled the door open and peeked inside.

The shoeboxes were gone.

'Shit.' Byrd frowned and spent the next several minutes looking around the room, opening and closing drawers, checking through the things on the desk. There was nothing left in his room that could help them at all.

Back downstairs in the dining room they found Anna staring into space, her hands cupped around the mug resting on the table surface in front of her, steam gently rising from it.

'Where's Ethan? At school?'

'I'll pick him up at three.'

'How's he coping?'

'He . . . he seems fine. I don't think he really understands yet. You see, Mark spent a lot of his time out and about. He spent most of his time at his friend's house, I think. Doesn't live far — on Craig Street.'

Byrd knew this from what Mac, the DFU guy, had said about the location of Mark's phone over the past few weeks. 'Do you know what number house on Craig Street?'

'I'm sorry, I don't.'

Byrd pulled out a chair and slowly dropped into it. 'Anna, when we carried out the post-mortem of Mark, we found something unusual.'

A look of concern washed over her face as her body seemed to tense. 'What?'

'The pathologist found marks on his back. They appeared to be whip marks. He had nine in total. The pathologist thinks some of them could date back more than two years. There's some that appear freshly done, probably done in the past few months. Do you know anything about them?'

She shook her head quickly and expressed a look of disgust. 'I . . . I don't know . . . Marks? On his back?'

Byrd nodded.

'He never mentioned anything to me about them.'

'Have you never seen them?'

'I haven't seen him without a T-shirt on for a few years. I . . . I never knew. God, who did that to him?' She raised a palm to her mouth, genuinely horrified by what Byrd was telling her.

'We don't know, Anna, but we'll do our best to find out,' Byrd said, then paused a beat. 'How long ago, just out of interest, did Mark begin spending his time at his friend's house on Craig Street?'

She shrugged, thinking hard. 'At least three years. I don't . . . I don't know them that well. I mean, I know a few of their names, ones that Mark has mentioned, but I wouldn't have thought they'd have done that to him.'

'Anna, what I've learned in this job, in over twenty years, is that people are capable of anything.'

Once finished, Byrd and Tiffin stood, made their way to the door, and headed back out to the car.

'We need to find out what's going on in Craig Street.'

41

Friday, late morning
Rise Junior School, Eldon Street

Tanzy stopped the Golf at the side of the road and turned the engine off. Annoyed there were no leads yesterday when Leonard and Weaver had visited the empty office of Cairnfield Developments on Duke Street, he'd spent time this morning trying to locate Andrew Cairn, but it was as if he didn't exist. After all, maybe Mr Cairn had nothing to do with the children going missing, but they couldn't ignore the connection and would continue to search.

While they waited for results on the search for Cairn, their next stop was the children's school. Someone must know something or the reason behind three children from the same class being taken.

Tanzy opened the car door, stepped out into the chill, and squinted up at the sun breaking through the clouds. It was bright but cold. His long, grey Parka jacket really came in handy on days like this. PC Andrews wore his standard black uniform, topped with a padded jacket they wore in the colder weather.

They crossed Eldon Street and passed the two bricked pillars into the rectangular car park, noticing an entrance door in the far corner with a sign above it stating 'Rise Juniors'.

The glass doors slid open on their approach and their focus fell on a middle-aged lady with short blonde hair sitting behind a desk. She wore thin-framed glasses and had something about her, something elegant. She looked up over the computer screen.

'Good afternoon, how can I help?' she asked evenly.

'Detective Inspector Orion Tanzy. This is PC Josh Andrews. We're here to speak to the head about the disappearance of three of your students yesterday.'

'Have they been found?' she asked, eagerness in her voice.

'Unfortunately, not yet,' Tanzy replied, sadly.

'Okay, I'll call him now.' She picked up the phone to her right, dialled a few digits, and put it to her ear. 'Hello, Mr Heslop. We have the police here to speak with you about Damien, Melissa, and Eddy . . . okay . . . yes, I will. I'll let her know too.' She hung up the phone. 'He's coming right now. I'm just going to contact their teacher as well, as she'd no doubt like to speak to you.'

'Thank you,' Tanzy replied, giving a brief smile. He turned away from her and studied the reception area. It looked new, modern and fresh, a total contradiction to its appearance on the outside. One wall was covered in children's paintings, evidently starting from the lower years on the left, through to the older children on the right. Another wall featured a large photograph of all the students, taken from a height somewhere in the playground, either by a drone or some mad man on the roof.

A minute later, a small, round man appeared in front of them, offering them both a firm handshake. He had a thinning bald head and bright-green eyes. 'I'm Fred Heslop, headteacher here at Rise Juniors. Thank you for coming in. Should we take a seat?' He motioned to their right towards a small table which was surrounded by low, deep, soft blue chairs. They all sat down and sank into the foam.

'It's awful what has happened to the children,' the headteacher started. 'When they didn't turn up for class, their teacher, Mrs Everitt, checked and counted the children again. At first she assumed they were ill, or maybe running late. But at half nine, she went to check with Alison—' he motioned towards the short, blonde-haired receptionist sitting at the desk behind them — 'who confirmed that there had been no phone calls from any of their parents indicating they wouldn't be in.'

Mr Heslop turned to the receptionist. 'Is Mrs Everitt on her way?'

She gazed over. 'I've let her know the police are here.'

He glanced down at his watch. 'She won't be a moment . . . I hope.'

There was a sound of spinning tyres coming from the car park, the sudden high-screeched noise coming through the closed glass entrance door.

'Give me a sec,' the headteacher said, frowning. He stood and dashed over to the door. 'There's a speed limit in the school car park. I've made that clear on several occasions!' Tanzy and Andrews jumped up and looked out of the window too. A blue Peugeot 307 was just disappearing through the exit.

'Who was that?' Tanzy asked.

'Someone leaving the car park quickly.'

'Whose car was it?'

'The children's teacher, Jane Everitt.'

Mr Heslop quickly pulled out his phone and put it to his ear. Tanzy and Andrews watched him, waiting.

'She isn't picking up. What's she playing at?' He turned to the receptionist, who was watching warily. 'Did you tell her the police were here?'

'Yes, yes. She said she was on her way.'

The headteacher sighed heavily.

'Where is she going?' Tanzy asked, staring out into the car park, thinking it was a strange thing for the teacher to do if she knew the police were here regarding three of her students.

'Why would she do that?' Andrews said. 'She knows we're here. Why would she go before speaking to us?'

'I . . . I . . . I don't know,' Heslop said. It was clear he didn't know and was flustered because of it. He tried her number again. 'Perhaps it's a problem with my phone. Alison, please try phoning Mrs Everitt.'

'It's going to her answering machine, she's not picking up,' Alison said from behind the reception desk, sighing heavily.

Fred Heslop huffed, his shoulders dropping an inch. 'I'll have to go to her classroom. She must have just left the students.' Then he shrugged at Tanzy. 'I don't understand this, Detective. I'm sorry.'

* * *

Nearly a mile away, in the blue Peugeot 307, Jane Everitt was hitting almost 50 mph as she approached the bottom of North Road. She was well over the speed limit, but she needed to get home as quickly as possible. There was no time to explain. After she'd spoken to the emergency services asking for an ambulance, she placed the phone down on the passenger seat and both hands on the steering wheel.

She took a right at the large roundabout at the bottom of North Road, the tyres barely gripping the wet tarmac. A car beeped to her left before she pulled onto St Augustine's Way towards Woodland Road.

She swung a right at the roundabout and put her foot to the floor. In front of her, a yellow Vauxhall Corsa slowed as the lights up ahead went from amber to red. There was no time to waste, so instead she veered around it, and headed straight over the busy crossroads.

* * *

The DHL van coming from the left ploughed straight into the side of the Peugeot, rolling the car twice until the roof was hard up against the now-bent metal barrier that bordered the footpath near the large block of flats. A woman beside the railing screamed and grabbed her five-year-old son in a panic.

All of the traffic on the crossroads came to a sudden halt, drivers' eyes wide and mouths open in shock. Several drivers got out of their cars and made their way over to the damaged blue Peugeot lying on its side. Through the smashed front windscreen, one man could see a woman in the driver's seat with her head tipped sideways, gravity pulling her long black hair towards the floor. He could see her face, covered in blood.

She didn't move.

'Jesus!' he gasped, jumping over the barrier and climbing up onto the car to open the passenger door, but it wouldn't budge.

'Just hold on, missus!' he yelled through the cracked window. Then he looked around at the people who had started to circle the car. 'Someone help me, I can't open the door. She's unconscious. Someone . . .' The people around started to panic a little. One man jumped up and tried to assist but the door wouldn't move. It felt like it was welded shut.

Then they heard a sound.

A ringtone.

Both men glanced at each other.

'Not mine,' one of them said.

'Not mine, either.'

They both looked through the cracked side passenger window. On the floor of the passenger footwell, there was an iPhone, the screen facing up in their direction.

'It's there,' one of them said, pointing.

The screen flashed and the phone vibrated, making tiny arcs of movement in the shallow sea of glass at the bottom of the car. The caller ID was Fred Heslop. Seconds afterwards, the call stopped. Then a text message appeared. It was from her husband, Brian.

They lowered their faces closer to the glass. It read: *I'm so sorry, Jane. You're too late.*

42

Friday, early afternoon
Darlington

The six children sat on the floor near the bay window of the huge bedroom. Melissa was next to Eddy, shaking, her face tucked into the middle of her bony knees, not quite believing that the other three had been there for fifty-nine days. Neither Melissa, Damien, nor Eddy had slept well last night, for obvious reasons.

'They haven't let you out, not once?' Damien asked Joseph, who was occupied with building a ramp for the toy cars on the floor in front of him.

Joseph shook his head but showed no sadness. 'Only to go to the toilet and to brush our teeth.'

'Your parents must think . . .' He trailed off, not wanting to say it out loud.

'That we're dead?' He looked away from Damien, tilted his head back, and observed the all-too-familiar white ceiling above them. His face was emotionless, as if he'd been in the room for so long, he'd accepted their situation.

'Have you tried to escape?' Eddy asked.

'Twice. I won't try it again.'

'Why? What happened?'

'Once, when the door opened at dinner time, which is half twelve every day, without fail, I waited next to it. Tess and John had agreed to sit on the floor against this wall and I packed my bed with their pillows, making it look like I was sleeping. When the man came in with a tray of food, I snuck out onto the landing. I got five steps, then an alarm went off. A loud siren. I panicked and, suddenly, the man who'd come in with the food was behind me. He was so angry and he pulled me back into the room. I saw a camera outside the door. That must have tripped the alarm.'

'When was the other time?' Damien asked. 'You said twice.'

'I climbed out of the window,' he explained. Damien, Melissa, and Eddy tilted their gazes at the window. It was square, with a lock mechanism at the bottom of it. The window opened from the top, with hinges that allowed it to swivel inwards.

'What happened?'

'We tied the bedsheets together so I could climb down. It's pretty high. Before my feet touched the floor outside, another loud alarm went off. The same sound as when I tried it the first time. I dropped to the floor and ran, but I'd hurt my ankle when I landed, so I didn't get far. Only to the driveway. I shouted but no one heard me.'

Melissa started to cry again. Eddy stared at the floor vacantly. Damien absorbed this information but tried his best to think of something, as he, too, glanced away from Joseph.

'Has anyone else been in this room other than you three?' Damien asked. 'Any other kids, I mean?'

'Yes.'

'Where . . . where did the others go?'

Joseph shrugged. 'We don't know. The men sometimes come in and choose one of us. Sometimes two. We—' he motioned to himself, John, and Tess with his hand — 'all arrived at the same time. We haven't gone anywhere yet.

As far as I know, we're safe in this room. We get food and water. We have beds to sleep in and we have toys. When we get picked, I don't know where we'll go, so without knowing what will happen, I want to stay here.'

'How many—'

Damien's question fizzled out when he heard something on the other side of the door.

A buzzing sound. Damien frowned at the door. It was almost like a hive of angry bees.

'Say goodbye to your hair,' John whispered.

Damien glanced his way. 'My hair?'

'Yeah . . .' Joseph said. 'Just before they cut your hair, a man stands on the other side of the door for a minute with the shears turned on. Then he comes in and shaves off your hair. Like I said, I've had mine done six times now.'

After the minute passed, the sound of the hair clippers stopped outside the door. Damien, Eddy, and Melissa glared with anticipation.

The door creaked open. Standing there, with a set of clippers, was a small stocky man with a greasy face and tanned skin. He entered the room, staring at them all.

'Who's first, then?'

Melissa dug her head deeper between her knees and started to cry.

The man holding the clippers started to laugh and went over to her first.

43

After getting Jane Everitt's address from the headteacher at Rise Juniors, Tanzy and Andrews made their way over to Claxton Avenue.

'There it is, small porch, white front door, wide window,' Andrews said, spotting the house number.

Tanzy checked the rear-view mirror and angled over to the kerb. There was a black Fiat Punto on the driveway. Tanzy recalled it wasn't the same car that Jane Everitt had left the school in less than half an hour before. He remembered the head had called her 'Mrs', so it could be her husband's. He opened the car door, the cold air fresh on his bald head, and reached up, scratching his throat from a faint rash caused by shaving earlier that morning.

Tanzy and Andrews stopped at the edge of the drive, assessed the house for a moment, and scanned the windows for any movement. They both moved down the side of the Punto and Tanzy, who was in front, placed his palm on the bonnet of the car. It was ice cold. The car hadn't moved for a while. 'Let's go see—'

A loud siren came from the left, cutting him off. They turned curiously at the noise, which was growing louder by the second.

An ambulance roared down the road towards them, coming to a stop in front of the house they were standing at. The paramedic in the passenger seat, a small, muscular, fit-looking woman, stepped out and studied them.

'Is he okay?' she shouted, rushing to the side door, and swinging it open. She grabbed a medical bag, slammed the door closed, and turned. 'Is he okay?' she asked them again.

Tanzy frowned at the paramedic. 'Who?'

'The caller's husband,' she said. 'Is he okay?'

Tanzy frowned.

'Who are you two?' she asked, noticing Andrews in a uniform.

'Detective Inspector Orion Tanzy. This is PC Andrews. Why . . . why are you here? What's happened?'

'I'm Jessie. He's Paul.' She pointed towards the ambulance at the male paramedic. 'We received an emergency call. An individual at this address requires immediate assistance,' she said, panting. From the back of the ambulance, the male paramedic, Paul, appeared. He was average height, quite stocky, with a kind face but hardened. Proof of years of experience involving these types of situations. He stepped down onto the driveway.

Paul noticed Andrews' uniform. 'Can you get us inside?'

'We've just got here. We're looking for a woman called Jane,' Tanzy explained. 'She was—'

'That's who made the call,' the man replied. 'We're here for her husband.'

Jessie used her hands as a visor and looked through the cold glass of the wide living room window. Her mouth opened in horror.

'What is it?' Tanzy said quickly, noticing her change in expression.

'You need to get us in there, now!'

44

Tanzy took a step back, lifted his right foot, and with everything he had, lunged forward into the white door. There was a loud crack as the lock snapped but the door didn't fully open. The metallic parts of the lock had bent. He tried again, and this time the door was flung open, pounding into the wall inside the hallway.

Jessie moved past Tanzy into the house.

'Hey, wait!' Tanzy gasped, trying to grab her shoulder to hold her back but missing. 'Wait, we don't know who's in there.'

She dashed down the hallway but abruptly came to a halt at the doorway to the living room.

Tanzy caught her up, Andrews just behind. Shoulder to shoulder, Tanzy and Jessie glared in horror at what was on the floor in front of them.

Blood. Plenty of it.

'Jesus!' Tanzy gasped, absorbing the scene before him.

Jessie stepped into the hot living room and stood over the man, carefully minding her footing near the blood surrounding him. The man lay on his back with his eyes wide open, staring vacantly at the low ceiling above. There was a smell in the air that was familiar to Tanzy. Pastry or croissants, something like that. There was also a faint smell of fabric softener coming from the damp clothes on nearby radiators.

Paul entered the room, stepping around Tanzy and Andrews.

'Good God . . .' he puffed.

'He's dead. I . . . I think this is a scene for you guys and forensics,' Jessie said, slowly standing. Paul agreed.

Tanzy turned to Andrews. 'Call it in, get the team down here immediately.'

Andrews pulled the radio from his belt and stepped back into the hallway.

'What do you think happened?' Jessie asked Tanzy, who was methodically analysing the scene. The man's head was near the door, his feet pointing in the direction of the corner just left of the window, where a flatscreen television sat neatly on a thick, expensive-looking wooden unit. The floor was a light wood, bordered by low, stylish skirting boards that ran around the outside of the room, and the walls were a light blue. Two light-brown three-seater leather sofas sat perpendicular to each other, one on the left side of the room facing the window, and the other on the right, facing the fire, which was just behind the man on the floor.

'Well,' Tanzy started, 'judging by that knife in his hand, chances are it could be self-inflicted.' Tanzy paused a beat, then faced Jessie. 'What was the nature of the call?'

'His wife rang for an ambulance, told the operator that he needed emergency assistance.' She gave a sad smile, looking down at him.

Tanzy peeled his focus away from Jessie and glared back down at the knife on the floor. 'Maybe that's why she left the school so suddenly,' he said to himself, working it out.

In the doorway, PC Andrews appeared, his complexion pale.

'They on their way?' Tanzy asked him.

'Coming now,' he confirmed, leaning to one side for support.

'You okay? You look like you've lost a little colour,' Tanzy commented, and, without making it obvious, both paramedics glanced his way, both understanding the situation.

'Think it was something I ate earlier. Stomach isn't right. I'll be okay soon.'

Tanzy nodded. 'Go outside. Have a breather.'

Andrews silently made his way to the door, stepping out into the cold, crisp afternoon. The skies above were still grey, the sun nowhere to be seen. It wouldn't be long until darkness was upon them and the frost would set in. They'd use portable lamps and UV equipment anyway, so Tanzy wasn't worried about it getting dark.

'Hey, what's that?' Tanzy said, pointing down at the front of the sofa, seeing something black on the floor, just next to the man's right hand. He tilted his head, aiding him to identify the object. Half of it seemed to be underneath the bottom of the sofa. 'Is it a mobile phone?'

'It could be, yeah,' Paul said, leaning over.

'We'll collect that soon. Forensics won't be too much longer.'

'There's something else,' Paul said, his finger angled further along the sofa. Another object. This was bigger and longer. He edged around the bloody body and lowered himself to his knees and bent forward. 'Looks like a laptop, maybe?'

'A laptop?' Tanzy repeated.

'Yeah — have you got a torch or a light? There's something white on top of it. Looks like paper?'

Tanzy reached inside his grey Parka and pulled out a thin, silver Maglite, then bent down, handing it over. 'Here.'

Paul turned on the light, lowered himself to the floor again, careful not to touch the feet of the man, and shone it under the sofa into the three-inch space. 'It's an envelope.'

'Okay, we'll wait for forensics to check for prints first before we touch it.'

Paul shuffled back from the body and stood up, handing the torch back to Tanzy.

'Really think it was self-inflicted?' Jessie asked, frowning down at the man.

'It could be. It would have been difficult, though. I wouldn't fancy doing it,' Tanzy admitted, wincing.

'Where are his clothes?' Jessie asked, looking around carefully.

Tanzy shrugged.

'Never mind his clothes,' Paul said, 'where is his penis?'

45

Friday afternoon
Claxton Avenue, Mowden

By the time that the forensic team had turned up, the afternoon sun had nearly gone. Tanzy had turned on the house lights and stood back, while Tallow, Hope, and Forrest, all dressed in white plastic coveralls and white face masks, stood around the body. Andrews was still in the hallway, struggling with the nausea he'd felt ever since he'd entered the living room.

Tanzy, now in overshoes and acting as first responder, stood at the far wall with a A4 clipboard, signing team members in and out. Not a job he usually did, but Andrews, usually very capable, didn't seem at the top of his game today.

'Where the hell is his dick?' Tallow said, slowly shaking his head at Tanzy in amazement.

'I haven't seen it, if you're actually asking me,' Tanzy replied. Then, to his right, he heard people enter the house, their footsteps echoing on the wooden floor in the hallway. It was Byrd, followed by DC Anne Tiffin.

'Welcome to the party, Max. What took you so long?'

'Reports and traffic. Usual shit. Is it bad?' He joined him in the doorway to the living room.

'Bad enough.' Tanzy moved aside, allowing Byrd to see into the room. The naked man was still in the exact position he'd been discovered. Forensics hadn't moved the body yet.

Tallow briefly smiled at Byrd before focusing back on his camera, taking some more shots, the brilliant flash lighting up the room like stabs of lightning.

Amanda Forrest was on her knees, next to the laptop, envelope, and phone. Tanzy had mentioned seeing it under the sofa so, very carefully, without touching the pool of blood or the body, they'd lifted the sofa upright onto its side, leaning it against the small space of the wall next to the window, giving them better access. Under the light of the temporary lamps situated around the room, Forrest noticed a name written on the envelope.

Tanzy, watching her from a distance, noticed her frown. 'What does it say, Amanda?'

'Jane.'

'That's his wife,' Tanzy said. 'A suicide note?' He turned his attention to the right of the room, noticing Tallow duck under the archway leading into the rear dining room. There was an old-fashioned dining room table with a polished sheen finish which reflected the glare of the temporary lighting they'd set up. On the far wall, there was a set of French doors that led out to a patio and garden. The left wall was filled with a brown unit with several shelves on. One was lined with four small six-by-four photo frames; the top two were filled with paperback books, all different colours, all different heights, a mixture of well-known and not so well-known authors.

'See anything?' Tanzy asked Tallow, watching him near the French doors.

Tallow paused, angled his gaze upwards. 'Come see this.'

Both Tanzy and Byrd moved under the archway into the dining room. 'What is it?'

'Look,' Tallow said. They moved around the table to where he was standing.

'Jesus . . . is that . . . ?'

Byrd saw it too. 'God . . .'

Tallow leaned over and, with gloved hands, picked up the object, then studied it for a few seconds. Stunned, he shook his head. 'Not often you find one of these at a crime scene.'

Tanzy padded over and stopped before them. 'He was blessed, wasn't he?'

'Seems that way,' Tallow replied, then looked into the living room. 'Hey, Hope.' She glanced his way. Holding the object for her to see, he said, 'I found the penis.'

'I don't want to see it,' she shouted, turning away, shaking her head at him. 'Bag it up. You can deal with that shit,' she replied, continuing to focus on what she was doing. Tallow gave Tanzy a half-smile and moved around the table towards the forensics kit, which had been left under the archway. He picked up a bag and carefully dropped the penis into it, running his thumb and index finger across the top to seal it.

'How are you doing, Amanda?' Tallow asked her.

She glanced up at Tallow and Tanzy. 'Should we . . . should we open this?' She held the envelope in her hands, aiming the question at either Tanzy or Byrd, hoping one of them would answer.

'Yes, open it,' Tanzy decided.

Judiciously, she turned the envelope and peeled away the seal, then pulled out the paper inside. All eyes were on her. She unfolded the paper, read the words, then said out loud: '*Jane, I'm sorry for the person I've become, I can't do this any longer.*'

'Maybe Jane can help us with what this means exactly,' Tanzy commented. 'We need to speak with her as soon as possible.'

'Sir,' Andrews said, appearing in the doorway, his face still pale. 'Just had a call through. There's been a serious RTC on Woodland Road near town. A woman has been badly hurt, currently unresponsive. Ambulance and police are at the scene.'

Tanzy waited for him to go on, wondering why he was eager to tell him.

'According to the driving license in her purse she's been identified as Jane Everitt.'

46

Friday night
Darlington

In his study on the first floor of the mansion, Jonny Feland was sitting at his desk looking through old photographs, reminiscing about the past. He studied a photo of his mother and father at Redcar, standing on the beach. The flat, dull sea was placid behind them, the sky pleasant but dotted with clouds.

Footsteps came from the landing. Feland looked up, seeing Jamie appear in the open doorway.

'Got a minute, boss?'

'Yeah, sure, come in.'

Jamie sauntered into his office and stood before him.

'What's happening with the next batch?' Jamie asked, looking down on him.

'It's being delivered tonight. I'll send some of the boys to go pick it up. We're going to try something different.'

Jamie frowned. 'Changing the supplier?'

Feland shook his head. 'No. He's cheap and the product is good. So no, we're not changing the supplier.'

'What about what happened last year? Did it come from him?'

Feland shrugged. 'These things happen, Jamie. If people want to risk having a good time and doing drugs, they have to accept the responsibility that sometimes there are consequences. Sometimes things go bad.'

'But it was our product.'

'I don't care. That young lass is no concern to me. As long as we get paid, I'm not bothered. Neither should you be. Why the sudden concern, Jamie?' Feland swivelled fully towards him, curious to know.

Jamie had Feland's undivided attention. It made him nervous.

'I think if we supply someone a service, that service should be a certain standard. I remember reading the report in the newspaper when the police found the girl. There was rat poison in the powder. I know we didn't put rat poison in. Why would we?'

Feland shrugged. 'Exactly, Jamie, why would we? We wouldn't. We send the product out there. People buy it. People like it. Then people come back for more. It's a simple process which has worked for longer than I've been in the game. Whatever happened to the girl was nothing to do with us.'

'But she bought it from one of us,' Jamie said.

Feland's face became more serious. 'Jamie, my boy, I need you to drop this.'

Just over a year ago, there had been a 999 call from someone at a party on Swinburne Avenue, saying his friend had gone missing just after midnight. Over two hours later the girl had been found in Stanhope Park naked in a pool of her own sick. The cocaine she had taken, according to medical reports, had contained rat poison. The amount of alcohol she'd consumed, which had thinned her blood, allowed the poison to hit her bloodstream quickly.

'Please drop it, boy,' Feland told him.

Jamie seemed unsure. 'I feel bad because I was at that party, boss. I'm the one who sold her the product.'

Feland slammed his palm onto the desk quickly, the sudden bang echoing around the room making Jamie tense.

'I won't tell you again,' Feland said, coldly. 'Do. You. Understand?'

Jamie sheepishly nodded and backed away out of the room.

Feland sighed heavily after he'd gone. In hindsight, the girl wouldn't have died that night if Feland hadn't handed out the product when he had. His supplier had told him there could be an issue with it, that he'd had the powder out on his table at home the same time he'd had an infestation of rats, and that he'd kept rat poison nearby. He admitted to Feland he'd spilled some rat poison on the table where the cocaine was and that it was unsafe to sell. Most of it would be fine but there was still a risk, the supplier had told him. Feland wanted the product anyway at half the usual price. The supplier didn't want to lose money on the product and had agreed.

Then a day later, the seventeen-year-old girl died.

Feland had read about it in the paper the following day. And smiled.

* * *

A few hours later, Feland was down in the living room, sitting with Thomas. The huge television was on in the corner, but they were discussing what to do with the children upstairs.

'Damien isn't well,' Thomas told him, looking at a folder of Damien on his knee. There were five other folders just like it, one for each child upstairs.

'How do you mean?' Feland asked.

'He keeps saying his heart hurts. That he needs medication.'

Feland stood up. 'Show me.'

A few minutes later they entered the bedroom and switched on the light. Tess, John, and Joseph were sound asleep. Melissa and Eddy were sitting next to Damien's bed, holding his hand, filled with worry.

Feland stopped next to the bed as Melissa and Eddy backed away quickly, returning to their own beds. 'What's up, Damien?'

'I have a pain in my chest and I feel sick. Really sick.' His voice was weak, his body frail and curled up. His face was as white as the bed sheet. 'I have a heart condition. I need my medication.'

Feland turned to Thomas. 'He doesn't look well.'

Thomas shook his head, a serious look in his eye. 'Can I have a word outside?'

Feland agreed then closed the bedroom door.

'Listen, Jonny,' Thomas started, 'no one is going to want him like this. We don't know how serious his heart condition is. He was fine a few hours ago. Last thing we want is a dead kid in the house.'

Feland mulled over his words for a few moments. 'But we have a buyer for him. A guy from Manchester is coming in the morning. He liked the look of his picture.'

'In my opinion if you sell him like this your reputation will suffer. He needs to go home, back to his mother, before he dies. I'm no doctor, but if he continues to worsen, he'll be dead before the morning.'

'Are you getting soft, Thomas?' Feland asked, frowning.

'I couldn't care less what happens to the kid but we can't sell him like this. As I said, your reputation will suffer. I'm not telling you how to run your business but you can't sell him. Why not offer Eddy plus one of the other kids?'

Feland's face hardened. The thought of one of his employees telling how to run things angered him, but he had a point. His face softened.

'Tell you what,' Feland said, 'I have an idea. Take the kid away. Tell the other kids you're taking him to get some medicine and that he'll be back soon. Do what you like with him. Just get rid of him.'

'I understand,' Thomas said.

'Good.' Feland turned and went back downstairs, leaving the problem in Thomas's hands.

Thomas returned to the bedroom with a smile on his face and stopped at the side of Damien's bed. 'Hey, Damien, we're going to take you to get some medicine. Okay?'

Damien half smiled and bobbed his head.

'Come on, let's get you up,' Thomas said, holding his arm and supporting his weight. Thomas collected his possessions and put his shoes on.

The security light flashed on outside, illuminating the garden and garage space. Thomas's red Mondeo was parked in front of the garage. With an arm over the young man's shoulder he guided him across to the car, opened the door for him, and gently put him inside.

'Am I going home?' Damien asked once Thomas had climbed into the driver's seat and closed the door.

'Yes. But we need to get you some medication first. I know someone who can help.'

Thomas guided the Mondeo down the side of the house onto the main road. Instead of going left, towards Damien's house, Thomas took a right.

Damien, crouched on the back seat behind him, stared through the passenger window in pain, watching the glare of the street lights they passed every few seconds. Then the sound of classical music started playing from the front of the car. Damien stiffened slightly, remembering that the man had played it yesterday morning when he had brought them to the house.

It wasn't long before the car took a right and the view out of the window changed, as if the street lights were set back a little from the road. Damien, using all of his strength, shuffled up and looked outside. They were on Coniscliffe Road heading out of town.

'Where are we going?' Damien whispered, slumping back down into the seat.

'To get you some medicine, Damien.'

A few minutes later Thomas slowed the Mondeo, took a left into Broken Scar, crawled up the steady incline, then down into the dark car park at the bottom. He applied the handbrake and switched off the engine.

'Where . . . where are we?' Damien asked, seeing nothing but darkness outside his window. He was terrified of the situation he was in, but he was too weak, too disorientated to do anything about it.

'The person who's giving us the medicine is going to meet us here. You'll be fixed up in no time.' Thomas got out then opened the back door and picked the nine-year-old up with ease.

In the darkness, with Damien in his arms, Thomas walked through the metal gate at the end of the car park, took a left, and walked along the man-made footpath for a few minutes. The river to his right almost looked picturesque under the moon. There were no sounds around them, apart from Thomas's shoes and the soft flow of passing water. It would be almost impossible to see if not for the moonlight, but Thomas knew where he was going. He'd been here before, doing this exact same thing.

'I don't feel well,' Damien managed, as Thomas made his way carefully down to the riverbank.

'I know, young man, I know,' he whispered.

'Where are we going?' Damien asked, suddenly feeling Thomas manoeuvring down the muddy bank towards the water.

'To fix you.'

Thomas stopped at the side of the river, watching the flow of water before them. Then without a second thought, he threw Damien into the river.

47

Friday night
Broken Scar, River Tees

'Shhhhh,' one of them said. 'Did you hear that?'

'Hear what?'

'Shhh.' The lad stared upriver, frowning.

His three friends, who were all drunk, glared at him as if he had three heads.

'Jake? Hear what?' a lad in a red jacket said.

'A splash. Just up there,' he said, pointing.

The four of them were up in a tree, listening to songs on their phones and drinking cheap lager. Jake had an infection and was on antibiotics for the next four days at least, so he was sober and alert. He'd just been about to choose the next song when he'd heard the splash upstream.

Jake moved off the thick branch, down the tree, until he reached the floor.

'Where are you going, Jake?'

'You wait here,' Jake said. Using the light from his phone, he cautiously stepped down the muddy bank. He flashed his light on the river. The sound he thought he'd heard was someone jumping in. He found it odd as they'd been the only ones down here for a while now, and the water wasn't exactly warm.

If someone had jumped in or fell in, they wouldn't last very long.

'Jake, get back up here, dude!' one of the lads in the tree shouted from behind him.

Jake watched the river for a moment. He couldn't see it, so turned—

'Whoa . . .' he gasped. 'What is that?'

Something floated downstream, but he couldn't work it out. Then he saw an arm move. It was a body. A child? He moved closer to the water's edge. Whatever it was, it was level with him now. Then it rapidly passed him. The speed of the current was frightening.

'Shit, shit,' he said, panicking. 'It's . . . it's a . . . ah, shit.' He dropped his phone on the floor and quickly took off his coat, then took a step towards the water.

'What the hell are you doing?' someone slurred behind him.

'There's someone in the river. I'm going in.'

Without saying anything else, Jake jumped into the river and went after the moving body. Immediately, he felt the current drag him to the centre of the river and he started to panic but tried to look downstream for any sign of the child. Just ahead, he could just about make him out, ten metres in front of him, his arms flailing side to side as he bobbed helplessly.

Knowing he didn't have long, Jake leaned forward and started swimming. The speed of the water helped him along until he banged his knee on a rock, sending a hot pain up his body, and he roared out in pain. He was sure he'd cut something and he wanted to stop but he needed to get the boy, needed to help him, so he powered on, his arms propelling him through the ice-cold moving water.

When he reached the boy he grabbed the hood of his coat and pulled him back, causing the boy to moan.

'Hey, I got you, I got you!'

Jake wasn't sure what he was going to do now. The water was too deep to stand and had a quick undercurrent. He tried to steady his frantic breathing and keep both their heads above the water. To their left, he saw the riverbank. He needed to get over there, get them to safety.

Starting to feel his own body tiring, he used his left hand to move towards the bank and pulled on the boy's hood with his right hand. After a few tries he realised he hadn't got far and the currents were too strong. Panic set in but he tried even harder, battling against the relentless power of the water, the lactic acid starting to build up in his muscles, clawing at his stamina and will to survive.

'Come on!' he screamed, dragging the boy as best he could to get to the bank. His left foot scraped the bottom of the river, and he felt the pull of the current lessen, a colossal feeling of hope growing inside. The idea of living almost overwhelmed him. In a tremendous amount of pain, he managed to pull the boy to safety, dragging him out of the river and placing him down on the stones. He stared down at him in the dark, hunched over himself, panting for a decent breath of air. He was freezing. They both were shaking.

It felt like a lifetime, but ten minutes later, his friends found them. Jake asked two of them for their coats while he took off the boy's clothes, leaving his pants on, and lowered his small body on one coat then placed the other over the top of him. He then told them to ring an ambulance.

It wasn't long before the sirens were heard in the distance.

The child was still and unresponsive. Jake leaned over and whispered in his ear, 'Hold on, little man. Help is coming now.'

48

Tallow and Hope had just arrived in the examination room of the pathology department. Arnold, with his assistant, Laura, had already taken Brian Everitt's body out of the body bag ready for the examination. In the time they'd spent waiting, they'd taken a blood sample, a urine sample, and strands of hair.

Byrd, Tanzy, the coroner Peter Gibbs, and PC Weaver were watching from a few feet away.

'We know what happened here,' Arnold started. 'The first obvious injury, as we can see—' he moved to his right towards Brian's head — 'is major bruising around his throat. It looks like a wire of some sort has caused this.'

After a moment, he went to the second obvious injury that Brian had sustained. 'Here we can clearly see the penis has been severed, cut off close to the base. We'll clean and examine the type of cut next. We're waiting on results from bloods and toxicology.'

'What was the official cause of death?' Byrd asked.

Arnold raised his finger, as if expecting the question. 'Good point. It appears from the bruising and the line around his throat that he was strangled but he didn't die from that. Because of the amount of blood, in my opinion, when his penis was removed, the heart was still pumping and pushed a large proportion of blood out of the wound. Then, if we look closely—' he pointed to the throat, and Byrd, Tanzy, and the senior forensics leaned in — 'you can see a different kind of bruising. It was caused by two hands squeezing the throat. I think that was the official cause of death.'

Byrd nodded. 'What else can you tell us?'

Arnold turned to his assistant, Laura. 'Shall we?'

She moved so she was level with his knees. Arnold grabbed the nearest arm and pulled him towards the edge of the trolley, then both of them turned Brian onto his front.

On his back the detectives saw a mark that appeared to have been done by a whip.

'How old is that?' Tanzy asked, wincing at it.

'Only a few weeks old at the most,' Arnold informed them.

Byrd's phone rang inside his pocket, disturbing the silence of the room. He apologised and stepped back to answer it.

'Mac has been through Brian Everitt's laptop,' PC Weaver said. 'I think it's obvious why the penis was cut off.'

49

Byrd and Tanzy returned to the station to find PC Weaver and ask her about Brian Everitt's laptop.

She to the right side of the room, her legs tucked in under her desk, her attention on the computer screen in front of her.

'Hey, Amy,' Tanzy said, pulling a chair out and sitting down next to her. Byrd took a chair from the next desk, which was vacant, dragged it over, and dropped into it.

'What do we have?' Byrd asked, wasting no time.

'Mac went through Everitt's PC. There was a substantial amount of child abuse images on there. Very disturbing stuff.'

'Jesus,' Tanzy said, shaking his head in disgust.

'I understand what the letter to Jane might have meant now.' He recalled the words on the paper found under the sofa at Claxton Avenue: *Jane, I'm sorry for the person I've become, I can't do this any longer.* 'She may have known about it,' he added.

Tanzy frowned at Byrd. 'It's unlikely.'

'Why?' Byrd asked, curious about his comment.

'The people who watch this stuff aren't quite wired properly. If she knew about it, with her being a teacher, she'd not only be disgusted but she'd have reported him. If I was in that situation, that's what I'd do.'

'It's never that simple, Ori, and you know it.'

Tanzy eyed Byrd curiously, not expecting him to say that.

Weaver picked up on their disagreement. 'We don't know either way. We'll find out when she wakes up from her coma.' Her words distracted the detectives, bringing them back to what was important.

'What else did Mac find on the laptop?' Byrd enquired.

'It seemed there were documents about Cairnfield Developments. Planning ideas and drawing designs. There were also documents containing costs and a folder containing photos from previous jobs. I also came across a folder which was named 'The Team', which contained around thirty individual documents. I haven't been through all of them but, from the first six or seven I opened, from what I can see, they contain information on individuals in the business trade. Two of them were plumbers, two others were electricians, one a plasterer . . . you get the picture.'

Byrd straightened his posture in the chair. 'We'll wait for forensics to get back about the house on Claxton Avenue. See if they spot anything left by the intruder. In the meantime we need to speak to the doctors at the hospital, see how Jane is doing. We need to speak to her about the missing children and, of course, about her husband, Brian.'

Tanzy stood up, ready for the day. He wasn't planning on being in all day because Pip had wanted to go somewhere with the kids. Eric wanted to go to soft play at some point over the weekend and Tanzy had agreed they'd all go. The last thing he needed was attitude and earache off Eric. In recent months, they hadn't done much as a family but he'd decided things would change.

As Tanzy went to leave PC Weaver's work area, DC Leonard appeared in the aisle before him, halting him in his stride.

'Boss, we got a call.'

'What is it, Jim?'

'Remember when we were knocking on doors in Claxton Avenue earlier, to see if the neighbours had seen anyone enter the property of Brian and Jane Everitt?'

Tanzy waited.

'And there was a house opposite that didn't answer the door. The house with an old red Rover and old-fashioned curtains.'

'I remember . . .' Tanzy said, but didn't, really wishing he'd get to the point sooner.

'We've had a call from her. Her name is Margaret Dawson. She has a camera on the front of her house that looks down on the driveway. Says the camera picks up the road and the house opposite too.'

'Does it show what car it is?'

'Better. It shows a man getting out of the car and walking into the house.'

Tanzy suddenly felt exhilarated. 'Come on, Jim, you're with me.' He patted his shoulder and walked around him, heading straight to the door and out into the car park.

50

Saturday morning
Claxton Avenue

Less than ten minutes later, Tanzy and Leonard pulled up at the house. The woman who'd made the call was watching them through the wide living room window. Tanzy noticed her snooping and she backed away and turned out of sight.

Before Tanzy had even stepped on her driveway the front door opened. Margaret Dawson waved at them, telling them to come inside. She was short and plump, in her late sixties.

'Please, come this way,' she said, her voice croaky.

Tanzy and Leonard followed her into the dining room through a haze of hanging cigarette smoke. Tanzy winced a little, noticing an ashtray full of cigarette butts on a large circular table surrounded by six chairs in the centre of the room. In the alcove to the left, there was a battered desk which had seen better days, supporting a large old computer monitor. Wires trailed from the back of it down behind the desk, connecting to an ancient PC.

Margaret apologised for the mess and took a seat in front of the screen. The chair looked weak, creaking under her weight, but she didn't seem concerned it would crumble under her.

Tanzy and Leonard stood behind her, waiting. To their left a set of wooden French doors led to a small decking area then, beyond that, an overgrown garden several weeks beyond needing a cut.

'I came back and noticed the people in the white suits. I asked a tall man what had happened but he ignored me,' she said. 'That's when I knocked on Mary next door. She told me what had happened. Just awful. Poor Brian.'

She clicked on one of the folders. There were hundreds of files, all with names that meant nothing to the detectives. 'Let me see,' she whispered, hovering the mouse over the colossal list. 'This one,' she said, finally settling on one then clicking on it.

The video file opened.

From the bar at the bottom, Tanzy noticed it was an hour long, and watched as the camera stared out onto the street. The primary focus of the camera was the old red Rover on the driveway and the path beside it, but the road and the house opposite were clear, and that excited Tanzy.

'Let me see,' she said again, using the mouse to scroll the time indicator forward until she stopped on seven minutes. 'This is it,' she told them, pointing to the screen.

Tanzy and Leonard watched intently.

At the top right part of the screen, a dark blue four-by-four appeared and stopped outside the house directly opposite. A Kia Sportage. Tanzy hid his excitement. Was it the same four-by-four as the one on the CCTV footage that had run down the naked man on Cleveland Street?

For around five minutes the man in the driver's seat remained inside the car, his focus on something down on his lap. Then he leaned to his left, disappearing for a few seconds to grab something from the glovebox. The details of his face were okay, but not brilliant. It was clear the man had short dark hair, and that he was white. It was difficult to tell his age from this view.

'Does he look familiar to you?' Tanzy asked Leonard.

'But you got him though, he's right there,' Margaret told them, stabbing the air in front of the screen, as if merely by seeing him on camera they would put him straight into prison.

'I wish it was that easy,' Tanzy murmured.

The man stepped out of the car holding a box and headed down the driveway to the front door. To the detectives he moved like someone would if they were between thirty and fifty. He didn't have that youthful bounce, nor was he slow and measured, just naturally relaxed going about his business. The door opened and there were a few words exchanged with Brian Everitt before Brian nodded and the man stepped inside.

'If he's just delivering, then why's he going in?' Leonard said, scratching the side of his forehead.

The man was inside the Everitt house for twenty-seven minutes before he returned to the car and drove off.

'No plates,' Tanzy said in frustration. The camera was positioned so the car had come in from the right and moved out of shot to the left, not allowing them to see any of the front or rear plate.

'Would you mind if we put this video on a memory stick and took it back for analysis?' Leonard asked Margaret.

'Please, help yourself,' she insisted.

Leonard pulled a USB stick from the inside of his black fleece and lowered himself to the PC to plug it in. Once retrieved, they thanked her and left the property, heading back to the Golf. Glancing over to the Everitt house, now cordoned off by plastic tape, Leonard said, 'Hopefully we can zoom in on the video. It's clear enough, just too far away.'

Tanzy agreed with him, and they headed back to the station.

51

The office was quiet.

Just the way Byrd liked it.

He sipped on his coffee, then placed it down on his desk. He was writing up his report from Brian Everitt's house yesterday. It was difficult to write about the child abuse images Mac had found on the laptop and harder to consider that Brian's wife, Jane, knew anything about it. When she was well enough, perhaps he'd find out the truth.

His phone to the right pinged with a text message. He moved it closer to him and opened it. It was from Claire.

Love you. Have a good day. Can't wait for our meal tonight. x

He'd completely forgotten they were going for a meal with her friend Alice and her husband Alex. Claire had booked a table at Uno Momento for 7 p.m. He placed his phone to the side and went back to his report. A few moments later he was disrupted by a ringing sound coming from Tanzy's desk phone.

'Hello, DI Byrd speaking.'

'I was hoping to speak to Orion Tanzy,' the caller said. The voice was male, well-educated and local.

197

'I'm a colleague of his. Who's calling?'

'My name is Peter Main. I have a graphic design office on Duke Street. Some of your colleagues came to my office on Thursday afternoon asking for Andrew Cairn of Cairnfield Developments?'

Byrd thought quickly, remembering DC Leonard had gone there with PC Weaver. 'Yes, go on, sir.'

'I was out at the time, but my assistant told me what your colleagues were looking for. They gave him this number in case I could help. The name on the card was DI Orion Tanzy.'

'Okay, go on,' Byrd encouraged him, taking his eyes off his screen. 'I can help.'

'Okay. Well, I haven't seen Andrew Cairn since I've been there so I can't help you with any information about what he does when he's here.'

Byrd felt a 'but' coming on.

'But,' Peter Main said, 'I have his number and an address for him.'

Byrd's eyes widened. 'An address?'

'Yes. A package was delivered and he asked me to post it for him as he couldn't make it down.'

'Could I have that address, please? It's very important we speak to him.'

Peter Main hesitated.

'Is he in some kind of trouble?' Peter asked, now starting to annoy Byrd.

'No, sir. We need to ask him something which could be fundamental to helping us find a missing boy.'

Main told him the address and Byrd quickly pulled a sheet of paper from the printer nearby, scribbling down what Peter had said.

'Thank you, Peter, this will help in our investigation.'

'My pleasure,' he replied, before hanging up.

Byrd pushed his chair out, stood up, and grabbed his coat. Across the office he stopped at PC Andrews' desk.

'You busy?' he asked him.

Andrews looked up. 'Just a report and a few phone calls I need to make.'

'Good,' Byrd said, 'you're coming with me.'

They left the office and headed across the car park to Byrd's X5.

* * *

The house was on Carmel Road North, roughly sixty metres up from the small roundabout at the end of Staindrop Road. It was colossal, with heaps of character. Byrd wasn't a property expert, but it was obvious it had been built before many of the properties in Darlington. He pulled up on the road, parking well onto the kerb to avoid disrupting the flow of traffic as Carmel Road was always busy. It was one of the main roads in Darlington.

On their way over, Byrd told Andrews the story and the reason why they were there.

They wandered down the driveway, watching the house carefully, eyeing the windows, looking for movement. It was a semi-detached property, three storeys, with a high-pitched peak at the top of the house. The brickwork had aged perfectly in time, and stood solid, as if it had been there for two hundred years and would stand for two hundred more. To the left of the house was a wide, double front door, which looked like it had been painted recently. The paintwork around the windows and windowsills also looked fresh.

Byrd noticed the driveway to the left continued down the side of the house to the rear of the property. Parked in front of a garage was a Silver Bentley, the registration F3L 4ND. Byrd knew who it belonged to but took out his notepad and jotted it down, then put it back in the inside pocket of his long coat. He could see no other cars, but there could have been more out of sight.

Byrd stepped up onto the extravagant semicircular doorstep and knocked three times, his knuckles feeling the cold against the solid oak.

They seemed to wait for ever until it slowly creaked open, and standing there was a man who appeared to be in his forties. He was smaller than both Byrd and Andrews and sported a scruffy beard. His hair was thinning, greasy, in desperate need of a shower.

'Andrew Cairn?' asked Byrd.

'He's not here at the moment. Can . . . can I help you?' he asked, eyeing them up.

'Good afternoon. I am Detective Inspector Max Byrd. This is my colleague PC Josh Andrews. Do you know where Andrew Cairn is at the moment?'

The small man frowned for a moment, his hand still holding the door. 'I don't know. I'm not his babysitter.'

'Then who are you?'

'Paddy' the man said.

Byrd smiled. 'Well, Paddy, do you know when Andrew will be home?'

The man shrugged again. 'I don't. I'm sorry. What is this about?'

'I need to ask him a few questions about his business. That's all, nothing major.' Byrd peered beyond Andy into the huge hallway.

Paddy edged the door closed a little. 'Well, like I said, he isn't here.'

'Would it be okay if we come in?' Byrd asked.

The man narrowed his eyes. 'Do you have a warrant, Detective?'

Byrd shook his head.

'Then no, it isn't okay for you to come in.'

A few seconds of awkward silence passed. 'Let Mr Cairn know we've been, and that we'll be back real soon. Okay?'

Paddy smiled. 'Sure thing.' Then he took obvious pleasure in slamming the door closed.

Byrd and PC Andrews turned, stepped down onto the driveway, and made their way slowly back to the car parked at the side of the road.

As they climbed in, Byrd pulled out his phone and found the number he needed.

'Who you ringing?' Andrews asked.

Byrd ignored him, listening to the ringing in his ear until it was answered by DC Anne Tiffin.

'Anne, are you near a computer?'

'I'm at my desk. What do you need?'

Byrd heard her tapping on the keyboard through the phone. 'I need you to run a check on a registration plate for me. It belongs to a Bentley.'

'Okay, go ahead.'

'F. 3. L. 4. N. D.'

'Hold on, sir.'

Byrd waited, staring out onto Carmel Road at the gentle flow of passing traffic.

'Got it. It belongs to a Jonathan Feland.'

'Jonathan Feland?'

'Yeah,' she confirmed.

Byrd sighed heavily. 'Thank you, Anne. How's it going at the office? Has Orion got back yet?'

'Just got back now. He got the footage from across the road at Claxton Avenue. The quality isn't very good so were going to speak to Mac to see if he can adjust it. You heading back?'

'Yeah. Mention to Orion about the registration and who it belongs to. I'll see you soon,' he said. He hung up, put the phone back into his pocket.

'Who is Jonathan Feland?' PC Andrews asked, eyeing him suspiciously, then glanced back to the house.

'Jonny Feland is one of the most dangerous men in this town. He deals in drugs and violence. In fact, he supplies most of the drugs in the area and has an extensive number of people working for him. We know what he's up to, but we've never got anything on him. I've certainly never known where he lived.'

They both looked back at the house. 'Seems to be doing okay for himself, doesn't he?'

'He does.' Byrd turned on the engine and glanced in the wing mirror before he pulled out. 'Chances are, there's no such person as Andrew Cairn, and he's using the name as a front.'

'Crafty bugger.'

'What are we going to do about Feland?'

Byrd's phone rang in his pocket. 'Hold on, Josh.' He pressed a button on the dash to transfer it to the car and pressed answer on the central console. 'Hello?'

'Sir, it's DS Stockdale. I had a call from Darlington Memorial Hospital earlier: it's good news and bad news. Damien Spencer's been found.'

Byrd absorbed his words. 'Go on . . .'

'He was pulled out of the river last night by a passer-by. He's alive, but it's been touch and go.'

'Jesus,' Byrd said. 'What happened?' He took a right at the small roundabout and clicked on his indicator, pulling over to the side of the road so he could concentrate on what his sergeant was telling him.

'According to the boy who saved him, who was there with his friends at the time, he heard a splash and saw Damien floating down the river. He dived in and went after him. A very, very brave thing to do.'

'Absolutely,' Byrd agreed. 'How did Damien get into the water?'

'We don't know that yet, neither does the young man who saved him. He just heard the splash. It was too dark.'

'But if he's been in hospital since last night . . . Why are we only just hearing about this now?'

'I think some kind of miscommunication at the hospital, sir.'

'One hell of a miscommunication — Damien's been all over the news since he went missing. His poor mother's been beside herself . . .' Byrd took a breath and started again. 'How's the passer-by who rescued him doing?'

'He's not that old himself — just seventeen. The river water was close to freezing. He was okay though, no damage done. I've taken a statement. And I've called Damien's family — his mother's with him now.'

'How's Damien? We'll need to speak to him as soon as possible — he's our best hope of finding the other children.'

'Well that's the bad news, I'm afraid.'

Byrd said nothing, waiting for the sergeant to tell him.

'He's in an induced coma. It was clear to paramedics he was not only suffering from hypothermia, but he was medically unstable. He has an issue with his heart and hasn't been getting his daily intake of medications.'

Byrd felt a pang of guilt. 'Okay, Stockdale, thanks for letting me know. We'll be in soon.'

52

Saturday afternoon
Darlington Memorial Hospital

Opening her eyes, Jane Everitt felt groggy and her vision was blurred. The two lights above her looked like flying saucers, moving side to side every time she blinked.

'Jane?' she heard a voice say. 'Jane, dear, are you awake?'

Her eyes fluttered and her vision improved enough for her to see a female nurse with short blonde hair, somewhere between fifty and sixty, standing beside her.

'Jane, can you hear me? Nod if you can hear me, dear,' said the nurse.

Jane Everitt nodded weakly.

'Good, Jane, that's brilliant. Are you able to sit up a little? There's some people here who want to ask you some questions.'

'Could I . . .' She trailed off, her voice weak.

'Sorry, honey, could you say that again?' the nurse asked, patiently.

'Water?' Jane managed.

'Of course. Let's sit you up and I'll get you a drink.' The nurse propped her up and placed a pillow behind her, then leaned over to the bedside table and poured a glass of water. 'Here you go.'

Jane's trembling hand took it, and she managed a sip before handing it back to the nurse.

'There's some people here that would like to speak to you,' the nurse repeated. 'Would that be okay?'

Jane blinked several times.

'Okay,' the nurse said, turning to the door. 'She says it's okay.' Then she turned back to Jane. 'If it gets too much for you or you feel unwell, press this button—' she lifted up a piece of plastic with a button at the top connected to a thin wire that ran along the bed towards a machine behind her — 'and I'll be straight back in, okay?'

'Okay.'

The nurse left the small room as two police officers came in.

'Good afternoon, Jane,' said the one who wasn't in uniform, stopping by the side of the bed. 'I'm Detective Inspector Tanzy and this is PC Weaver. How are you holding up?'

'I feel . . . I feel sore.' She tried to move but winced.

'Hey, let me,' Tanzy insisted, getting her more comfortable.

'Thank you,' she whispered in pain. 'I feel like I've been hit by a wall.'

Tanzy stepped back, giving her some space. 'Can you remember what happened?'

She narrowed her eyes in thought. 'I was at the school. My husband texted me . . . He . . . He needed help.' She glanced to the window, piecing the story together in her mind. 'Then I left.'

Before he came in to see her, Tanzy had spoken to one of the doctors, who'd confirmed that there might be confusion about what happened. Tanzy was also aware Jane didn't know about her husband's death and he would have to break the news the best way he could.

'Can you remember driving on Woodland Road?' Tanzy asked.

'I . . . I don't . . . What happened?' Her eyebrows furrowed in confusion.

'You were involved in a car crash. A vehicle hit the side of your car, flipping it twice. The fire brigade had to break into the car to get you out. Thankfully, the only damage is that broken arm you have there and a bit of concussion.'

She only noticed the pot on her arm when she looked down. Her face was blank. 'I don't understand . . .'

'We came to see you at the school about the disappearance of the missing children. We were waiting in the reception area for you, but you got into your car and sped away, heading for home.'

Her memories flooded back.

'Oh, God . . .' She raised a hand to her mouth. 'Brian. I was going home to Brian. He needed help. Is he okay?'

Tanzy smiled sadly. 'We need to tell you something about Brian.'

She frowned. 'What?'

'Brian's dead, Jane. His body was found in your home yesterday.'

'God . . .' She held her breath, brought her hands to her face and sobbed. 'How?'

Tanzy explained the scene they discovered but sugar-coated it the best he could while she quietly sobbed and shook on the bed. PC Weaver leaned over and held her hand for some comfort.

'Why?'

'I don't know. We're collecting evidence and will find out what happened and who was responsible.'

Jane lowered her hands and stared out the window with tears streaming from her face. 'I should have been there. He needed help.'

'Why did he need help, Jane?'

'Brian hadn't been feeling well in recent weeks. Not physically, but mentally. He's had it before but not as bad as this.'

Tanzy frowned.

'Depression,' Jane said weakly, filling in the blanks for him. 'He's on tablets for it. Sometimes it helps, other times it doesn't. Over the past few weeks, I've noticed a change in him. He's shut himself away, spent more time on his laptop working. God knows what he was doing on there.

'I've learned to cope with him though, as he tried to commit suicide a few years back. After his mother passed away, he couldn't cope living without her. They were close, you see. Cancer took her in the end.' She glanced away vacantly towards the window, going back to the sad time in her head.

'Jane,' Tanzy said. 'Is there anyone your husband had any disagreements with recently? Anything at all you can think of?'

She slowly shook her head, still gazing absently through the window.

'I'm so very sorry for your loss.'

Happy that Jane was unaware of the material on her husband's laptop, they left her to digest the news she'd just been told.

53

'God, that was hard,' Weaver said, standing outside the pae-diatric ward with Tanzy, feeling sorry for Jane Everitt, while they waited for Byrd to show up.

'How'd it go with Jane?' asked Byrd.

'Tough. Very tough. She's absolutely devastated.'

Byrd said nothing, expecting as much.

'How'd it go at Andrew Cairn's house?' Tanzy asked, scratching his goatee.

'Interesting,' Byrd said. 'Turns out he wasn't in, accord-ing to the bloke who answered the door. But I did see a Bentley down the side of the house and checked the reg.'

Tanzy smiled. 'I saw your message. The infamous Mr Feland.'

Byrd smiled briefly. '*There's* a name we haven't heard for a while.'

'I haven't missed it.'

Byrd agreed and told him that the man at the door had denied them access and told them to come back with a warrant. 'Feland is probably using the Cairnfield business for his own financial reasons.'

'The man is like Teflon. Nothing will stick to him.'

'See what Damien says. Might give us enough to get a warrant if he's the man responsible for this.'

PC Weaver left and returned to the office to file her report before heading home. Byrd and Tanzy pressed the button on the intercom on the floor.

There was a short crackle, before a voice said, 'Can I help you?'

'Detective Inspector Max Byrd with Detective Inspector Orion Tanzy,' Byrd said, showing his ID to the small camera on the wall. 'We're here to see Damien Spencer.'

The doors gave a loud continual buzz until Byrd took the handle and pulled it open.

A nurse, who appeared to be around the age of forty, slim with dark long hair and blue eyes, appeared in the corridor to meet them. 'Damien is down the hall, room sixteen. His mother is there with him. He's currently being treated with medication but is unresponsive. So if you're here to ask him questions, it won't be much use, but you can speak to his mother if you'd like.'

They went towards room 16, passing several open doorways where patients were, some awake, some asleep, some with family with them, while others were alone.

The door to the single room Damien was in was open a few inches.

The nurse knocked twice. 'Hello.'

Inside the small room there was a bed to the right. On the far side were machines and a cluster of complex wiring, some attached to Damien, who was lying on the bed. Mandy Spencer was on a chair beside him, her face puffy and her eyes red, full of tears.

'Hey, Mandy,' Tanzy said, approaching her with a sad smile.

'How's he doing?' Byrd asked, stopping at the foot of his bed.

Damien had a mouthpiece over his face which had a long flexible grey hose trailing from the bottom to the right of the bed.

'He's alive,' Mandy said, 'and that's all that matters right now.'

Byrd smiled, feeling a lump forming in his throat.

After a few moments, they left to speak to one of the doctors in the corridor, who told them he'd contact them as soon as Damien woke up but was unsure how long that would be. Damien's body had some repairing to do and, in his opinion, it would be a few days before he'd be well enough to speak to anyone. They thanked him and left.

'I hope he wakes up soon, Max,' Tanzy said on their way back to the car. 'The sooner we can speak to Damien, the sooner we can locate the other children.'

'Let's hope it's soon, Ori,' said Byrd. 'Their parents are worried sick.'

54

Saturday night
Uno Momento, Darlington town centre

'What time are they getting here?' Byrd asked, a few minutes after they'd sat down.

Claire was dressed in a white tight-fitting dress, her hair down to her shoulders. 'They're dropping Callum off at Alice's parents,' she added. 'They should be here any minute now.'

'You look stunning tonight.' Her lips reflected the soft lighting coming from all areas of the room.

'You're not too shabby yourself, Mr Byrd,' she said. He wore a dark blue suit jacket over a light-blue thin jumper, dark slim-fitting jeans, and the brown shoes which Claire had bought him a few weeks before. After telling him he needed some new clothes, she had bought him some more jumpers and several pairs of jeans. The half-decent clothes he had didn't fit him anymore and he looked utterly ridiculous because of the weight he'd lost.

Byrd smiled, then glanced down at his wristwatch. It was nearly quarter past seven. 'By the way, where did you put the letter you mentioned from the DVLA? On the microwave?'

'Yeah. Just on top of your car magazines.'

'I couldn't see it the other night,' he said, shrugging.

'I'll find it tomorrow,' she reassured him.

Positioned in a good spot at the back, he glanced around, absorbing the noisy restaurant filled to the brim.

'Who you looking for?' Claire asked him, frowning.

He met her gaze. 'No one.'

'Max, you're not on duty now. Relax, okay?' She placed her hand over his.

'Hold on a sec,' he said, pulling his phone from his pocket.

'You're not going to be on that all night, are you?'

She was half joking, half serious.

'Of course not, just checking something before—'

'Hey, Claire,' an excited voice said behind them, followed by a clatter of high heels.

Claire recognised the voice, turned, stood up and gave Alice a firm hug. She appeared so different to when Byrd had seen her a few nights ago. Her hair was curled, her make-up perfect; dark mascara made her green eyes shine like glowing emeralds, grabbing the attention of every man in there.

She released herself from Claire and, as Byrd stood up, she placed her arms around him and squeezed. 'Hi, Max. Thanks for coming out.'

'I didn't have a choice really,' he said, grinning. The playful joke was followed by a gentle slap on the side of his arm. Then she moved to the opposite side of the table, took her coat off, and put it on the back of the wooden chair. 'Max, this is Alex.' Her palm angled towards the man at the edge of the table. He smiled at Byrd and held out a hand.

'Detective . . . it's nice to meet you.'

'Please, call me Max,' he said, taking his firm grip. 'Hey, I like that shirt.'

It was black, slim-fitting, and appeared to be made from silk.

'The boss's choice,' Alex replied, nodding towards Alice.

Byrd laughed. 'I know exactly what you mean. Please take a seat.' It wasn't long before a waiter came over with some menus and ordered them some drinks.

A minute later the waiter came back with the drinks and placed them down on the table, and informed them their food would be coming soon. The four of them talked about their days so far. Byrd missed out some of his day so they could enjoy their meals without feeling queasy.

The conversation they were having was drowned out by a noise nearby. Four men were arguing about something. Byrd couldn't quite hear what the conversation was about but he could tell it was getting tense. He heard one of them talking about money and another calling one of the other men a liar. The people around them stopped their conversations to also look their way. The men, aged between thirty and forty, didn't realise they were the focus of the restaurant, until a waiter approached their table.

One of them looked at the waiter, frowning in anger.

'Excuse me, sir,' the waiter said politely. 'Would it be possible just to turn the volume down a little? There are other people who I'm sure would like to enjoy their meals with a little less noise.'

The man raised his palm. 'Yeah, no problem, we apologise.' He glanced around the tables near him and apologised once more.

'Thank you.' The waiter turned and made and his way back down to the front of the restaurant.

'Some people just don't give a shit,' Alex whispered, making sure only their table heard. Then he glanced at Byrd. 'So, Max, how long have you been in the police?'

Byrd puffed his cheeks out for a moment. 'Nearly twenty-three years. Went in when I was eighteen.'

'Good effort, that.'

'It pays the bills,' he replied before swigging his pint of lager.

'Is it exciting?' Alex asked, picking up his own drink, taking a sip, then placing it down.

'Sometimes. There's a lot of paperwork involved but that comes with most jobs now, I guess.'

Alex nodded, as if he knew what he meant.

'What is it you do, Alex?'

'I'm a business analyst.'

'That sounds . . . interesting,' Byrd said, but it was more of a question.

'It can be. Depends how much you like facts, figures, and formulas. It can get boring sometimes but it's all part and parcel of the job.'

Byrd took another swig. 'Been doing it long?'

Alex smiled. 'Ever since I left the army.'

'How long did you serve?'

'Ten years,' he replied.

Byrd raised his glass to him. 'Why the change?'

'I missed home too much. I missed Alice.' He glanced over and she paused her conversation with Claire and smiled at him. 'I missed the kids too. Only being off for a few weeks at a time and then back for six-month stints was too much. I know a lot of people do it, but I couldn't cope any longer. I'd been doing business analysis before I went in and wanted to see if I could make something from it.'

'Fair enough,' Byrd commented. 'How many kids you got?'

'Two. Boy and a girl. Callum, who's twelve and knows everything, and Lisa, who's eighteen and knows even more.'

'Where are they tonight?'

'Callum is at Alice's mother's and Lisa is doing her own thing.' He took another swig. 'Do you have kids?'

Byrd shook his head. 'No . . .' He felt Claire's gaze drift over to him. 'Not yet anyway . . .' She returned her attention to Alice.

'Even at forty-one, there's always time.'

Byrd didn't respond to him. His attention was fixed on the window at the front of the restaurant. A man was standing on the other side of the glass staring right at him. Byrd held the gaze and, after a few seconds, even Claire had noticed his strange behaviour. 'Max?'

He looked her way and smiled. 'What?'

'Why are you staring?'

He focused back on the window, but the man had gone.

Byrd frowned. 'Sorry, I was lost there.' He picked up his drink, took a long swig, then placed it back down. 'How do you know my age?'

Alex smiled at him. 'You said you'd been in the force nearly twenty-three years and went in when you were eighteen. Simple mathematics.'

Byrd smiled, tilting his head, appreciating the obvious.

They shared a laugh and both picked up their drinks. Moments later the meals arrived. Byrd had ordered pizza and Claire had chosen lasagne. 'Looks amazing, thank you,' Claire told the waiter, who bowed his head at them and walked away.

'Here, mate, fuck you!' a voice shouted from their left.

The restaurant became quiet, everyone looking at the four men sitting at the table at the back. One of them stood up, knocking his chair back with the hind of his knees and threw his white fabric napkin down on his chair. He then headed into the toilet, leaving the three men at the table.

Two waiters appeared from the steps, staring towards the back of the room. Byrd didn't really want to get involved tonight. The past week had been one of the most hectic in his life. If he could have just one night off that would be brilliant.

The level of noise returned to normal soon enough and everyone carried on with their meals.

'Excuse me,' Alex said, pushing himself out from the table and standing up. 'Quick toilet break, two minutes.'

Byrd, Claire, and Alice continued eating. Byrd joined in with their conversation about a building development somewhere on the edge of town. Darlington was continually growing all the time. You couldn't drive anywhere in the town without passing some roadworks causing diversions or building sites or renovations.

Byrd noticed Alex had been gone longer than it would take for a swift toilet visit and looked towards the doorway leading to them while Claire and Alice continued talking.

'Excuse me,' he said, standing. 'Just going to the toilet.'

He passed two of the four men sitting the at table causing the noise disturbance earlier but didn't look at them; he was off duty tonight, he told himself. Whatever it was it was their business.

Byrd took a left, opening the toilet door, and froze in the doorway. His eyes widened. 'Alex?'

Alex was standing by the sink with blood on his hands and the front of his clothes. Down on the floor was the man from the loud table and a knife a couple of feet from him, smeared in blood.

'Max, help me,' begged Alex.

'Alex, what on earth happened?'

Alex, shaking, told him.

Byrd shook his head in disbelief. 'I'll call it in.'

55

Saturday night
Uno Momento, Darlington town centre

It wasn't long before PC Weaver and DC Leonard appeared, together. Neither were wearing their uniform.

'Sir,' Leonard said to Byrd, focusing on Alex, who Byrd had brought to sit back down at the table. The people nearby had all panicked and moved away, giving Alex and Byrd some space. The two remaining men sitting at the table of four had disappeared like a shot when Byrd was in the toilet discovering Alex. 'Max, what happened?'

'You two got here fast,' said Byrd, frowning their way, unsure why Weaver wasn't in uniform. 'I've only just called it in.'

Leonard, glancing at Weaver for a split second too long for Byrd not to notice, said, 'We're not on duty, sir. We were passing, heard the commotion. What's happened?'

Byrd told them both what he knew, about discovering Alex inside the toilet covered in blood, but Alex was so shaken up he hadn't been able to relay exactly what happened, so Byrd had sat him down and got him a drink of water.

Leonard glanced to a different table where Claire was sitting, comforting Alice, who'd got upset after seeing Alex appear distraught and covered in blood.

A few moments later, two paramedics arrived, and lowered to Alex to check him over. Byrd stood back and heard footsteps behind him. PC Andrews and PC Timms appeared up the steps, eyeing the scene, particularly Alex at the table, smeared in blood.

'Hey, boss.' Timms nodded at Byrd. 'What on earth happened?'

'Let me show you,' Byrd said, heading for the toilets. Timms and Andrews followed him, while Leonard and Weaver, although not officially on duty, stayed with Alex and the paramedics to make sure things were okay.

They entered the small, cold corridor. The toilets were on the left but there was a door ahead of them, swinging open in the stormy night, where rain pelted down, bouncing on the ground outside, the sounds distracting them. Several bins were up against the brick wall at the back and not much else.

PC Timms, with his baton in his hand, passed Byrd and peered outside. There was a door swinging open leading to an exit, but he didn't know where it went. There was no sign of anyone.

Byrd, slowly followed by Andrews, went cautiously into the toilet. Down on the ground near the urinal was the man he'd seen before. He recognised his red T-shirt as one of the men sitting at the table causing the disturbance earlier. The man hadn't moved. The pool of blood around the body had grown, as if making its way to the door. The knife was near the sink, pointing towards the cubicle at the back of the small space.

'The fuck happening here?' Andrews asked, peering around Byrd.

'God knows.' He turned to him. 'We need forensics ASAP. Call it in, will you? I'll tell those paramedics to come through here once they've finished with Alex.'

'God, there's never a dull moment in this town.'

'You've been spending too much time with Orion,' replied Byrd, then slowly backed out, leaving the scene for forensics to examine. Hopefully Alex had calmed down as he was the only one who knew what really happened.

The paramedics were satisfied Alex was okay and had sustained no injuries to be concerned with, so Byrd sent them through to the bathroom to administer to the dead man. Byrd had asked the manager to keep all the diners inside, so one of the PCs could speak to them, get a better idea of what went on.

Claire and Alice were still sitting on a different table, curiously eyeing Alex, who was sitting by himself, his focus absently down on the table in front of him.

'Alex, I need to take you to the station to get a statement on what happened. You think you're able to do that?'

Alex, with his gaze still on the table, said nothing.

Byrd helped him up and led him to his car. So far, Alex was their prime suspect.

56

With another night interrupted with work, DI Byrd peered through the one-way mirror in one of the interrogation rooms back at the station. Standing next to him was the smartly dressed DC Leonard, arms folded, leaning against a filing cabinet.

'What do you think?' Leonard asked, turning his head to Byrd.

Byrd shrugged. 'I don't know what to think, to be honest.'

Claire had gone home, taking Alice with her, who said she wanted to be with someone until Alex had been interviewed. Byrd had kissed Claire and told her he'd find out what's going on and be home soon.

PC Weaver had left Leonard and headed home, thanking him for their evening.

'Amy, eh?' Byrd said, angling towards Leonard, who turned his way and smiled but said nothing.

On the other side of the glass, sitting at a table positioned in the centre of the square room, was Alex Richards.

After arriving in Byrd's car, he had been told to remove all of his clothes apart from his underwear and he was now wearing a plain white T-shirt, a black jumper, some grey jogging bottoms and some spare trainers while forensics took samples of the blood. Amanda Forrest, the only forensic officer in the lab, had swabbed the blood on his hands to ensure it matched with the blood on the shirt. Tallow and Hope were at the restaurant, working the crime scene, and would be busy for a few hours at least.

DC Anne Tiffin had volunteered to work late to cover a few PCs who'd taken holidays, and was sitting opposite Alex.

'So, what happened?' she asked.

'I walked into toilets, went to the cubicle. There was a man at the urinal. A moment later, the toilet door opened, so I assumed someone came in as I could still hear him peeing. They were talking, one of them saying something about the other should've accepted the deal. Then I heard a scuffle and a loud grunt, followed by the door opening. I left the cubicle and found him in the middle of the toilets, staggering. He then fell into me, hence the blood all over me.'

She digested the story.

'Did you see the man who walked in?'

Alex sighed. 'No, I didn't. How many more times do I need to say it? By the time I came out of the cubicle, he'd gone. There was only the man who was attacked. He stumbled into me and I had nowhere to go.'

Tiffin made notes.

'Can I go now?' he asked. 'My wife is waiting for me.'

There was a knock at the door.

'Come in,' Tiffin said loudly.

PC Andrews entered. In his hand, there was a small fingerprint scanner, which he placed on the table.

Tiffin thanked him before he turned and left.

'What's that?'

'A fingerprint scanner.'

'I don't even know why I'm here,' he said, slamming his palm onto the table. 'I'm innocent.'

The words and sudden change in movement took Byrd by surprise.

'Then you won't mind me taking your fingerprints so we can eliminate you from the suspects?'

He seemed to think about the request and sighed heavily. 'Am I under arrest?'

Tiffin shook her head. 'No, you know you're not. But you can't argue with how the situation looks.'

Alex considered her words. 'As the law states, don't I need to be under arrest before you take my prints?'

Tiffin explained it was standard procedure to take prints at a crime scene to rule out suspects.

Byrd sighed on the other side of the glass. 'Come on, Alex, don't go down this road.' He knew, if he chose not to give his prints, then he may have to be arrested.

'Why is he being awkward?' Leonard asked Byrd.

'I don't know.'

Tiffin stared at Alex. 'What's it going to be?'

'Fine, I'll give you the prints.'

Tiffin turned on the machine and asked him to place each finger and thumb on it one at a time. Reluctantly, he did so.

'Thank you,' Tiffin said, pulling the scanner back to her side of the table.

Alex nodded. 'Can I go now?'

'Not just yet.' She stood. 'I need to check something.' She left the room, closing the door behind her.

A minute later, she appeared in the room that Byrd and Leonard were in.

'Got there with the prints eventually?' Byrd mused, smiling.

'Awkward one, your friend.' She stopped at the glass and studied Alex.

'It wasn't him,' Byrd said.

'How can you be so sure?' Tiffin asked, frowning.

'Because while you were in there, I got a phone call from the manager of Uno Momento. He checked the camera in the corridor outside the toilets, which shows Alex going in, followed by another man, who appeared tense. Less than a minute later, the man ran out, took a left, and went out the door that led to the yard.'

'Is there a way out from there?' Tiffin asked.

'There's access to a back alley.'

'Okay. It coincides with his story, then.'

Byrd agreed. 'I'll take him back to mine. That's where his wife is.'

'Any idea who the murdered man is? You mentioned the four men at the back table?' Tiffin asked.

'Yes. One of them was the victim. When I went to the toilet to check on Alex, there were only two people at that table. The third man was missing. My guess is that he's our guy.'

'We need to find out who was sitting there.'

'The manager confirmed the booking was under the name of Carrington. Anne, look into males aged thirty to forty with the surname of Carrington.'

'No problem. How long will forensics be at the restaurant?'

'A few hours at least. Tallow and Hope should be able to confirm Alex's story from what they find. They'll be able to decipher the blood spatter.'

'The manager has emailed me the footage, which I'll take a look at first thing tomorrow when I do my report.' Byrd yawned. 'There was me thinking I'd be able to go for a quiet meal and relax. I should've known better.' They all shared a smile. 'Right, I'll take him. Thanks for dropping in.'

'I suppose even when you're off duty, you're never really off duty,' noted Leonard.

'You're getting the hang of this detective thing, huh?'

Leonard smiled and left the office. Byrd made his way back to his car with Alex Richards. As they got in, Byrd's phoned beeped. It was a text message from Keith. It read: *Still no sign of Lyle, mate. I'm getting very worried now. Have you seen him?*

'Not yet, old friend, not yet,' Byrd said to himself, as he turned the engine on and headed for home with Alex.

57

After they returned home from soft play yesterday, Tanzy had bathed the kids, put their pyjamas on, and they'd all watched *Toy Story 4* together in Eric's room.

With the kids asleep, Tanzy and Pip ordered a takeaway and decided to watch *The Equalizer* with Denzel Washington, one of Tanzy's favourites. Pip had never seen it as she was more of a romcom type. They rarely watched films together because they always bickered about what to watch.

Later, in bed, he had stared at Pip, watching the way her hair fell to one side and the way she breathed. She was a beautiful woman. Tanzy seldom stopped to admire her, normally too hung up on things at work, but, in that very moment, he felt all the love in the world for her. He was proud of her too. He'd never been dependant on drugs or alcohol but, in his line of work, he'd seen hundreds of people that were. Many of them failed when they tried changing things but Pip had gone over five months now free of alcohol, and he was proud of her achievement.

Now at the station, he watched the footage of the man getting out of the dark blue Kia Sportage at the Everitt house. He felt like he knew him, that he looked familiar in some way, but he couldn't place it. Mac had done a great job cleaning up the image but the quality still wasn't great and it wasn't as clear as he'd hoped. It was unlikely they'd get facial recognition from it.

'Why did you go inside?' Tanzy asked the image.

He'd rung Byrd earlier, apologising for waking him and also for not replying to the text message Byrd had sent him last night about what had happened at the restaurant.

He played back the video again from Claxton Avenue, watching the man in the green high-vis vest go inside.

'If I was getting something delivered, what reason would someone give to come in?' he whispered. Then he realised it could only be one thing. He picked up his phone, found the number and pressed CALL.

'Orion, you do know what time it is, don't you?' Jacob Tallow, the senior forensic, asked.

Tanzy glanced down at his wrist. 'I do. Twenty to nine.'

'Exactly. And it's a Sunday morning! What do I owe the pleasure, mate?'

'It's about Claxton Avenue.'

'Go on.'

'I was wondering why Brian Everitt let the guy in. There's only one thing I can think of.'

'Which is?' Tallow said groggily.

'To use the toilet,' Tanzy said.

'And you're going to ask me if I dusted the toilet door handle for prints aren't you?'

'I am,' Tanzy said.

'Shit . . .'

Tanzy fell silent for a moment, surprised by that. 'Would it be possible at some point today to get the prints off the door handle? I can get the key and meet you there.'

'Give me an hour, Ori, I'll see you there.'

'You're a good man.'

'I know,' he said, hanging up.

Tanzy finished his coffee, stood up, grabbed his coat, and headed out into the cold.

* * *

An hour later Tallow turned up in his black Volvo XC60, pulling up behind Tanzy's Golf. He stepped out with a small briefcase. The air was fresh, clear, and still. There wasn't a cloud in the sky.

Tanzy met him at the end of the driveway. 'Jacob, thanks for coming.'

'Anything for you, Ori, you know that.'

They walked down the slight slope, careful of their footing on the icy paving slabs, and stopped at the door. Tanzy pulled a key from his coat, placed it in the keyhole, turned it and edged the door open slowly.

Inside the hallway it felt colder than outside as Tanzy padded along the hall towards the closed toilet door.

'Did either you or Hope go in the toilet?'

'I did. I remember opening the door to see what it was. I checked for any signs or prints. But, for some reason, I didn't check the handle.' A tinge of embarrassment crossed his face.

'Happens to the best of us, don't worry about it,' Tanzy reassured him. 'The saving grace is that everyone will have worn gloves yesterday, so, if the man's prints were there, they still will be.'

Tallow lowered to his knees in front of the closed door, opened the lid of his black case, pulled out a small tub of powder, and opened the lid. With a brush, he dabbed it into the powder then, slowly and carefully, applied it to the brass handle of the door.

'From the video, he didn't wear gloves when he entered the house,' Tanzy said, 'so if he did use the toilet, there's a good chance he used the handle to open it.'

Tallow carefully brushed the powder onto the handle, revealing several thumbprints. He placed the brush down on the lid of his kit and picked up a roll of special clear tape, and delicately pressed down on the print, then peeled it away. He repeated the process for the underside of the handle where he would expect to find fingerprints. In total he managed to get eight prints.

'Brilliant, Jacob,' Tanzy said, standing a few metres back watching him.

'Chances are that some of these will belong to Brian and his wife Jane.'

'But there's a chance they won't.'

'Always a chance.' Tallow stood up, his head almost catching the ceiling pendant above him. 'I'll take these back to the lab and run them. I'm meant to be going out today with the missus, so hopefully it won't take too long.'

Tanzy wasn't a stranger to work getting in the way of home life. He smiled. 'Appreciate that, thanks man.'

58

Sunday evening
Craig Street, Darlington

'Which one do you think it is?' Weaver asked Leonard.

'I haven't got a clue. Just keep your eyes peeled.'

They'd been instructed by Tanzy to sit in Craig Street and keep an eye on any suspicious activity. They knew, from the location tracker on Mark Greenwell's phone, he'd spent a lot of time in this part of the street. The problem was that they didn't know which house. Mac, from DFU, had done his best, but scoping the street out was the best option for now.

'Hey, look . . .' said Leonard, pointing.

Weaver followed Leonard's finger across the street.

Two teenagers strutted down the path, stopped at a house, and knocked on the door. A moment later, it opened, and they disappeared inside. Ten minutes later they watched a hooded male stop at the house, knock on the door, and eventually go inside.

'Think we've found the house.' Weaver turned to Leonard.

Leonard agreed with a nod. 'We'll sit a little longer, see what happens, and report back.'

Almost twenty minutes later, after several teenagers had come and gone, they saw car headlights in their wing mirror. The car passed them, then slowed, pulled over, and stopped directly in front of the house.

'You seeing what I'm seeing?'

'A red Mondeo.'

Shortly afterwards, another car passed them. It was a dark blue Kia Sportage, but neither Weaver nor Leonard noticed it as their attention was on the red Mondeo. The Mondeo's lights went off. The driver stepped out. He was tall and thin, wearing a long coat that draped down to his knees.

'You getting this?'

Weaver captured the images on her camera.

The tall man made his way around the front of the car and knocked on the same door.

* * *

The dark blue Kia Sportage passed the red Mondeo, reached the end of the street, and took a right into Greenbank Road. The driver grabbed the object from the passenger seat, opened the door, and stepped out into the cold, then made his way back to the corner of Craig Street and watched the house from there. The object was small enough to be concealed in his pocket so anyone watching wouldn't suspect anything.

He ambled down the street, stopped at the red Mondeo, and lowered himself by the side of the car as if doing up his shoelace. In one fluid movement, he pulled the object from his pocket and placed it under the wheel arch. He then stood and carried on walking until he'd made his way around the block back to where he'd parked.

* * *

'Who's this guy?' Leonard asked.

Weaver was still snapping pictures. 'Not sure. I've got him on camera though.'

'What's he doing?' Leonard said, noticing the man behind the Mondeo.

'Doing his shoelace? I don't think he's one of them. He didn't even look at the house.'

Leonard picked up his phone and called Tanzy's number.

'We're just at Craig Street, boss. Seems to be a lot of activity at a particular house. Several people coming and going. Thought I'd let you know that a red Mondeo pulled up and the driver went into the house too. Can you remember the registration plate that the old guy on Brougham Street gave? The red Mondeo that took the kids?'

'Hold on,' Tanzy told him. 'Yeah, it's NA66 CFD.'

'Ahh, this one's different. They don't match,' Leonard told him.

'It doesn't mean they haven't been swapped though.' Tanzy had a good point. 'Sit tight. I'll get a warrant on that property immediately. What's the number?'

Leonard glanced to his left, across the road, and noted the house number, then counted the houses down until he reached the one they were watching and told him.

'Okay, good. The missing children, Melissa Clarke and Eddy Long, could be in there. Stay where you are and don't leave the car, okay? Backup is on the way.'

'You got it, boss,' Leonard said before hanging up.

Just as Leonard put down the phone, the door to the house opened. The tall man who had arrived in the Mondeo was at the door telling one of the teenagers something. Whatever it was, it seemed to be an order, the boy nodding several times.

The tall man returned to the car and got in, turned on the engine and edged out onto the road.

'Do we wait for backup, or . . .' Weaver was unsure.

'No, we follow him,' Leonard said, starting the car.

59

'Here, phone Orion back.' Leonard threw his phone onto Weaver's lap. 'He'll be the last caller.'

Leonard put his foot down, accelerating up to 40 mph. The red Mondeo took a right, so Tanzy did the same.

'Hey, Orion,' Weaver spoke into the phone. 'The red Mondeo has moved. We're currently in pursuit. Going up Greenbank Road in the direction of town.'

'Okay, stay with it, don't do anything too rash. Keep a safe distance but don't lose it. The driver should be considered very dangerous.'

'Okay, we understand.'

'Just to update you, I've called dispatch. They're arranging an armed response vehicle to go to Craig Street and they'll be there within twenty minutes.'

'Should we continue to follow the Mondeo?'

'Yeah, stay with him. Make sure you have his description noted down as well.'

'Already done, sir.'

'Good work. I'm leaving the house. Should be in Darlington within ten minutes. If anything happens, ring me.'

'Understood,' she said before ending the call.

The Mondeo reached the cross-junction traffic lights at the end of Greenbank Road where it met Woodland Road. When the lights turned green, the Mondeo went right, followed by Leonard, maintaining that safe gap. The Mondeo continued driving down Woodland Road, passing the petrol station on the left. It wasn't long before he hit the small roundabout at the end of Woodland Road and took a left, then another left at the next roundabout.

'Where's he going?' Weaver said.

The Mondeo accelerated up the bank, then slowed a little and pulled over to the side of the road. The hazard lights came on.

'What's he doing?'

'He knows we're following him. He wants us to overtake him.' Leonard was in two minds. 'Orion told us not to lose him.'

'What are you doing?' Weaver asked, as he slowed and pulled over behind the Mondeo. 'James, what . . . what are you doing?'

'If this is the guy who's responsible for taking those kids and killing Sheena Edwards, he isn't getting away with it. We need to bring him down. Ring Orion now. Tell him he's pulled over and we're approaching the vehicle.'

They came to a halt behind the Mondeo and Leonard put the handbrake on firmly to prevent it rolling back down the inclined road.

Weaver glanced his way nervously and shook her head. 'He's not answering.'

'Come on,' Leonard said, 'let's go.'

Both Leonard and Weaver opened the door and stepped out. It was bitterly cold now. As they approached the Mondeo, there was classical music coming from inside.

'You hear that?' Weaver asked, frowning. Leonard nodded, approaching the driver's side, but before he got there, the door was flung open and the tall man got out. He was six or seven inches taller than Leonard, who glared up at him.

The man stared down at Leonard. 'You seem to be following me?'

'I need to ask you some questions down at the station,' Leonard said.

'You can ask me questions here.' His voice was cold and flat. He wasn't intimidated by either Leonard or Weaver, who kept her distance at the opposite side of the car.

'No can do, sir,' Leonard advised. 'We're taking you to the station.'

Weaver pulled out a set of handcuffs and held them for a moment so the man could see them, but all he did was smile at her.

'Sir, we need to take you in!'

'Are you arresting me?'

'I am.'

'On what grounds?'

Leonard got the handcuffs from Weaver and took a few steps forward.

The man reached inside his jacket and pulled out a gun.

Leonard froze to the spot, unable to take his eyes off it. The man raised it and pulled the trigger. The bullet hit Leonard in the side of the chest and he fell onto the floor, wailing in pain.

Weaver threw her hands to her mouth and gasped.

The shooter very casually placed the gun back into his long coat, turned around and got into his car. A moment later the Mondeo pulled away up Carmel Road and out of sight. Weaver rushed over to Leonard, pulled her radio from her belt, and pressed the red button on the top of it, then requested immediate medical attention. Code Red blocked all other police radios in the area and left hers open, so everyone was aware of what had happened.

60

Sunday evening
Carmel Road, Darlington

Tanzy was there within minutes of Weaver informing him that Leonard had been shot and that the Mondeo had gone.

On his way he'd contacted dispatch telling them to send a unit in the direction of Carmel Road South and to request air support. He knew that the closest police aviation centre was near Newcastle but, as this man was linked to the kidnapping of three children and the murder of an elderly lady *and* the shooting of DC Leonard, it should be treated as a priority, so to send helicopter assistance was a very reasonable request.

Tanzy pulled over at the side of the road behind Leonard's car. He couldn't see Leonard or Weaver. He turned off the engine and jumped out.

'Just hang in there, Jim, hang in there,' Tanzy heard Weaver say to Leonard as he noticed them at the front of the car. Tears streamed down her face as she leaned over him, holding his head off the floor. There was a pool of blood underneath him and his black fleece was saturated.

'Jesus,' Tanzy said as he lowered by her side, noticing Leonard's gaze faintly switch to him. 'Where's he shot?'

'I don't know,' Weaver confessed. 'I—'

'Just try and relax, Amy, an ambulance is coming.' Tanzy lifted Leonard's arm an inch to get a better look at the amount of blood he'd lost. 'Is he wearing a vest?'

Amy shrugged.

He looked into Leonard's vacant eyes. 'James, are you wearing a vest, buddy?'

Leonard struggled to maintain eye contact with Tanzy and looked into the dark sky above. His chest was rising and falling rapidly as he struggled for breath.

'Where did it hit you?' Tanzy asked. Leonard couldn't answer. Then to Weaver: 'I can feel the stab vest. Bullet can't have penetrated that, so it must have entered through his arm or armpit. Help me lift him and take off his jacket.'

'We should wait for—'

'Amy, he's losing blood too quickly. We need to find out where it's coming from and stop it the best we can. Help me.'

They pulled him up slightly and Tanzy carefully peeled Leonard's arms out of his jacket and managed to pull it off. Leonard winced in pain. 'We need this off too,' he said, referring to the stab vest and T-shirt. It took a little while but they managed it.

'You got your light?'

Weaver found her torch from her belt and passed it to Tanzy. 'Here.'

'We need to turn him onto his side a little,' he told her. 'To get a better look at this.'

After they turned him over, Tanzy shone the light down onto his left side. 'This might hurt, Jim. Just bear with me, mate.' Tanzy took hold of his left forearm and, very slowly, started to raise it a little, causing Leonard to scream out in pain. 'Sorry, sorry, mate, just hold on — where's that fucking ambulance at!' The light from the torch showed the bullet hole just under Leonard's armpit. 'I'm going to put your arm across your body.' Tanzy guided Leonard's arm across and placed it on the middle of his vest. 'It'll give the paramedics a better look when they get here.' He turned his attention to Weaver. 'Amy, how many times did the guy shoot?'

She frowned. 'Just once.'

'He didn't shoot at you?'

She shook her head quickly. 'No, no.'

'Okay.'

The wail of distant sirens ripped through the air. 'Will he be okay?' Weaver asked.

Tanzy wasn't sure but had to remain positive. 'Yeah, looks like the bullet went straight through. I don't know why he's being so dramatic, to be honest.'

Weaver smiled sadly and placed her hand on top of Leonard's. 'Hang in there, Jim, help is coming now,' said Weaver. 'Can you hear the sirens?'

When the ambulance arrived, two paramedics, a man and a woman, jumped out the back with a stretcher, and placed it down near Leonard.

'What happened?' asked the man.

Tanzy explained. As he did, Weaver remained quiet, watching the paramedics check him out. After a few minutes, they lifted him onto the stretcher and put him in the back of the ambulance.

'I'm going with him,' Weaver told Tanzy.

Tanzy watched her climb into the back and a paramedic lean out and pull the door closed. Then the ambulance disappeared down the road, taking a right at the roundabout towards the hospital.

Tanzy took a deep breath and returned to his car. On his way to the incident, he'd spoken with Sergeant Jack Tunstall, the sergeant on shift, about the raid at the house on Craig Street. Tanzy had suggested an armed tactical unit to handle it as he considered these were dangerous people they were dealing with. Tunstall agreed and informed Tanzy that he would arrange it.

As Tanzy turned the key to start the engine, his phone rang. It was PC Josh Andrews. He knew Andrews was on shift and was heading to Craig Street.

'Josh, what's happening there?'

'Ori, you need to see this,' Andrews said. 'I've seen nothing like it in my life.'

'I'll be straight over. Sit tight.'

61

Sunday evening
Craig Street, Darlington

Tanzy pulled up near the house on Craig Street, noticing light shining brightly from every window. Two police vans were parked directly in front of the house, and two police cars were parked across the middle of the road. The street was full of officers, some in tactical gear holding weapons and others milling around, taking notes, and speaking with neighbours. Most of the neighbours were either out on their doorsteps watching or peering through their windows to see what all the fuss was about.

Through his windscreen he noticed PC Andrews standing a few feet from the front door. He turned the engine off and opened his door, a rush of cold air seeping in, and got out. He moved around the car and stepped onto the path, making his way towards the house.

'Hey, Orion,' PC Donny Grearer said, hearing his approach.

'How's it going?'

'I'll let *you* decide that one. Go have a look in there,' he said, smiling. 'We've hit the jackpot.'

Tanzy drifted past him, approaching Andrews.

'Josh,' Tanzy said, nodding.

Andrews had finished a conversation with one of the neighbours and turned to face him. 'Hey, boss.'

To their right, they heard shouting, screaming, and swearing. 'They in there?'

Andrews nodded to the police vans. 'Both are full, as well as the cars.'

'Jesus,' he gasped. 'What did you find?'

Andrews waved him on. 'Come on, I'll show you.'

Tanzy followed Andrews into the terraced house, stepping up into a narrow hallway lined with grubby cream wallpaper that used to be white, and a dark brown carpet clotted with stains. They passed one door and took the second, Tanzy noticing it had a few holes in the base of it, as if it had been subject to a good kicking in the past. In the dining room, on a square table that was placed against the chimney breast, there must have been over two hundred bricks of white powder, roughly six inches by four, all solid.

Tanzy froze on the spot. 'Jesus fucking wept!'

Andrews smiled at him. 'Jackpot.'

Tanzy exhaled as he padded closer to the contents on the table.

'How much you reckon it's worth?' Andrews asked him.

'No idea at all.'

They heard footsteps behind them. Tanzy turned to see Sergeant Jack Tunstall walk in. He was short but wide, with a scar on his cheek from a knife attack during the last week of his initial ten-week training as a constable. It hadn't improved his looks, that's for sure.

Tanzy shook his hand, matching his equally firm grip. 'Hey, Jack. Hit the jackpot, I think.'

'About time these fuckers were found out. I reckon they were running the whole town's drug supply. We'll take them all down the station and question them. Good tip-off from Mac in DFU. I heard what he did with Mark Greenwell's phone.'

'He knows his stuff.' He turned to PC Andrews. 'Can you take more photos of this and start bagging it up, please? I'll send someone else in to help.'

Andrews nodded to his sergeant and took out his phone to take some photos.

Tanzy patted him on the back. 'Good work, Josh.' Then Tanzy followed Sergeant Tunstall out into the hallway. 'He's a good lad,' he said to the sergeant.

'He is. One of our best, is Josh.'

They both stepped outside into the cold and noticed the street was busier than before. Tanzy glanced to his left, seeing a news van and, just next to it, a reporter, standing in front of a camera with her back to the house.

He wanted to go home, get a shower, and go to bed. He decided to ring Weaver when he got home and check up on Leonard. He was sure, from his own experience, that Leonard would pull through no problem.

Despite Leonard's injury, it had been a successful day for the police. Tomorrow might be different.

62

Monday morning
High Row, Darlington town centre

'Graham, the thing is,' the taller of the two men said, 'if we tell him the things we've missed, we'll be gone. You know that as well as I do.'

Graham pressed his lips together. 'It's a tough one, Pete. He might already have evidence about what we haven't done. He knows the regs inside out, that's why he's the boss.'

'We'll see what he says. We could plead ignorance?'

'Always an option.'

They continued walking along the top of High Row, passing Greggs on their left. The time on the town clock showed them it was just before seven. If they got there with plenty of time, they could prepare for the director's arrival and attempt to cover all bases.

Up ahead they saw something at the bottom of the Joseph Pease statue.

Pete pointed, laughing. 'Looks like he's had a good night, doesn't it?'

Graham was focused on the window of Waterstones to his right, then glanced up ahead. 'Who?'

'The guy up there, look.'

They noticed a man sitting on the floor with his back against the thick concrete block at the base of the statue.

'What's he doing?' Pete said, squinting to see better.

'Is he naked?'

'God, I think he is,' Pete said. 'It's bloody freezing. What's he playing at?'

'Why is he sitting like that?'

They were roughly forty metres away now but angled their walk over to the statue to get a closer look.

'We should check if he's okay, Pete. He'll bloody freeze to death.'

Pete agreed. 'Must have had some wild . . .' He trailed off and stopped, as did Graham, when the scene at the base of the statue finally became clear.

'What. The. Actual. Fuck.' Pete stared, trying to make sense of it. 'Graham, why's he like that?'

Graham couldn't take his eyes off him and stayed silent.

In front of them, sitting at the base of the statue, was a naked man, with his arms pinned to his sides with what seemed like some kind of rope wrapped around his wrists going around the statue's base. His face and hair were white as if covered completely in powder, so much so they couldn't see his features very well. There was something around his neck too.

'What is this?' Pete whispered.

'Is this real?'

Barbed wire was wrapped around his throat and neck. From his mouth, foam leaked and had hardened on his chin.

'Is this a fucking wind-up?' Pete shouted, then looked around.

Graham said, 'We need to ring the police, now.'

242

63

The first PCs to arrive on the scene were Weaver and Grearer. Shortly after, further PCs, CID, forensics, and an ambulance turned up, although it was clear the man was beyond the help of paramedics.

It was an early start for them, but what better way to start a fresh Monday morning than being thrown in at the deep end.

They'd set up a huge perimeter with tape, preventing access for dozens of workers who'd joined the growing crowd, questioning why they couldn't get to work. It was PC Weaver's duty to take charge as first responder to the scene, as well as monitoring personnel who entered through the tape.

Tallow and Hope decided to set up a tent around the body, giving them a little privacy and at least preserving the scene if the heavens started to open, which looked likely.

Very soon afterwards, as if they'd timed it, Byrd and Tanzy arrived separately, both parking up on the footpath opposite Burger King.

'Just what we need. Perfect start to our Monday morning.' Tanzy shook his head, making his way across the concrete with Byrd.

Standing at the tape was Weaver. 'Morning,' she said.

'What do we have, Amy?'

'I can't really describe it,' she explained, frowning. 'Think it's better for you to see for yourself. Here, put these on.' She handed them some blue overshoes.

The tent that the forensics had set up resembled a gazebo, but with only two sides to it. Four lots of barrier tape had been set up in the area, preventing people seeing into it.

Byrd and Tanzy heard talking inside the tent as they approached.

'What do you think that is?' Hope was asking Tallow.

Tallow was taking photos, the flash of the camera hitting the plastic sheeting like stabs of lightning before they faded away.

'Could be talc . . . could be cocaine . . . could be fake snow,' he said.

Byrd and Tanzy stopped at the side opening of the tent. 'Safe to come in?' Byrd asked.

'Not just yet, unless you have overshoes on. I need to check for prints,' Tallow replied.

'Jesus Christ, what happened to him?' Tanzy said, scratching the side of his head.

Hope, dressed in her disposable plastic suit and white face mask, shrugged. 'What's your opinion on this one, Orion?'

Tanzy sighed a little, absorbing the scene for a moment, then looked back to Hope. 'I have nothing yet. What're your thoughts?'

'I think it's spiritual,' she said, glancing Tallow's way, who shook his head, clearly disagreeing with her idea.

Byrd and Tanzy, despite the forensic team moving around and occasionally stepping in their line of sight, considered the naked man for a long time.

'Do you think it's him? Lyle Wilson?' Tanzy said, glancing Byrd's way.

'No idea.' He looked at Tallow. 'It's clear he hasn't been here for long because someone would have seen him, but is there any indication how long he's been dead?'

The man's face was covered with white powder but the rest of his body was clear to see. Tallow lowered himself, looking at the skin, how it had bloated and the odd skin colour. 'Almost three days?'

'Emily, what would you say?' Byrd asked.

She put the hair sample she'd cut from the man's head into a small, clear bag, then moved back a little, analysing him. After a few moments, she said, 'I'd have to agree with Jacob. It's also obvious that he wasn't killed here.'

Byrd looked at Tallow. 'Would it be possible to clean his face a little? I want to know if it's Lyle Wilson or not.'

'Sure.' Tallow let the camera hang from a lanyard around his neck, shuffled outside the tent to where their kit was and pulled out a small brush.

Byrd frowned at the naked man as he waited for Tallow.

'What's up?' Tanzy asked, noticing his expression.

'If this is the guy who was knocked over, I'm just wondering why he's turned up now and not yesterday, or the day before, or the night he was knocked down on Cleveland Street.'

'Think it's the same person who killed the others?' Tanzy asked.

'I assume so. Lyle Wilson was clearly associated with Mark Greenwell and spent much of his time around the Denes park. There's also a common link with Brian Everitt as both were strangled with something. I think the killer is responsible for all three deaths.'

'What's their link?' Tanzy asked, his eyebrows furrowing.

'Mark and Lyle, if this is Lyle, are similar in age. The anomaly is Brian Everitt and how he fits into it. But if Mark and Lyle spent a lot of time at the house on Craig Street and were a part of that drug operation, then chances are they were working for Jonny Feland.'

'It's a shame we have nothing to nail the bastard with,' Tanzy sighed.

Byrd raised a finger. 'We will, don't worry. We need to speak to Damien to see how the Mondeo fits into this and to locate the house he was taken to. We're still looking for Melissa and Eddy so, as soon as he's well enough, we'll head over there.'

'If this is linked to Jonny Feland, the question is why is someone doing this to his men?' Tanzy said. 'An enemy? Someone he's pissed off in the past?'

'Maybe,' Byrd replied, looking down at the body. 'What's your first impression here, mate?'

'I think someone killed him elsewhere, then brought him here. Then he put him in that position, tied his hands up like that, placed barbed wire around his neck, and poured the powder on him.'

Byrd tilted his head. 'Okay.'

'You?'

'Yeah, the barbed wire is just for show. However he died, he wasn't strangled with it.' He looked at Tallow, who'd returned to the tent and was now bent over the body. 'You think it's cocaine?'

Before Tallow brushed away the white powder, he pinched a little of it from the man's hair and rubbed it between his index finger and thumb. 'Same consistency as cocaine, Max. We've already got a sample of it and we'll test it at the lab later.'

Tallow carefully started brushing away the powder from the man's face and the features became clearer.

Byrd knew straight away it was Lyle Wilson. The thought of telling his friend Keith made him feel physically sick.

Byrd took a few steps back until he was outside the tent and bent over slightly. Tanzy came out and placed a palm on his back.

Byrd took a lungful of icy air, closed his eyes, and eventually breathed out. 'I *fucking* love this job.'

Tanzy gave a sad smile, then left him to have a moment to himself. After he'd done a slow three-sixty sweep, he counted four cameras in view. He'd go see Jennifer Lucas at the town hall to have a look.

'You okay, Max?'

Byrd nodded. 'Feel a little light-headed but I'll survive.'

'What's left to do?' Byrd asked Tallow and Hope.

'Plenty,' Tallow answered, a little frustrated.

Byrd noticed it. 'Everything okay, mate?'

Tallow took a deep breath. 'Yeah, fine, sorry. It's just the last thing we need first thing on a Monday morning.'

'I know,' Byrd replied, shuffling his feet. 'Other than the obvious cust from the barbed wire around his neck, do you think he's sustained any other injuries? Not including obviously any possible injuries when he was run over?'

'He does have deep ligature marks on his wrists. But I know what you're thinking, Max. You're wondering if he has whip marks, aren't you?'

Byrd smiled at Tanzy.

'Peter's on his way,' Tallow said, glancing down at his watch. 'I don't want to move him until he's here. Then we can remove the rope and have a closer look.'

* * *

Almost twenty minutes passed before Peter Gibbs, the coroner, turned up. PC Weaver had signed him in at the tape and provided him with some overshoes to enter. He stopped a few feet into the tent and glared down at Lyle Wilson.

'Do we know him?' Gibbs asked no one in particular.

'We do,' Byrd said. 'He's a friend's son. I've known him for years. He went missing three nights ago. His phone was found at the scene where Mark Greenwell was found in the Denes park.' He paused for a moment to collect his thoughts. 'It's definitely Lyle Wilson.'

Tallow and Hope moved back to allow Gibbs to have a closer look. He made some notes and took several photographs. 'We'll take the body to pathology, see what Arnold and Laura come up with.'

'Are we okay undoing the rope tying him to the statue?' Tallow asked Gibbs.

'If you have everything you need, I don't see why not.'

'We need to get a look at his back,' Tanzy said.

Tallow went around the back of the monument and released the single knot in the rope. 'Undoing it now. Mind he doesn't drop forward.'

Hope held up his weight, her palms on his shoulders. 'Go on, I've got him.'

Hope gently lowered him to the ground, turning him over as she did so they could see his bare back. 'Come and see this,' she told the detectives.

On his back, there were seven whip marks: some faded, some fresh. They all ran from the rear of his right shoulder all the way down to his left hip.

'We need to stop this fucker ASAP,' Byrd shouted.

'I'll go see Jennifer Lucas,' said Tanzy. 'I'll meet you guys later at the hospital for the post-mortem.'

Gibbs nodded. 'I need to prepare some paperwork for this.' Then he looked at Tallow and Hope. 'You guys do what you need to do and give the paramedics a shout when you're done, then we'll take over.'

Byrd and Tanzy left the scene, ducked under the tape, and headed back to their cars.

'I heard what happened to Leonard,' Byrd said. 'How's he doing?'

'I spoke with Amy last night. She says he's still in hospital but is doing okay. She stayed with him for a few hours until the doctors told her he needed to rest.' They stopped at the cars. 'The bullet went straight through, just missing his vest by . . .' He made a very small gap between his thumb and finger. 'He was unlucky, but it isn't life-threatening.'

'Good,' Byrd said. 'I heard you had air support. Did anyone pick up on the Mondeo?'

Tanzy shook his head. 'Unfortunately not.'

'You heading over to see Jennifer?'

'Yeah. If any of the cameras can tell us something, she's the one who'll make it happen.'

'Okay. I need to contact Keith before this gets out.'

Tanzy's face softened. 'Good luck, Max.'

'Thanks, I'll need it.'

64

Tanzy knocked on the door and stepped inside the dark control room. Most of the light came from the cluster of screens to the left of the room. The chair in front of the screens was empty.

'Hello, Orion,' said Jennifer, over to the right of the room, placing something in one of the drawers. 'To what do I owe the pleasure today?'

'I need your skills,' he said.

She pushed her lips out and elegantly moved across the room to her chair. 'Go on.'

Tanzy explained the crime scene at the statue and that it had happened in the last twelve hours.

Jennifer took hold of the mouse and navigated the cursor where she needed to. 'There are six cameras on High Row. From where you're saying, at least three of them should have a view of what you're after.'

'I counted four,' Tanzy said.

'Well, aren't you clever?' she said, focusing back to the screen.

He smiled.

'From what you've described this is probably going to be the best one, but I can change it depending on what we see.' The angle appeared to be above Burger King facing north. The Joseph Pease monument was in darkness and there was no sign of Lyle Wilson's body at the base of it. The time display showed 9.01 p.m. last night.

'Whoever put it there will have done so in the early hours when no one would be around. Scroll forward to two in the morning, please,' Tanzy said.

As she scrolled along the time bar at the bottom of the screen, Tanzy glanced down at her. Her hair, her skin, the slight arching of her lips.

Stop it, he told himself, focusing back on the screen.

'Okay, this is two in the morning,' she said.

Still no body.

'Go to four in the morning.'

The body at the base of the monument.

'Go back, please, Jen.'

At 3.07 a.m., a dark blue Kia Sportage appeared in the right bottom corner of the screen, slowly crawling across the square until it stopped in front of the monument.

'Pause it there.' Tanzy squinted, then pointed. 'Can you zoom in on the registration plate?'

She dragged the rear of the car into focus. The letters and numbers were very clear. Tanzy took out his phone, found the number he needed, and put it to his ear.

'Yeah, it's Detective Inspector Orion Tanzy, can you run a plate check please?'

'Go ahead,' said the operator.

'N. U. 1. 3. P. T. X.'

'Hold on.'

After a few moments, the operator said, 'Detective Tanzy, are you sure that's correct?'

Tanzy frowned, looking towards Jennifer. 'Can you enhance it?'

She did.

'Yeah, I confirm it's NU13 PTX.'

'I'm sorry, that plate doesn't exist on the DVLA database.'

'Okay, thanks,' Tanzy said, hanging up before the operator could respond. He turned to Jennifer. 'It's a fake.'

She focused on the screen and pressed play. The driver of the car got out. The camera picked his head and shoulders up over the roof of the Sportage but there was something odd about him.

'Pause it. Zoom in on his face.'

She did.

'What's he wearing?' Tanzy asked, unsure what he was looking at, then it made sense. 'Balaclava?'

Jennifer tilted her head. 'Looks like it.'

'Great . . .' Tanzy sighed. 'Play it. See what he does.'

The man went to the back of the car, opened the boot, leaned in, and pulled something out. It was a naked body. He carried it around the side of the car which they couldn't see.

'Any cameras on the other side?' Tanzy asked.

From another camera, they saw the Kia Sportage crawl into view from the top left of the screen. The masked driver got out, went to the back of the car, dragged out the body, and carried it over to the monument. He returned to the boot of the car and grabbed a bag and some rope, then lowered to the naked man and tied the rope around one of his hands, then walked around the base of the statue until he was back where he started. He took a step back and admired his work, coming back into view of the camera.

He then placed a ring of barbed wire around Lyle's neck.

'What is this guy doing?' Jennifer asked, her palm over her mouth.

He pulled out another bag, similar in size to a carrier bag. It was full. He then lifted the bag above the man's head and poured its contents over his head and face.

'What . . . what on earth is that?'

'We think it's cocaine,' Tanzy told her. Then at 3.22 a.m., the man put the bag in the back of the car, climbed into the driver's seat, and drove out of sight.

'Can we try and see where the car goes?'

She manoeuvred the mouse until she found a north-facing camera near the town clock. She scrolled the time along to 3.21 a.m. A minute later, the Kia Sportage came into view and casually rounded the bend down towards St Cuthbert's Way.

Tanzy smiled.

'What's funny?'

'He isn't even rushing to get away. It's as if he has all the time in the world.'

Jennifer found the next camera. They watched the Sportage pass and disappear at the bottom of the screen.

'Where did he go?'

She found the camera at the end of Crown Street, fixed to the side of the library.

'Let's see if he comes this way,' she said, carefully watching the screen.

The car turned, passing the William Stead pub, then, strangely, it slowed and pulled up behind a black Jaguar that was parked on the corner of the *Northern Echo* building.

The Kia Sportage flashed its headlights at the Jaguar. The driver of the Sportage stepped out and waited. The driver's door of the Jaguar opened and another man stepped out, dressed exactly the same as the man from the Sportage. He was the same height and build, also wearing a balaclava. They spoke for a few minutes, then got back in their cars and vanished into the night.

'Hold on, we can see the plate of the Jag.' Jennifer dragged the time bar. 'See?'

Tanzy leaned closer to the screen. 'Yeah. I'll call it in and get a check on the plate.' He pulled his phone back from his pocket and called PC Cornty.

'Sir?' he answered.

'Phil, are you at the station near a computer?'

'Yeah, I'm at my desk now. What's up, boss?'

'I need you to check a plate for me: S. B. 1. 3. M. T. P. Got that?'

'Yeah, hang on.' There was some background noise. 'Why are we checking this plate, sir?'

'It belongs to a car that's possibly owned by someone responsible for the murder of Lyle Wilson. Anything?'

'Erm . . . it's er . . .'

'Is it fake?'

'No, it's registered.'

'Come on, Phil, who's it registered to?'

'It's registered to Detective Inspector Max Byrd.'

65

Monday morning
Darlington Town Hall

'Can you say that again, Phil?'

'The Jaguar is registered to Max Byrd.'

Tanzy was stunned. Jennifer glared up wondering what he'd been told.

'I . . . I don't . . . I don't understand,' he muttered. 'He doesn't have a Jaguar.'

'The car's registered to him. It says right here.'

'How long has he had the car?'

'The date of registration for the ownership of that vehicle was just over three weeks ago. It matches up with his address in Low Coniscliffe. He's the owner.'

Tanzy was lost for words, digesting the absurd information.

'Sir?'

'Okay, thanks,' snapped Tanzy. 'Say nothing, Phil, leave it with me.'

'But shouldn't we—'

Tanzy hung up quickly, placed the phone on the desk, and dropped his face into his palms.

'What's happened?' Jennifer asked softly, taking a gentle grip of his forearm.

'I need to go. Thanks for your help.' He pulled himself away from the table and made for the door quickly, his head swimming with this new information. Within two minutes he was sitting in his Golf, rubbing his hands together and breathing heavily. He considered the men on the CCTV screen. Could one of them be Byrd? He had lost weight and could fit the image, but who was the other man?

Was he working with someone?

He pulled his phone out and decided to call Byrd, to give him a chance to explain what was going on; there had to be a reason.

The phone rang twice then Byrd cancelled the call.

He tried again.

It went straight to voicemail. Byrd had turned his phone off. Why on earth would his phone be off?

'Max, what are you playing at?'

He threw his phone onto the passenger seat so hard it bounced up onto the floor. Sighing, he banged on his steering wheel so hard that the horn sounded in the car park and people passing by frowned at him.

He leaned over, picked up his phone, and found PC Josh Andrews' number.

As soon as it was answered, he said, 'Have you seen Max? I need to speak with him immediately.'

'I'm at the office, boss. Cornty has just told me about a car being registered to Max. What's going on?'

Tanzy clamped his eyes shut and tipped his head back onto the head rest. 'Listen, keep this under wraps. DCI Fuller does not find out about this yet. Tell Phil that he needs to keep his big mouth shut. Who else knows?'

Andrews hesitated, then admitted, 'A few of us.'

Tanzy sighed. 'Find Phil. I need to speak to him.'

'Okay, hold on, he's on his way to Fuller's office.'

'Get to him before he gets there, quick!'

Andrews started to pant a little. 'Phil, Phil. Here, Orion's on the phone, he needs to speak with you.'

'Yeah?' Cornty said into the phone.

'Phil, what are you playing at?' said Tanzy.

'I . . . I don't know—'

'You *do* fucking know,' Tanzy barked. 'You need to keep this quiet until I've spoken to Max, okay? Stay away from Fuller's office. That, DC Phillip Cornty, is an order from me, your superior. Do you understand that?'

Cornty gulped. 'I understand, sir.'

'Let me speak to Max first,' Tanzy told him. 'I'm sure there's a reason for this. Pass the phone back to Josh, please.'

Andrews came back to the phone.

'Sir?'

'There's another problem, Josh,' Tanzy said. 'It isn't only one guy we're looking for, it's two.'

'Jesus.'

'Yeah. Listen, keep it quiet. I need to speak to Max first. I've known him for years. I owe him that.'

'Yeah . . . okay.'

Tanzy heard something in his tone. 'What is it?'

'Nothing, sir, I—'

'Tell me,' demanded Tanzy, cutting him short.

'I just think DI Byrd has been different recently. A few of us have said it.'

'Different how?' Tanzy heard no reply. 'Josh, speak to me. Different how?'

'Not quite himself. Reserved somehow.'

Tanzy thought about his words, considering them, but personally, hadn't noticed anything different about the colleague he'd known for years.

'Sir, you there?'

'I'm here,' replied Tanzy, coming out of his thoughts. 'His parents have passed away recently. He's bound to be different in some way.'

Andrews remained silent, realising Tanzy wasn't willing to see anything bad in Byrd.

'Let me speak to Max, we'll get this sorted.'
They disconnected and Tanzy tried calling Byrd again.
Straight to answerphone.
'Where the fuck are you, Max?' he whispered.

66

Monday afternoon
Carmel Road, Darlington

Jonny Feland was sitting at his kitchen table when Andy rushed in, pulled out the chair next to Feland, and opened the laptop.

'You need to see this, boss.'

'What is it?'

Feland had watched the footage from the camera above his office on Duke Street earlier, picking up a man and a woman breaking into his empty office. The rent was cheap enough to run without actually using it, which disguised him as a legitimate businessman with a registered business address. For those in his circle, they knew he used his home for the real work — the stuff he wanted to keep private, away from prying eyes.

He'd also watched the news about the police hitting his property on Craig Street and seizing a substantial quantity of drugs. A huge setback but not the end of the world. Being in the game for so long, he had other properties with stock; he wasn't stupid enough to keep all of his merchandise in just one place. It did mean he'd have to redirect the flow of product before setting up another location.

'What is it?' Feland asked Andy, the laptop now fully open.

'Just watch.' Andy clicked on a video file. 'I remotely hacked Brian Everitt's laptop to transfer all of the business documents and information and found this . . .' He pointed at the screen. 'Just watch.'

For the next three minutes, they watched the footage closely, Andy keeping an eye on his boss's reaction.

'Play that again,' Feland said, coldly.

On the video feed, they watched Brian casually return to his laptop, and a moment later a man wearing a high-vis vest entered the room, placed a wire over Brian's head, and pulled it tight around his throat, then dragged him back off the chair down to the floor. For a minute, no one was on the screen, until the man stood up.

'How are we watching this?'

'All of our laptops are set up with an internal recording device. While the user is logged in, a camera records what's going on. I had a look back to the day he was murdered.'

Feland studied the man from the still shot on the screen. 'I know him. He's familiar.'

'Who is he?'

Feland opened up the internet and typed something in the search bar, then pressed ENTER, revealing a string of results. The first link took him to the *Northern Echo* website. He scrolled down a few pages and stopped.

'That's him,' Feland said. 'That fucker's just made the biggest mistake of his life.'

67

Alice Richards' phone rang on the worktop. Drying her hands after washing up, she placed the folded tea towel neatly on the drainer.

'Hey, Alex,' she answered.

'Hey yourself. You all right?'

'Yeah, I'm good.' She left the kitchen, turned off the light, and headed to the stairs.

'How's Callum doing? He didn't seem very happy when he got in from school. Sorry I didn't get chance to see him. I needed to finish an important report.'

'He said one of the boys at school was calling him names or something. I told him I'd speak to his teacher tomorrow. What times your football game?'

'Starts in ten minutes. Just pulling up now.'

She fell silent for a moment.

'What's Cal up to now?'

'Just in his room, on the PlayStation.' She started climbing the stairs. 'It was mad what happened on Saturday at the restaurant, wasn't it? I was thinking about it earlier.'

'I know, I can't believe they thought I had something to do with it.'

'You can't blame them. They're just doing their jobs.'

'Hey, I was thinking . . .'

'Thinking what?'

'Hold on,' she said.

'What?'

'Shh . . . I think I heard something,' she said.

'It'll be just Cal—'

'Shh . . . There's someone outside,' she whispered.

'There's what?'

'Someone outside the back door.' Alice froze on the landing and peered over the handrail down into the well-lit hallway. Behind her, she heard Callum on his PlayStation through his closed bedroom door.

'Alice, is this a joke?'

She didn't reply.

'Alice, are you being—'

There was a loud crack then a bang.

'The back door in the kitchen is being smashed in, Alex! Alex, the back door . . .' She trailed off, moving quickly into Callum's room and closing the door immediately. 'Callum, Callum! Get up, get up off the bed now!'

Callum looked at her strangely, wondering what on earth she was doing.

'Callum, up now!' She threw the phone onto the floor and, using all the strength she had, pulled Callum's bed towards the closed door.

'Alice, what the hell is going on?' Alex shouted down the phone.

'Mam, what is—'

'Help me move this. Quick!' she begged Callum.

He pulled his headset off, threw it down onto the floor, and dashed over to help her.

They could hear heavy footsteps climbing the stairs.

'Alice!' Alex cried. 'Hold on, I'm coming home!'

'Mam, is that Dad?'

Footsteps pounded on the landing outside the door and, before she could push the bed against the door, it was booted open, colliding into the side of the bed.

A man pushed his way in, dressed in black and wearing a smile from ear to ear. There was a knife in his hand.

'Hello, Alice,' he said.

Alice grabbed Callum and backed into the furthest corner from the doorway. Both of them started to cry.

68

Monday evening
Low Coniscliffe, Darlington

Tanzy hadn't wanted to do it, but he felt he had no other choice. He'd tracked the location of Byrd's phone, which was at his home. He'd tried calling throughout the day, but Byrd's phone had been turned off.

Byrd hadn't turned up for the post-mortem of Lyle Wilson, which Tanzy thought was strange because Byrd said he'd be there. Nevertheless, whatever the reason, Tanzy had made an excuse for him, telling forensics and the pathologists he was busy attending something else but didn't say what exactly. From the post-mortem, it was clear Lyle had been strangled with a very thin, sharp wire and had sustained several broken bones and fractures when he'd been run down by the Kia Sportage. Consistent with the other victims, Lyle Wilson had seven marks on his back, most likely done with a thin whip. Two of them were fresh, and in the opinion of the senior pathologist, Dr Hemsley, Lyle has suffered these within the last two weeks. The hardest part of Tanzy's day was speaking with Fuller, who had asked him what was happening on the case. Tanzy didn't tell him about seeing two men on the CCTV and about the black Jaguar that was registered to Byrd.

Tanzy pulled up outside Byrd's house, blocking in Byrd's X5 on the driveway. The street was quiet and dark.

He got out of the car and closed his door gently, taking a lungful of cold, quiet air. He stared at Byrd's house for a moment, thinking hard about the conversation he was about to have with him. There was light coming through the curtains in the living room and through the bathroom blinds just above the front door.

There was no Jaguar in sight as he looked up and down the street.

He wasn't sure how he was going to approach this one; it was a situation he'd never been in, especially with someone he'd known for so long.

He ambled up the driveway and lightly knocked twice on the door. A moment later, he heard footsteps and Claire opened the door, smiling.

'Hi, Claire. Is Max in?'

'Yes, please come in.' She stood back and held the door for him. 'It's been a while, Ori.'

Tanzy stepped into the warm hallway. 'It *has* been a while, Claire. You okay?'

Claire closed the door. 'I'm good. How's Pip and the kids doing?'

Tanzy looked down the hall, then focused on her. 'They're good. Where's Max?'

'He's just in the kitchen. He'll be happy you called.' She made her way to the kitchen. Tanzy followed.

At the table, there was an empty glass with a half-full bottle of whisky next to it, but the kitchen was empty.

'Max?' said Tanzy.

Claire frowned, looking around. 'Max, you in here?'

'In the garage,' they heard him say from the door off the kitchen. 'Is that you, Ori?'

'Yeah,' Tanzy replied, loud enough to be heard.

'Can I make you a tea or a coffee?' Claire asked, heading for the kettle.

'I'm okay, thank you.'

A minute later, Byrd stepped through the door from the garage, then closed and locked it. He placed the key on a key hook fixed to the wall.

Tanzy watched him carefully.

'How you doing, Ori?' Byrd said, turning to him. 'Thanks for dropping by.'

Tanzy frowned at the man he'd known for as long as he had been in the police force.

Byrd narrowed his gaze. 'To what do I owe this pleasure, Ori?'

Tanzy smiled. 'I found out something very interesting today.'

'Oh yeah?'

'Yeah,' said Tanzy, then fell silent.

Byrd turned to Claire. 'I'll have one too. Thanks.' He tiredly made his way over to the kitchen table, pulled out chair, and dropped into it with a sigh. He focused on Tanzy. 'What was it, Ori?'

'Did you kill Mark Greenwell?'

'What?' Byrd scowled at the question.

'What about Brian Everitt?' Tanzy added.

Byrd, with a perplexed look on his face, was stunned.

'Well, did you?' Tanzy persisted, his eyes wide.

'Now listen, Ori, you've known me for years. Are you really asking me these questions or is this some big wind-up?' Byrd leaned back as if checking for cameras.

'People are saying you've been acting differently.'

Claire said, 'I don't understand all this. Different? What people?' She took a step towards the table. 'What the hell is going on here, you two?'

'Which people?' Byrd said.

'Where were you when I went to the post-mortem?'

Byrd didn't answer.

'It isn't a game, Max. We can't argue with the facts here. Did you kill them?' Tanzy stood up.

'I don't know what you're getting at, but if you ask me that again, you're going on your arse.' Byrd also stood, facing him. 'You hear me?'

Tanzy smiled and shrugged. 'Really?'

'You can count on it.'

'Go on then, give me your best shot . . .'

69

Monday evening
Stonedale Crescent, Darlington

Alex Richards slammed the brakes on outside his house, bringing his car to a screeching stop in front of his driveway. The phone call with Alice had ended seconds after he'd heard her and Callum screaming.

He jumped out, ran as fast as he could to the front door, unlocked it, and barged it open with a shoulder.

'Alice!' he shouted. 'Alice!'

The house was pitch black. He pressed the switch to his right, the hallway erupting in cold harsh light.

'Callum!'

The house was silent.

He raced up the stairs, taking the steps two at a time, until he reached the landing and froze. Through the open bathroom door he could see something written on the mirror.

Too Late.

His heart missed a beat and his stomach flipped. He sprinted to Callum's bedroom, barging into the door until it bounced off the side of Callum's bed and rebounded back into him.

He turned on the switch on the wall and the room filled with light.

'Jesus . . .'

There was blood all over the white carpet.

He looked around the messy room. The bed was pushed over by the door. Callum's chair was tipped over next to his broken desk. His wardrobe door was barely hanging on by one hinge, the other door had come off and was against the wall to the left. Callum's clothes were all over, small piles scattered around.

He saw Alice's body slumped against the wall in the corner, a pool of blood underneath her, the bottom of her dressing gown saturated in it.

'Alice?' Alex said quietly.

He climbed over the bed, went over to her, and placed his hand on her shoulder to pull her back to see her face. He screamed and threw his hands to his mouth. Letting her go too quickly, she dropped to the floor with a thud, her body twisting, glaring up at him with wide, vacant, bloodshot eyes.

Her dressing gown was pierced in several places. He took a few steps back, stumbling on the floor. The tears fell as he shook with anger.

He turned his attention to the landing, but after carefully checking the house, he couldn't find Callum. He had to assume he'd been taken.

He moved to the kitchen, opened up a cupboard, grabbed a bag from the bottom, and went out the back door towards his car, determined to settle the score with the man responsible for this.

70

Monday evening
Low Coniscliffe, Darlington

'You don't want to do this, Max.' Tanzy shook his head a little, knowing he could handle Byrd if it ever came down to anything physical.

'You're the one who stood up first, Ori.' Byrd shrugged, his face now serious.

'What's going on here?' Claire pleaded. 'Will you two just talk about this?'

'I'm trying to find out what's going on, Claire,' replied Tanzy, keeping his focus on Byrd, who stood a few feet in front of him. 'Why don't we go down to the station and have a chat about it?'

Byrd burst into laughter. 'You want to take me in?'

'Come on,' Tanzy said, leaning forward, grabbing his forearm.

Byrd shrugged him off. 'Get the fuck off me! You're not taking me in.'

'If that's what it takes to find out what you've done, then yes, I'm taking you in.'

Byrd's face reddened and he lunged forward with a straight jab. Tanzy was quick, but not quite quick enough as Byrd's knuckles caught the side of Tanzy's nose. He stumbled back a step, surprised at the speed which Byrd had delivered it.

'Not bad,' Tanzy said, rubbing the tip of his warm nose with a finger.

'Not just a slow old man after all, eh?' Byrd shouted, his fists raised high.

'Please, just stop!' screamed Claire, only metres away from them, her palms pressed against her face as if hiding from what was going on.

'You only had one shot,' Tanzy told him.

Byrd lunged forward again with the same jab but Tanzy saw it coming a mile away and ducked, driving a right hand into his kidneys. Byrd slumped over in severe pain, the sudden wince telling Tanzy he'd done damage.

'Why did you do it, Max?' Tanzy shouted.

Byrd didn't answer. Instead, he composed himself and straightened up, then threw himself at Tanzy, trying to grab him with flaying hands. Byrd almost grabbed Tanzy's throat, but Tanzy used his hands to deflect this attempt, turning Byrd side on, which opened up an opportunity for Tanzy to come in from the side and get him in a choke hold, squeezing tightly. Byrd was tough, but Tanzy had grappled with much bigger men in his judo training and knew it would be only a matter of time.

Byrd struggled until his body became limp. Tanzy lowered him to the floor slowly and turned him over, grabbing a pair of handcuffs and both of his hands.

'Detective Inspector Max Byrd, I'm arresting you on the—'

Tanzy felt an excruciating pain at the back of his head before he lost consciousness and passed out on the floor next to Byrd with a thud.

* * *

271

His eyes fluttered open. He didn't know where he was. The pain in his head made him feel sick. Lying on his side, he brought his hand up and touched the top of his head, feeling the hard lump rising.

He gazed up, focusing on the light above him. As the dizziness faded, he turned onto his front and looked around.

'Where . . . where . . .' he tried to say, then fell silent, his head pounding.

To his left, sitting on a chair facing him, was Byrd holding a baseball bat, ready to use it if necessary. Claire was opposite him, watching Tanzy in anticipation.

'Orion, first of all, keep calm,' Byrd said, 'because I genuinely don't understand why you came here tonight or why you asked me the questions you did. I've had a pretty shitty day too, so—' Byrd shuffled slightly in his seat — 'for the benefit of the friendship we've had for nearly twenty years, I need you to stay calm and relax. Come and sit down and explain to me what's going on.'

Tanzy very slowly stood up, a rush of blood finding his head. He looked at Claire. 'What did you hit me with? A hammer?'

She pointed to the frying pan on the worktop to her right.

'Nice,' Tanzy sighed, steadying himself.

'Please, come and sit down. No more fucking around and fighting. Talk to me,' Byrd insisted.

Tanzy padded over to the table, disorientated, and dropped into the seat next to Byrd.

'Would you like some water, Orion?' Claire asked.

He nodded to her. She grabbed a glass from the cupboard and filled it at the sink.

'Ori . . . what's happened?'

'You *really* don't know?'

Byrd shook his head. 'Enlighten me . . .'

'Do you own a black Jaguar? Registration plate S. B. 1. 3. M. T. P.'

Byrd frowned at him. 'You know what car I drive, I—'

'Just answer the question,' Tanzy told him.

'No, I do not own that vehicle.'

'Okay.'

'What's so special about this car?' Byrd asked.

Tanzy told him about the video where the Kia Sportage stopped behind the car. He mentioned the two men on the camera footage.

'I checked the registration plate with the DVLA. You're the owner. It's registered at this address, Max.'

Byrd scrunched up his face, then looked over to Claire, who was similarly confused.

Tanzy shrugged. 'Any explanation how that is possible?'

'Honestly, Ori, I don't understand this. Have you got the video?'

Tanzy pulled out his phone to show him. Claire came over to watch it too.

'And . . . that car's registered to me?'

'According to the DVLA, it is.'

'DVLA?' Claire said. 'The letter.'

'What letter?' Tanzy asked.

Byrd remembered. 'I didn't read it. Where did you say you put it?'

She went over to the microwave and sifted through the random pile of envelopes, takeaway leaflets, and magazines. 'I put it on here. Except . . . it isn't here. Where is it?'

'When did this letter come, Max?' Tanzy asked.

'Three days ago,' Claire replied, confidently. 'Yeah, one hundred per cent I put it on there.' She checked through the pile again. 'It's definitely not here.'

'If what you're saying is true, Max, and trust me, I want to believe you, then it seems someone has set you up. That letter from the DVLA could have been the logbook for the Jag. The date of the registration was less than three weeks ago.'

Byrd mulled over his words, trying to think of anyone who would — and could — do such a thing.

'I want to apologise for coming in like that and not giving you the chance to explain,' Tanzy said. 'I've known you nearly twenty years. I'm sorry.'

Byrd smiled. 'Don't worry about it. I won't go so easy on you next time,' he added, with a wink.

'Sorry for hitting you over the head, Ori,' Claire confessed, wincing. 'Instinct took over.'

'Max is rubbing off on you.'

71

Tuesday morning
Stonedale Crescent, Darlington

Byrd and Tanzy, along with forensics and a small team of PCs, arrived at the Richards house.

Byrd and Tanzy were informed what had happened in the boy's bedroom and were standing in the doorway, looking in.

Byrd shook his head. 'Well, this explains it.'

'Explains what?'

'Claire tried calling Alice last night but she didn't answer.'

Tallow, Hope, and Forrest were inside the room, dressed in white disposable suits and face masks. Hope was crouched down near Alice, taking a sample of her blood. Tallow stood back with his camera in hand, studying photos he'd already taken. Forrest was to the left, making notes on the blood spatter.

'Seems she was stabbed multiple times here,' Forrest said to Tallow, who put his camera down to give her his full attention. 'See the thicker lumps there. And there.'

Tallow nodded.

'This is where she was wounded, then she stumbled into the corner. Can you see that pattern across there? It seems she put up a good fight.'

Byrd scanned the wall, where the plaster had been dented in various places. Forrest turned to him. 'I'm assuming this is one of her children's rooms?'

'He's called Callum,' Byrd said. 'He's twelve. And they have a teenage girl, Lisa, who's just turned eighteen. *This* is Alice Richards. She's a friend of my partner. Her husband was involved in the incident at Uno Momento on Saturday night.'

'Does your partner know about this yet?'

'No,' he said, then turned his attention to Hope. 'Emily, how long has she been dead?'

'At least twelve hours,' she said confidently.

'Who called it in?' asked Tanzy.

'One of her work colleagues that normally picks her up. She waited and called several times, then decided to knock and open the door. She came upstairs to this.' Byrd pointed to the mess of the room.

Once Hope had moved away from the body, Tallow took photos of the whole room and then a short video. He placed his camera to one side and, with help from Hope, pulled Alice away from the corner and placed her down on her back. They lifted up her soaked vest and counted six stab marks to her stomach.

Byrd clamped his eyes shut for a second, struggling to get the images of what had happened out of his head.

'Who the hell did this?' Tanzy said.

'Where's the husband?' Tallow asked. They'd checked the house. There was no sign of Callum, Lisa, or Alex. Byrd shook his head.

From the landing, PC Cornty called out, 'The media's here.'

Tanzy said, 'Keep them back. Make sure Weaver and Andrews stay at the tape. This is really going to piss Fuller off.' He sighed and looked at the floor. 'This town is going to shit.'

Byrd said, 'I need some air.'

Tanzy watched him walk slowly down the stairs, his body slumped and shoulders dipped, then turned back to the room, watching Tallow put something in a plastic clear bag.

Hope faced Tanzy. 'Where's the children and husband?'

'That's what we need to find out, because at the moment, despite Max knowing him, our prime suspect is Alex Richards.'

72

Tuesday, late morning
Beechwood Avenue, Darlington

Byrd needed to find Alex Richards. He'd got his number after their meal on Saturday, just in case Alex ever needed a football player if they were short.

Sitting in his car, he called it. Straight to answerphone.

PC Weaver was sitting next to him, relaxed, her hands down on her lap. They'd spoken to one of the PCs at the station, who'd told them Alex's dad, Patrick, lived on Beechwood Avenue, just opposite the primary school.

'Come on,' Byrd said, opening his door. Weaver did the same and made her way around the rear of the car. The chance that Alex was here was slim but they needed to try.

Byrd opened the metal gate, approached the door, and knocked several times.

Weaver, standing behind him, shivered in her uniform. It was a few degrees lower than yesterday, but it was bright, the sun shining low in the sky.

The front door opened, revealing a man in his seventies. He was of average height, had long whispery hair and a beard that Santa would be proud of.

'Can I help you?' he asked.

Weaver asked him if he was Patrick Richards.

Patrick's eyes narrowed. 'Yes?'

'Have you seen your son Alex?'

His eyes shot left, then right. 'Not in a few weeks, no. We had a falling out a few months ago. He only comes over when he needs something.'

Byrd nodded. 'Can we pop in for a moment? I have some bad news, I'm afraid.'

Patrick digested his words and moved aside. 'Sorry about the mess.'

Byrd and Weaver walked into the large, wide hallway. The décor was in dire need of some TLC. No women lived there, Byrd decided.

'Is there a Mrs Richards here?'

Patrick shook his head sadly. 'Passed away three years ago. Cancer.'

Weaver smiled sadly and followed him down the hall.

'Please, sit in here.' He motioned to the living room. The ceiling was high, the walls were painted a faded duck-egg blue, and the carpet was black. A sofa was to the left near an old fireplace which looked older than he did and a television in the corner near the window, but not much else, leaving an empty space to the right. 'I used to have another sofa, but I sold it,' he explained, pointing to where it used to be.

'We're okay standing,' Byrd said.

'What's this about, Detective?'

'Unfortunately, we have some very bad news. Your daughter-in-law, Alice Richards, has been murdered.'

Patrick threw his hands up to his mouth in shock. 'What . . . what happened?'

'We're currently investigating that, but we need to speak to Alex. I've tried phoning him but there's no answer.'

'*You* have his number?' his father said, frowning.

'Yeah. Alice was a good friend of my partner.'

'I see . . .' Patrick said. 'Do you want me to call him?'

'If you could, yes please,' Byrd said, appreciatively.

Patrick went over to the mantelpiece and grabbed his phone, then took his time finding his son's number, as if not quite sure how to use it.

'Just calling him,' he told Byrd and Weaver, who exchanged a quick glance towards each other — it was so loud they could hear it themselves.

'No answer. There's a voice that comes on saying to leave a message or something.' Confusion enveloped his face for a moment.

'Okay, thank you for trying,' Byrd said. 'Can you tell me about Alex? Anything about his military service or his current job that might help us find him? Any friends or places he might be?'

Patrick scrunched his face up, unsure where to start. 'He's thirty-eight, was in the army for ten years.'

'What did he do in the army?'

'Everyone thinks he was front-line personnel, even Alice did, and his kids. But he wasn't.'

'He . . . wasn't?'

'No,' he said, shaking his head. 'He was a part of an SAS unit. He's . . .' He looked away. 'I shouldn't be telling you any of this.'

'We need everything you've got. Finding Alex is our priority here, Mr Richards. Please,' said Byrd.

'I'm the only one who truly knew him. Alice doesn't know. No one.'

'Go on.'

'Alex is very dangerous. He's very highly skilled and has concentration like nothing I've ever seen. Even as a child, he was so focused and driven.'

'What did he do in the SAS?'

'Detective, you know that's confidential.'

Byrd and Weaver stayed silent to encourage him to continue.

'He'd spend months at a time wherever the government sent him. He spent a lot of his time over in Costa Rica working in a small team, bringing down foreign officials planning

280

attacks on the UK and US. They needed a family member to be aware, in case they needed to contact someone close to him if things went bad.'

Byrd didn't know what to say.

'Have you spoken with their daughter, Lisa?' Weaver asked.

Patrick frowned and shook his head. 'What do you mean?'

'She may have phoned you?' Weaver offered.

'Lisa is dead . . .'

Byrd and Weaver fell silent, digesting the information.

'Alex was talking about her the other night, saying she was busy doing her own thing?'

'Alex can't accept what happened to her. That's why he came out of the army. He couldn't cope being away from his family any more. He blames himself for not being here for her.'

'*What* happened to her?'

'She was at a party with friends.' He sighed, looked away. 'She went missing. A few hours after, she was found dead in a park with no clothes on. Alex believes if he was home he could have helped her. No one knows who gave her the drugs that killed her. I know deep down it's played on his mind all this time. If he ever found out who was responsible, God, I don't know what he'd do.'

After Mr Richards tried calling Alex again with no joy, Byrd handed him a contact card. 'If you do see him or speak with him, tell him to call Max. He knows who I am.' Byrd went to turn and walk out the door.

'Detective . . .'

Byrd turned.

'Please, under no circumstances underestimate him. He's unlike anyone I know.'

Byrd gave him a long stare, processing his words, then turned and followed Weaver outside into the cold.

73

Tuesday afternoon
Carmel Road, Darlington

In the huge living room, sitting on the wide sofa, Jonny Feland was watching the television. He was sipping coffee when the programme was interrupted by breaking news.

A reporter was standing at a semi-detached house in Stonedale Crescent, a cul-de-sac off Milbank Road in Darlington. Feland picked up the remote and turned up the volume.

The reporter said, 'We're standing in a quiet cul-de-sac in front of a home where a woman, thirty-eight-year-old Alice Richards, has been found murdered. At the moment, the whereabouts of her husband, Alex Richards, and their son, Callum Richards, aged twelve, is unknown.'

'Don't worry,' Feland said to the television, smiling, 'Callum's safe upstairs.'

The reporter went on: 'Police and detectives are very keen to speak to Alex Richards. He hasn't been seen since yesterday. Mr Richards has spent more than ten years in the army, and if anyone knows his whereabouts, please contact the police immediately.'

'Army, eh?' Feland said, looking to his left towards Thomas.

'This is Abigail Trent, ITV News,' the reporter said, before the camera cut off and returned to the studio.

'Army,' Feland said again.

Thomas shrugged.

'And you killed his wife and brought his son here.'

He shrugged. 'Don't worry about it. I can handle him.'

'You see, Thomas, that's what I like about you. No task is too difficult.' Feland stood up and looked out of the impressive bay window onto his front garden. The sky above was clear blue; there wasn't a cloud in sight. 'It's a lovely day today.' He turned back to Thomas, whose dark eyes were watching him. 'Do you think he knows his son is here?'

'I doubt it,' Thomas replied. 'What are you going to do with Callum? He's older than the children we normally deal with.'

'He is. But he's handsome, isn't he? There'll be someone out there who wants him. We'll just sell him for a reduced price.'

Feland went back to the sofa and sat down with a worried expression.

'What's with the face?' Thomas asked.

'I keep thinking about something.' He fell silent for a moment. 'The night his daughter died was the night of that party, right?'

Thomas nodded.

'Mark Greenwell, Lyle Wilson, and Brian Everitt were all there. Now they're all dead, Thomas. He knows what happened to her. At first, I thought this could be the Farlans or the Haleys, but it's not gang- or drug-related, is it? It's pure revenge.'

'Who else was at the party that night?' Thomas asked.

'Jamie was there. He was talking about it a few days ago, feeling all sad about it for some fucking reason.'

'Who else? Were you there?'

Feland shook his head. 'No. All the people who've been killed worked for me in some way. Why now? Why, a year after her death, are these things happening? Someone's been talking to him, someone's told him what happened.'

'Did you say Jamie was there?'

Feland nodded. 'I suppose he's not dead yet.'

'Maybe Jamie's the one who's been talking?'

'That's ridiculous, Thomas. Jamie's solid. I've practically raised him as my own. I've offered him a home, money, anything he wants.'

'Where is he?' Thomas asked, standing up.

'I haven't seen him all day,' Feland admitted, watching Thomas head for the door. 'Do you honestly think Richards knows where I live?'

Thomas smiled. 'Well, we'll soon find out. How could he know, though? Unless he's put a tracker on one of our cars.'

Tuesday afternoon
Darlington Memorial Hospital

Byrd met Tanzy at the entrance to the paediatric ward. They explained to the nurse at reception they'd received a call from Damien Spencer's mother, Mandy, informing them Damien had woken and was okay to speak to the police.

'What's with the iPad?' Byrd asked, noticing it tucked under Tanzy's arm.

'You'll see,' he replied.

The nurse led them down the brightly lit corridor. It was lined with children's drawings and paintings of the nurses who had helped them. The children had signed their names and drawn smiley faces. It was a nice touch.

Before long the small, silver-haired nurse took a left through an open door. To the left-hand side of the room, sitting up in the bed, was Damien Spencer, with his mother sitting beside him; they were laughing about something. Byrd smiled inside, happy he was okay.

The nurse introduced the detectives to Damien and then left, telling them to let her know if they needed anything.

Mandy smiled at Tanzy.

'How you doing, Mandy?'

She nodded.

'It looks like you're feeling much better, Damien,' Tanzy said, switching his attention to the boy.

Damien gave an overexaggerted nod.

Byrd and Tanzy found two chairs and sat on the opposite side of the bed to Mandy.

'How you feeling, Damien?' Byrd said.

'I feel good.' Damien glanced at his mother to see if that was the right answer. She smiled proudly at him.

'Good, that's brilliant,' said Tanzy. 'Now, would it be okay if we asked you some questions?'

Without looking towards his mother, he nodded confidently.

'Brilliant. Now, if there's a question you don't understand or don't want to answer, that's okay, Damien.' Tanzy placed the iPad on the bed next to him.

Another nod. He glanced down at the tablet near him. 'I have one of those,' he told them.

'Really? Well, lucky you,' replied Tanzy. 'Then I guess you'll know how they work and do just fine with this.'

Byrd smiled, impressed with how Tanzy communicated with the boy. Being a father, he obviously knew how to interact and build a rapport with children. He watched Tanzy lean closer, hoping one day he'd be able to possess that skill.

'Okay, we know what happened to you. We know that you were taken to a house, weren't you?'

Damien bobbed his head.

'Good. What I would like to do is try and find that house. Do you think you can help us do that? Then maybe we can find your friends too.'

'I'll do my best,' he said, softly.

'That's great.' Tanzy looked at Mandy. 'That's okay, isn't it, Mum?'

'Of course, Detective.'

He smiled, then leaned in towards Damien again, placing the iPad on his bed covers, on top of his legs. 'Have you heard of Google Street View?'

His face lit up. 'Yeah, I've seen my house on there.'

'Have you?' Tanzy's eyes widened. 'Do we think we can go to a place on Google Street View, and from there try and find out where the man in the red car took you? Do you think we can do that?'

'Yeah, okay,' he said, smiling.

'Brill.' Tanzy typed *Woodland Road, Darlington* into the search bar and tapped ENTER. The screen showed the roundabout at the end of Woodland Road, which happened to be exactly where Tanzy wanted it to be.

He lifted it up so Damien had a better view. 'Do you know this roundabout?'

He nodded.

'When you were in the car, which way did you go?'

'That way.' He pointed left. Tanzy tapped the arrows on the iPad, angling the focus of the 3D virtual image to the left, the screen appearing at the next small roundabout.

'Why are you starting there?' Mandy asked, confused. 'We live on Brougham Street.'

'Through CCTV we tracked the red Mondeo to this spot then we lost it.'

She nodded.

'So, Damien, do you remember if the man went left or right?'

'He went left.'

Tanzy double-tapped the screen, taking the view up Carmel Road North.

'Do I keep going?'

Damien leaned forward, taking over, double-tapping the screen, then again, then he stopped. He dragged the focus of the screen ninety degrees to the right, so the screen faced a huge house with a long garden.

'Is that the house?' Tanzy asked him.

'Yes.'

Tanzy angled the screen and showed it to Byrd. He recognised it as the same house he'd gone to in an attempt to speak with Andrew Cairn of Cairnfield Developments.

Byrd pulled out his phone and rang PC Weaver. 'Amy, listen, we need a meeting in half an hour at the station. Round people up. Tell them Orion and I need to speak with them immediately. Get Fuller in there too. And get in touch with Sergeant Tunstall. I want him sitting in for this one as well.'

'Okay, sir.'

'And another thing,' said Byrd. 'I'll need two officers to go to the house and keep a look out while we prepare. Up for the task, Amy?'

'Absolutely. I'll let everyone know about the meeting and I'll grab one of the PCs and head over.'

'Thank you. We won't be long.' Byrd ended the call and placed the phone back into his trousers.

'Do . . . do you know who lives there?' Mandy asked from across the bed.

'We do,' Byrd confirmed. 'And believe me, the person responsible will be going straight to prison for this.'

Byrd and Tanzy thanked Mandy and Damien for their time and left the room, walked down the corridor, and signed out at the reception of the paediatric ward. Within five minutes, they were back in their cars, heading for the station.

75

When Byrd and Tanzy entered the meeting room, it was jam-packed; PC Weaver had done a great job rounding people up before she left. Judging by the people there, it looked like PC Timms had gone with her.

Tanzy took hold of the small black remote and pressed the button. 'Hey, everyone, thank you for coming.' He looked over to Jack Tunstall. 'Thank you, Jack. And your team. We've just been to the hospital to speak to Damien Spencer. He hasn't been strong enough to speak to us before now, but I'm glad to say he's much improved. According to him, when he started getting sick one of his kidnappers told him they were taking him to get medicine, but instead he was taken to Broken Scar and thrown in the river during the middle of the night and left to drown.

'He's just confirmed the address where he was held, along with five other children — the two kidnapped with him, and another three who had been there much longer, he says. It's the address of a man called Andrew Cairn, but we strongly suspect this is a cover name for Jonny Feland.'

Muttering swept across the room.

'I know, we can finally nail this piece of shit.'

Sergeant Tunstall joined Byrd and Tanzy at the front and, over the next five minutes, they came up with a plan of attack to take down Jonny Feland at his property. Feland would be armed and not alone. Bearing in mind what Damien had told them they'd have to be careful to avoid harming any children that may still be inside.

'So,' said Tanzy, 'three things we need to do to make today a success. One: arrest Jonny Feland. Bring this fucker down and get him behind bars. Two: get those kids to safety. This bastard has caused too much pain to too many families. And three: complete the first two tasks in the safest, most practical way possible.'

Everyone in the room nodded, indicating they were fired up for the task.

'Before we all go,' DCI Fuller said, from the left, 'has anyone located Alex Richards?'

'Nothing yet,' Tanzy replied. 'The media are showing his photo across multiple networks and social media applications.'

Byrd said, 'At the moment, Alex Richards remains the prime suspect in his wife's murder and the abduction of his son.'

'Anything else?' asked DCI Fuller.

Tanzy this time. 'We picked up a registration from the dark blue Kia Sportage which we caught on CCTV. The plates came back fake. Take a look.' He pulled a memory stick from his black jeans and placed it in the side of the laptop they used for their presentations. A moment later, after clicking through a few files, he clicked on an image which showed the Sportage's plate: NU13 PTX.

'We checked this plate,' Tanzy told them. 'Fake.'

DC Anne Tiffin raised her hand. 'Something isn't right with that, boss.'

'What's that, Anne?'

'That registration implies it's a 2013 model. That model Sportage is newer than that, I'm sure of it.'

She stood up and went over to one of the desks, grabbed a pen and notepad, then returned to her seat. She wrote down the reg: NU13 PTX and stared at it for a few moments.

'What you thinking, Anne?' Tanzy asked her.

'I think the real plate is NU18 BTX. He's altered the eight to make it look like a three and the B to make it look like a P. Can someone check this please?'

'I'll do it,' Byrd said, pulling a chair out in front of the laptop.

The door opened to their left and Tallow walked in.

He noticed everyone staring at him but focused solely on Tanzy. 'Ori, I finally finished running the prints from Saturday night at Uno Momento. One of them matches the prints I got from the handle on the toilet door at Brian Everitt's house.'

'Who's our guy?'

'Alex Richards,' he said.

Tanzy nodded. 'Right, lets pack up and—'

'Hold on, Orion,' Byrd said. 'Just confirmed, the owner of a blue Kia Sportage with the registration NU18 BTX is Alice Richards.'

'Okay, thanks, Max.' Tanzy turned to face everyone. 'We execute this plan, we get Feland, we find the children. Then we find Alex Richards. Any questions?'

Silence.

'Okay, good, let's get going!'

76

Tuesday, early evening
Carmel Road, Darlington

Alex Richards had been parked on the corner of Thornberry Rise for nearly twenty minutes. He could see the driveway of Jonny Feland's house through the front passenger window. On his phone, the magnetic tracking device he'd placed under the wheel arch of the red Mondeo told him the car was at Feland's house.

When Jamie had come to see him a few weeks ago, he'd been told everything about the night his daughter had died, everything about Feland, including the men who worked for him.

'Why are you telling me this?' Richards had asked him nearly a month ago, when Jamie had appeared outside of his home after he returned from football.

'Because I'm sorry for what happened to your daughter. It wasn't my fault, but I was there. We were all doing drugs but hers had been contaminated with poison.' He had paused, unsure whether Alex was going to hit him. 'It's going too far now,' Jamie added. 'I can't take any more of it. What Feland does to families is unforgiveable. He needs to be stopped.'

Alex stared at the tracking app he had open on his phone. The red Mondeo hadn't moved since he arrived.

According to Jamie, Thomas carried a gun on him at all times and wouldn't hesitate to fire. He'd also informed Richards about the children, how they were taken and kept at the house until they were sold and shipped off to buyers across the country. What the buyers did with the children after they were sold was something Feland wasn't interested in. All he cared about was the money.

Alex knew Callum was in there.

His phone on the passenger seat lit up and vibrated. He read the text message from Jamie. *Thomas is going out.*

'Good.' Alex opened the tracking app. The Mondeo's location marker moved, joining Carmel Road, and took a right in the direction away from him.

It was safe to go in.

He crossed the dark road, studying the house next door. The neighbour's driveway sat in total darkness. He took a right through the neighbour's open gates and lightly made his way along the gravel to a tall row of hedging that separated the gardens. Any cameras that Feland did have wouldn't have spotted him. Jamie had informed him this would be the safest way.

He stepped around a Black Volvo XC90 and kept low, making his way around the side of the house.

When he found himself in total darkness, he pulled a small torch from his pocket and shone it down at the floor. He stopped at the back corner of the huge house, poking his head around to look into the garden. There was a dim light on in the kitchen.

Staying low, he quietly passed the window until he reached the fence that divided the properties and peered into Feland's dark garden, seeing a security light fixed to the wall. He struggled over the top of the fence and quietly dropped down onto the other side. Crouching, he made his way under several windows until he reached Feland's back door. He glanced up, eyeing the camera fixed high on the wall, overlooking the gravel near him.

This would be the moment of truth. Had Jamie been honest with him or was this one big trick? Would a swarm of guys loaded with weapons appear from the darkness or would he get straight in undetected?

He grabbed the handle of the back door, very slowly pushed it down and edged the door open an inch. His heart was pumping so hard in his chest, it felt like it was going to explode. He opened the door further, revealing the most extravagant kitchen he'd ever seen. Everything was brand new. The worktops were made from marble. The under-cupboard lights were something you'd only see in a magazine.

Thank you, Jamie, he thought to himself.

He quietly closed the door, then turned, his body low until he found himself behind a huge island situated in the centre of the enormous space.

The phone in his pocket vibrated twice. A text message. As quietly as he could, he pulled out his phone. It read: *JD living room.*

How long will Thomas be? he replied.

A while.

Sit tight. Act normal.

He placed his phone back in his pocket and peered over the island. The kitchen was empty. He heard faint music coming through the open doorway, presumably from the living room.

He pulled out his phone and sent a text to Jamie: *How many in the house?*

Seconds later, it vibrated: *Feland and me downstairs. Paddy and Eric upstairs. And children upstairs.*

Alex lowered himself behind the island and returned the text: *Get JD to come in kitchen.* He pressed SEND and waited.

* * *

Jamie was sitting on the sofa closest to the door with an empty bottle of beer in his hand. On the other sofa, Feland took a last swig of his own, then lowered it to his knee. They were watching some documentary about planes; Feland was fascinated with them for some reason. The way the wings were shaped to keep them in the air. Jamie couldn't care less, but it was best to smile, agree, and go along with him.

The whip marks on his back were sore, the flesh was tender and open. In private he'd asked Andy to put some Vaseline on it and bandage it up, just like he had last month. If Feland knew, there'd have been another mark alongside it; he said to his boys they had to take what they deserved and deal with it like men.

If you make a mistake, own it. Pay the price and face the consequences, were his words.

Feland turned away from the television and looked at Jamie. 'You're quiet tonight, Jamie?'

Jamie focused on the floor and didn't look up.

'Don't ignore me, son,' Feland said, sternly.

'I'm . . . I'm tired, that's all,' he replied, glancing up briefly to meet his dark eyes.

Feland nodded. 'You want another beer, son?'

Jamie bobbed his head.

'I'll get you one,' Feland insisted, standing up.

Jamie watched Feland wander towards the door. He sighed a little, the wounds on his back uncomfortable. This time, the whipping had been for the police raiding the house on Craig Street. Feland had told him to manage the house, keeping the operation clean and simple, causing no suspicions or unusual activity. Feland had lost a lot of product so he had vented his anger on Jamie.

Jamie had heard the stories from the others about the whippings. Most of them hadn't believed it until it was too late, until they were in too deep to get out. They were threatened that their families would pay the ultimate price if they tried to leave and they all knew Feland was capable of anything.

'You stay right here, little Jamie.' Feland stopped at the door and turned to face him, smiling.

77

Tuesday, early evening
Carmel Road, Darlington

Alex Richards hid behind the kitchen island. His phone buzzed. *He's coming now,* the text from Jamie said.

He heard footsteps on the tiled floor then the bright lights above came on, the place flooding in white brilliance. Alex's heart was beating quicker than it ever had. Finally, he was in the same room as the man responsible for his daughter's death.

From the sounds he figured Feland had gone over to the fridge positioned to the left of the kitchen, something he noticed when he entered minutes earlier. After the door closed, Feland moved a few steps and pulled open a drawer, then one by one, opened the lids of the beer bottles.

'Bin open,' Feland said.

Alex frowned, then a second later, to his right, the lid of the bin raised with a quiet mechanical sound.

One bottle cap was thrown in. And then another, but the second one hit the rim and fell down on the tiled floor with a series of pings until it settled.

'Ahh, fuck,' Feland said, placing the bottles on the side and making his way over.

It was only a matter of seconds before Feland passed the island and picked up the cap. If Alex didn't move, Feland would see him, and would be in a vulnerable position.

Alex knew Feland was dangerous. He'd heard a story that Jamie had passed on, that he'd hit a man so hard in the face, he'd cartwheeled. He knew he'd have to be on his game; Feland certainly wouldn't go down easily.

As the footsteps were approaching to his right, Alex silently shuffled to the left, and moved around the side of the island. The size of it was roughly two metres by four, so there would be a lot of ground to cover to do what he planned in his head.

Feland picked up the bottle cap and stood, raising his hand in the air, like he was taking a shot with a basketball, and threw it.

Alex, now at the opposite side of the island, tiptoed around to the side Feland was on.

The bottle cap hit the back of the bin and Feland raised his arms in the air like he'd netted a three-pointer in an NBA game. 'He shoots and he scores.'

Then he stopped dead, staring at the back door.

Alex was a metre behind him, keeping low, ready to pounce. 'What the . . .'

Feland padded over to the back door, noticing it wasn't fully closed. Frowning, he opened it and peered out, curiously checking around the gravel and across the garden, which sat in silent darkness. Alex, two feet behind him, was setting himself.

'No one would dare . . .' Feland whispered, then edged back, but as he did, an arm came around him at lightning speed and dug under his chin, crushing his throat. Then he felt another arm from the left. Feland was extremely strong but even he couldn't release himself from the grip.

His first thought was Jamie. He knew Andy and Eric were upstairs.

'Jay . . .' he coughed, saliva spurting from his mouth as he fiercely scratched at the forearms and hands of Alex. His windpipe was being crushed by the powerful force and, after a few more seconds, his world went dark.

Alex stumbled back a little, breathing heavily, and lowered him to the floor. He went over to the drawers near the cooker and pulled open the third drawer. Jamie had told him he had left him some thick cable ties there. Alex had made it clear he wanted to speak to Feland first.

Killing him straight away would be too good for Feland. Alex needed him to confess. And he wanted the satisfaction of seeing Feland's life drain from him right after.

He grabbed the pack of cable ties, closed the drawer, went back to Feland, brought his wrists behind his back, and secured three cable ties around them, pulling them as tight as he could, so tight that the plastic dug into the skin.

Then he put Feland's feet together and tied his ankles, restricting his movement for when he woke up, which, Alex knew, wouldn't be long.

* * *

Feland was sitting on his sofa in the living room when he opened his eyes. His head was pounding and his shoulders were screaming in pain. He realised his hands were somehow behind him, tied together.

He tried to separate his legs, but he couldn't. Then saw the cable tie around his ankles and realised why.

'The fuck is this?' he shouted, glaring around the room. 'That you, Jamie, fucking around?' The television was on in the corner and the fireplace in front of him was still burning away. He felt hot and uncomfortable. And angry.

'Jamie!' he shouted.

'Jamie won't help you, Jonathan.'

The voice came from behind him.

Feland turned his head as best he could but his view was restricted. He certainly didn't recognise the voice. 'Who the fuck is that? Untie me now. I'll fucking kill you,' he spat.

Alex checked his phone and noticed Thomas's red Mondeo was now somewhere across town.

'You there, you coward? Attacking a man from behind. Must be proud of yourself?'

'Where's my boy?' Alex asked, getting closer to him.

'If you've figured out how to get in here and tie me up, I'm sure you're clever enough to find him.'

Alex moved out from behind the back of the sofa and stood before him, glaring down at Feland. He then lowered himself to his knees and smiled.

'The fuck is funny?' Feland spat.

'You've always been so careful, haven't you, Mr Feland? Always been hiding in the shadows, carrying out your operations, ruining the lives of teenagers and addicts in this town. Everyone knows it's you, but the police can't do anything about it. But now . . .'

'Now . . . what?'

'You killed my wife.' Alex leaned in closer and stopped when he was within a few inches of his face.

'You have nice eyes, Alex,' Feland commented. 'I think if—'

Alex headbutted him hard, the momentum sending him into the back of the sofa with a loud groan. Instantly, blood poured from his nose, down his chin, onto his T-shirt.

'I do have nice eyes,' Alex replied, grinning, waiting for him to get over the blow.

'Cheap shot, eh? Is that all you got?' Feland asked him, licking the blood around his mouth. 'Mmmm, tasty. What's next? I have things to do.'

'You killed my daughter last year. Your product killed her. That means *you* killed her.'

'And what are you going to do about that?'

Alex, astounded at the audacity of the man, pulled the knife from his pocket, leaned forward, and pushed it against his throat—

'Whoa, whoa, it wasn't my product!' Feland said quickly. 'It's not my product. My supplier brought over the gear direct to the party. I had no idea it was poisoned.'

Alex held the knife hard against his throat, the tip piercing the skin so a drop of blood appeared.

'You're talking shit,' Alex said.

'I'm not a liar. When your daughter died, I spoke to my supplier. He confirmed there could have been a chance the cocaine was contaminated. He told me the next five loads would be at half price as a sweetener if I didn't mention it. I'm a businessman, what can I say . . .'

'You're a waste of space.'

'Look around you, I don't seem to have done too bad for—'

Alex put more pressure on the knife, silencing him, a trickle of blood now running down the blade.

'Who was the supplier?'

Feland didn't answer.

'I might let you live if I get a name.'

'You're killing me either way. I know what you're capable of, so you might as well just—'

Richard drove his knife straight through Feland's throat. He looked him in the eyes and watched his life ebb away.

It was one of the most satisfying things he'd ever done.

78

Out in the hallway, Jamie waited for Alex. He hated Feland but he couldn't watch him die, although it was no less than he deserved in Jamie's opinion. He was a monster.

'All done?' Jamie asked, nervous in close proximity to Alex, the bloody knife still in his right hand.

Alex nodded. 'Where's my son?'

'I'll take you,' he said. 'Follow me.'

Jamie led Alex up the huge, wide staircase. When they reached the top, he took a right, then another until he arrived at a closed door. Jamie pulled out a set of keys and unlocked the door.

The room was dark and silent. Jamie went in first, flicked on the switch, the room filling with a cold, harsh light. Alex followed him inside and saw six beds, three on either side, with a walkway down the middle of the room.

The sudden bright light woke each child and they groggily sat up, rubbing their eyes. On the closest bed to the door was Callum, his son.

Alex gasped and ran over to him, dropping the knife on the floor. He picked Callum up, hugging and kissing him over and over. 'Are . . . are you okay?'

Callum started to cry but managed a nod before he dug his head into his father's shoulder. The other children watched in awe, unsure what was going on, exchanging glances with each other and obviously wondering who this man was.

'Right, let's get out of here,' Alex said, turning towards the doorway to the landing.

Jamie stood holding the knife that Alex had dropped. Alex came to a halt and eyed him curiously. After a few moments, Jamie spun the knife around and offered the handle to him. 'You dropped this, Alex.'

Alex let out a small sigh as he took the knife. 'Thank you, Jamie, for what you've done. You need to get out of here before the police come. Get a fresh start somewhere.'

Jamie smiled, shaking his head. 'I've done too many bad things to make a fresh start anywhere. Like Feland always told us, we must own our mistakes and face our consequences like men.'

'Feland is gone . . .'

'Come on, I'll show you out,' Jamie offered.

Alex and Callum, along with the other children, followed Jamie downstairs. Reaching the bottom, the greasy-looking IT guy, Paddy, stepped out from the kitchen, and they all stopped.

'Where on earth are they going?' he asked Jamie, frowning in confusion.

'They're going home.'

'I . . . I can't let them leave,' he told him. 'Feland will kill us.'

Jamie smiled and took a few steps towards him. 'Andy, go have a look in there. Go on.'

Paddy moved back so he would have a clear view of the living room. On the sofa near the bay window, he saw Feland, his hands tied behind his back and his face, neck, and clothes covered in blood.

'Jesus!' Paddy gasped, glaring back at Jamie.

'You see, he's gone now,' Jamie said. 'There's no reason for us to keep living like this. The monster is dead.'

'Just wait till Thomas finds out about this.'

Jamie turned and grabbed the knife from Alex. Paddy burst out laughing.

'And what on earth are you going to do with that, little boy?'

Jamie, without answering, stepped forward and stabbed him several times in the chest. Alex put a hand over Callum's face and stood in front of the other children to mask what was happening.

When Paddy had slumped to the floor, Jamie turned and handed back the knife to Alex.

'Before you go,' Jamie said, 'is it true what Feland said about the supplier knowing the cocaine was poisoned?'

Alex mulled over his words. It seemed his revenge wasn't complete. 'You got a name?'

'I do,' said Jamie, then told him the name and address.

Somewhere in the distance, they heard the sound of sirens.

'Go,' Jamie told him, 'go!'

* * *

Curled up on the hall floor behind the front door, Paddy coughed up blood. He heard Alex and the children escape and Jamie go upstairs. He slowly pulled his phone from his pocket, raised it to his face, unlocked it with his bloody fingers, and found the number he needed. He pressed CALL, then tapped on the speaker button.

'Yeah,' said the voice.

'Thomas, it's Paddy . . . Feland is dead. Alex Richards was here. He took the kids.'

'All of them?'

'Yes.'

'Where are they now?' Thomas asked calmly.

Paddy remembered overhearing what Jamie had told Richards a few moments before he left and, in his last breath, he told Thomas where they had gone.

79

Tuesday, early evening
Carmel Road, Darlington

Armed response and an array of police vehicles sped down Carmel Road towards Feland's house. The first vehicle turned in, drove down the driveway, and stopped before the front door. A second vehicle entered, followed by a third, then a fourth.

Byrd pulled up on Carmel Road, halfway up the pavement. He and Tanzy got out and briskly walked down the driveway towards the house. A team of armed officers were entering through the open door, followed by a cluster of PCs, Amy Weaver and Josh Andrews being among them.

They heard a gunshot from inside the house, causing Byrd and Tanzy to drop to their knees.

'Inside!' Tanzy shouted. 'Come on!'

Byrd and Tanzy cautiously peered into the hallway. Down to their right, a man lay on his side, covered in blood. PC Andrews lowered to him but, from the sea of blood beneath him, it was obvious he was dead.

Byrd and Tanzy heard footsteps in the living room to their right. Slowly, they focused on the man on the sofa, awkwardly leaning back, blood covering the front of his body. The armed response officer shouted, 'Clear,' before he left the room and went onto the next.

The detectives entered the room.

'That's Feland,' Byrd said, nodding over to the sofa. Tanzy recognised him too, although it'd been a while since they'd both seen him. Six years earlier the police had been called when Feland had allegedly punched someone, knocking several of their teeth out. However, several people in London had vouched that Feland was down south when the fight occurred so they removed him from their enquiries.

Now he stared vacantly up at the ceiling, covered in his own blood.

There was a sound in the doorway behind them.

'Boss!' PC Weaver shouted. 'Upstairs. We found something.'

Tanzy and Byrd left the living room and followed Weaver, climbing the stairs quickly. They passed several armed response personnel who were sweeping the rooms upstairs. They'd come across one of Feland's men, a forty-something guy who went by the name of Eric. He was claiming his innocence, that he'd done nothing wrong. PC Josh Andrews had cuffed him and was leading him out. Weaver and Byrd and Tanzy stepped aside, allowing them to pass on the landing.

They continued, stopping at an open door, where they saw several armed responders standing over the body of a young male lying on his back. There was a gun in his hand and blood covering his face. It was obvious he'd done it to himself.

'Have forensics been called?'

Weaver turned. 'Yes. And an ambulance too.'

'Good work,' Tanzy said to her.

'Come on,' Weaver told them, ignoring the praise, heading along the landing, and taking a right, then another.

They arrived at the doorway to the children's room and stepped inside.

'It looks like where they kept the children,' Tanzy said, looking around. The beds were unmade. Toys were on the floor. 'Where are they?'

Byrd didn't answer as he stepped further into the room, peering around. He lowered and checked under the beds in case anyone was hiding, but the room was empty.

'Sir?' someone said from the doorway. They all turned to PC Andrews. 'There's something you need to see.'

* * *

Byrd and Tanzy followed PC Andrews down the stairs and through the open front door to the driveway. Standing half-way down, beside one of the police cars, was a woman in her sixties with short silver hair and five children, all appearing timid, nervously looking around at the sea of police around them, unsure what was going on.

'Are they the missing children?' asked Byrd.

Andrews turned and nodded as they walked. 'The woman rang it in just now.'

They stopped before them. Byrd smiled. 'What's going on?'

'There was a knock on my door ten minutes ago,' the woman said frantically. 'It was a man. He had these kids with him. He told me to ring the police immediately and tell them these kids have been keep hostage.'

'Where's the man now?'

The elderly lady shrugged. 'He left with one of the boys, drove off in a car which was parked over the road from my house. I rang the police but saw the cars here.'

'There were six children?'

She nodded.

Byrd moved towards them. One of the kids backed away, almost cowering. 'It's okay, you don't need to be scared.' Byrd raised a slow palm and lowered to his knees to make them feel at ease. 'I'm with the police.' He showed them his warrant card. 'Detective Inspector Byrd. Are you all okay?'

A collection of nods followed.

Tanzy smiled, appreciating Byrd making the effort with them. The children all wore grey pyjamas and their heads were shaved.

'Is one of you called Melissa Clarke?' Byrd asked. He knew which one was Melissa, but he wanted to see her smile with happiness when she heard her name being called.

Melissa raised her hand quickly. Byrd said, 'Your mother and father will be very excited to see you.' Smiling, he turned away and then asked, 'Do we have an Eddy Long here?'

The boy closest to the woman raised his hand quickly. 'I'm Eddy!'

'Good, it's nice to meet you!'

He looked at the other three but didn't recognise them. 'What are your names?'

'I'm Joseph Cameron,' the boy on the left said. Byrd picked up a Glaswegian accent straight away. He pointed to the boy on the other side of Eddy. 'This is my twin brother, John.'

'And what's your name?' Byrd asked the girl who hadn't spoken yet.

'I'm Tess Longstaff,' she said, her accent similar to the boys.

'Everything is okay and you guys are all safe,' Byrd assured them confidently, making a note of them on his phone. He then nodded at Tanzy, taking a few steps back. Tanzy angled over. 'We'll get them checked out by paramedics. They look in good health but you never know. Then we'll start making some calls, see if we can find their parents.'

Tanzy went back to the children. 'Well, it's very nice to meet you all. Do you think it would be okay if you waited here while we got a doctor to come and check you're all okay? Then, after that, we can get you back home.'

They all nodded at him, excited by the news.

'Amy,' Byrd said to Weaver, grabbing her attention from the front door step. 'Can I have a private word?'

Weaver walked with him down the driveway. 'What's up, boss?'

'I need you get some more information from the children — find out where they're from, then get in touch with the police in that area, see if they've been reported missing. Get straight on it.'

As Weaver made her way towards the children, Byrd's phone pinged with a text message.

It was from Keith: *I really need to speak to you about something important, mate. As soon as possible.*

Byrd frowned, not knowing what it was or what it could be. He pressed the CALL button and put it to his ear. He was assuming it would be about their conversation yesterday when Byrd had told him they'd found Lyle.

'Keith, what's up? I'm busy . . .'

'Max, I need to tell you something important,' he said.

'I'm listening.'

'I need to tell you in person. You have to come to my house as soon as possible.'

'Listen, Keith, I'll be tied up for a little while. I'm at a crime scene . . .'

'I need to see you. I haven't been totally honest with you about things.'

Byrd glanced around. 'Can it wait?'

'No, Max, it can't. It's urgent. I'm in trouble,' he replied. 'I'll be waiting.' Keith hung up the phone and the line went dead.

Byrd wondered what on earth he was talking about. Whatever it was, it seemed important and Keith was obviously distressed. He *was* one of his oldest friends, after all.

Byrd pushed his phone into his trousers and waved Tanzy over. 'Can you handle things here?'

Tanzy frowned. 'Why?'

'Keith Wilson says he's in trouble, he needs to speak with me now.'

'Can't it wait? We're busy here, Max.'

'I know but there's practically all of the station here, minus DCI Fuller,' Byrd explained. 'An ambulance is coming. Forensics are coming. There are three dead bodies who aren't going anywhere and five children that we've saved. One less old detective won't be missed.'

'Will you be long?'

'Doubt it, although I'm not sure what he has to say. Ring me if there's any updates.'

Tanzy watched Byrd run down the drive, back to his car.

80

Tuesday, early evening
Willow Road, Darlington

Once Alex Richards dropped his son off at his grandfather's, he drove on to the house. He pulled up and turned off the engine, got out of the car, and stepped up onto the path.

Standing at the gate, he could see the number on the wall near the window. It was the address Jamie had given him. The living room curtains were closed but there was a light on behind them. The room directly above the living room was also lit, presumably the man's bedroom.

He opened the gate and walked to the front door, pushed down on the handle and was surprised when it opened. Once inside, he closed it gently, trying to keep as quiet as possible.

There was a light coming from the room at the end of the short hallway where he could see a table and a long narrow kitchen beyond it. To his right, there was an open door into the living room. He pulled out the bloody knife from his jacket and took a few steps inside, but no one was there.

He slowly backed out and glanced up the stairs, which were in darkness. He silently moved towards the dining room at the end of the hall, and saw a man sitting at the table, focusing on the phone in his hand.

Next to the phone was a block of white powder.

The man noticed Alex out of the corner of his eye and looked directly at him.

Alex walked in, holding the knife by his side.

'You?' the man asked, an expression of shock over his face.

'You know who I am?' Alex asked.

'I . . . I saw you on the news. The police want to speak to you,' the man told him, his voice almost breaking.

'You recognise me?'

The man at the table nodded.

'So, you know why I'm here, then?' Alex asked him, padding closer to the table. He glanced around, trying to locate any weapons that the man might be able to reach before he got to him, but he saw nothing.

The man nodded. 'I'm genuinely sorry for what happened to your daughter. And your wife too. I saw that part on the news.'

'I don't need your sympathy. If you were that sympathetic and decent, you would have disposed of the poisoned product before my daughter put it up her nose.'

The man dipped his head for a moment. 'I know.'

Alex slowly moved closer to him, cautious of what the man might do, but the man stayed where he was. He didn't try to move, nor did he make Alex change his mind about what he intended to do.

As Alex stopped beside him, the man glanced up, staring into Alex's black eyes.

Alex tightened his grip on the knife but froze when he heard someone enter the room behind him.

'Keith, what's going on?' Byrd absorbed the scene, seeing Alex Richards standing beside his friend with a knife in his hand. 'Alex . . .'

81

Tuesday, early evening
Carmel Road, Darlington

Tanzy watched the paramedics check over the children. He smiled, happy they were now safe. PC Weaver appeared by his side. 'I've been in touch with a sergeant from the Greater Glasgow Division — that's where the three non-Darlington kids are from. I explained the situation and gave him the names of the children. He confirmed the children were taken roughly two months ago. They'd suspended the investigation and limited their use of resources, assuming the children were gone for good.'

Tanzy knew, after twenty-four hours of a child or adult going missing, statistically they were usually found. However, after forty-eight to seventy-two hours, it was rare that a child would be found alive.

'Feland was a bastard,' Tanzy said, then glanced down to the floor.

'He was,' she agreed.

Tanzy looked away, frowning in deep thought.

'What's up?' Weaver asked him.

'Max got a text from Keith Wilson saying he needed to speak to him urgently. Max went to his house but said he'd be back soon.'

'When did he go?'

'Not long, but I have a bad feeling. Something isn't right. I'm going to head over.'

'I'll go with you,' she said.

Tunstall called over from the front of the house, 'Where you guys off to?'

Tanzy was already halfway down the drive. He turned back to the sergeant. 'I have a bad feeling about something. It could be nothing, but I need to check.'

'You need any help?'

'Amy and I should be fine,' Tanzy said, turning back towards the road. 'We'll go in your car, Amy. I came here with Max.'

As they reached the end of the driveway, they heard the sergeant shout, 'Wait!' Tanzy and Weaver turned, frowning. Tunstall waved at them, then pointed at one of the tactical response officers, Jericho. 'He'll go with you.'

Jericho was tall and wide, packed with muscle; tattoos covered his arms. He carried a gun down by his side. He nodded at Tanzy and Weaver. 'Let's go.'

The three of them got into a marked Astra and joined Carmel Road North, heading for the house. Turning left at the roundabout at Woodland Road they noticed a red Mondeo coming from Cockerton, turning left into Deneside Road.

'There!' Tanzy shouted.

Jericho was alert in the back seat. 'What?'

'The red Mondeo!' Tanzy informed them.

Weaver caught a glimpse of the reg plate as it turned into the road. 'It's him, the man who shot Jim Leonard.'

'Okay, okay,' Tanzy said. 'Let's all keep calm. We'll follow him.' Tanzy took a right turn into Deneside Road and followed the red Mondeo, which took the left into Newlands

Road, going out of sight. As they turned, they saw the car half-way up the street, approaching Willow Road. At the junction, it went right. Tanzy accelerated to the junction and, glancing right, noticed the Mondeo had stopped a few houses down.

A tall man stepped out of the Mondeo holding a gun in his hand and went through the open gate of a house. Then he opened the front door and stepped inside.

Tanzy recognised the dark blue Kia Sportage and Byrd's X5 on the road.

'What the hell is going on here?'

He stopped behind the Mondeo and they all climbed out. Jericho, with his gun ready, went through the gate first. Tanzy and Weaver followed.

That's when they heard the gunshot from inside the house.

82

'Keith, tell me what's going on.' Byrd looked from his friend to Alex.

Alex Richards stared at Byrd for a long time, until Byrd moved forward. 'Alex, I'm going to need you to put down that knife.'

Alex said, 'No fucking chance. He killed my daughter.'

Byrd frowned at his words, then glanced down at Keith. 'I . . . I don't understand.'

Alex glared down at Keith. 'You want to tell him?'

Keith told Byrd about the drugs, that he'd been having issues with rats and that he had accidently knocked over the tub of rat poison which had mixed with the cocaine.

'Cocaine?' Byrd shook his head. 'What cocaine?'

'The cocaine I sold Feland last year. The stuff he sent his boys out with, the same stuff that Lisa Richards used a few hours later.'

'What . . . what? Hold on a minute,' Byrd said, unable to get his head around this. 'Keith?'

'I've been a dealer for years, Max,' he confessed. 'You see that plumbing van outside?'

Byrd nodded.

'I haven't touched a spanner in years. That's what I wanted to speak to you about. Alex found out from one of Feland's men that his daughter had died from the product I'd supplied, Max. All of this is my fault. Mark Greenwell, Brian Everitt, and my own son. I killed my own son.'

He dropped his face into his hands and started to cry.

'Fucking man up!' Alex screamed.

Byrd kept a close eye on the knife in Alex's hand, knowing that if Alex decided to cut Keith's throat, there'd be nothing he could do to stop him. Without a weapon Byrd tried a different approach.

Moving to his left, he pulled out a chair at the opposite end of the table and sat down. Both Keith and Alex watched him closely. He was about to say something when he heard a sound to his right.

Standing in the hallway, with a gun in his hand, was a man he'd never seen in person before, but he'd seen his mugshot — Thomas Thorne, Feland's enforcer.

Byrd jumped up the same time as the man raised his arm and fired the gun at him.

83

Tuesday, early evening
Willow Road, Darlington

Byrd instinctively threw himself forward, then dived to the left, behind the table.

The sound of the gunshot from the hallway took Alex by surprise so he darted to the left towards the wall for more protection but kept his eye on the doorway, ready for whatever was coming through it. Thomas entered the room holding the gun at arm's length, and Alex crouched and threw his knife at him, piercing his forearm and causing Thomas to drop the gun.

Alex charged towards him, going in low with his right shoulder into Thomas's midsection, driving him back and slamming him into the wall with a sickening thud.

Thomas pulled the knife from his arm and let it fall to the floor, then began to hit Alex on the top of his head with his elbow. After the sixth strike, Alex's grip loosened and Thomas rolled him away then crawled across the floor to reach for his gun.

Byrd, from Thomas's left, kicked him in the side of his face, which barely seemed to affect him, although Byrd felt like it should have taken his head off his shoulders. Byrd tried again, bringing his right leg up, but Thomas grabbed it and stood up, lifting Byrd up with him like he weighed nothing, and with unbelievable strength, Thomas threw Byrd onto the table with so much force, Byrd smashed through it and landed on the floor with a loud thump.

Thomas casually bent down and picked up the gun, then stood up straight, facing Keith Wilson. He raised the gun at Keith's chest—

The sound of a gunshot echoed loudly.

Thomas stumbled and turned to his right. Along the hall near the front door, Jericho had fired a shot at him. His first bullet had caught Thomas in the right arm. Thomas turned fully towards him and raised his gun, but Jericho's second bullet hit Thomas in the centre of the chest, causing him to stagger back and collapse on the floor near Byrd.

Alex pulled himself onto his hands and knees, feeling disorientated from Thomas's blows.

* * *

Jericho, Tanzy, and Weaver charged down the hall and entered the room.

Looking quickly around the room, Jericho could see Byrd on the floor. Keith, sitting at the table, had watched the whole thing without moving a muscle. Seeing no immediate threat, Jericho picked up the radio from his belt and called for backup.

Tanzy lowered himself to Byrd to check if he was okay. Byrd winced in pain.

'Where are you hurt?'

'My back,' Byrd said. 'I can barely move.' Byrd attempted to get up.

'Just stay there!' Tanzy ordered him. 'Backup is coming.'

Tanzy looked up to Jericho, who was standing over them. 'Call for medical attention too, Max is injured.'

'What about Alex?' Byrd whispered.

'What about him?'

'He's over there on the floor,' said Byrd, pointing to his right.

Tanzy looked to where Byrd had pointed.

'There's no one else here, Max.'

84

Tuesday, early evening
Willow Road, Darlington

'Then where the fuck is he?' Byrd shouted in frustration, looking around the room as best he could.

Tanzy looked up at Jericho and signalled towards the back door. Jericho nodded and dashed into the narrow kitchen with his gun raised high, feeling cold air drift in through the open back door.

Alex Richards had escaped.

Byrd reached for Tanzy's hand and squeezed it. 'We did good, didn't we, Orion?'

'What do you mean, Max?'

'The kids from Glasgow, we found them,' Byrd said quietly. 'And . . . and . . .' He trailed off in pain.

'Hey, don't talk. Just try to relax, Max,' Tanzy said softly.

'Melissa Clarke. Eddy Long. Even Damien Spencer. We found them, Orion.'

'We did,' Tanzy said, squeezing his hand, grinning proudly. 'We got them.'

Tears formed in Byrd's eyes as he rested his head back to the floor and stared at the ceiling.

'Don't be getting all soft on me, Max. Tonight isn't over! We have a long night ahead of us. We need to find Alex Richards.'

Byrd told Tanzy to help him up to his feet.

'Careful, take it slow.' Tanzy helped him up. 'You all right?'

Byrd rubbed the back of his neck where he felt a little blood. 'Just a cut, I'll be fine.' He turned to Thomas, dead on the floor. 'Tough one, that guy!'

'They all go down eventually, Max, you know that,' Tanzy said, winking.

Then they both looked at Keith, who was still sitting on the chair.

'Why did you come here, Max?' Tanzy asked. 'What did he want so badly?'

Byrd explained about the drugs, the rat poison, and the deaths it had caused. He turned to face Keith.

'Come on, Keith,' Byrd said. 'I'm taking you to the station. Out of respect for our friendship, I'll take you in.'

Keith nodded in agreement, stood up slowly, and, without hesitation, placed his wrists together in front of Byrd, who cuffed them. Then Byrd read him his rights and told him what was going to happen. He turned to Tanzy. 'I'll take him in my car. Backup will be here any minute, but I'm not wasting any more time on this. We need to get back to Feland's house — it's a mess over there. And we need to wrap things up.'

'Sure, I'll wait here. I'll report it. You guys go,' he told Byrd, then watched him lead Keith into the hallway and out the front door towards his car. He turned to Weaver, who looked tired. 'You okay, Amy?'

'What a day, Orion.' She sighed lightly. 'Ready for my bed.'

'You and me both.'

Weaver let out a tired sigh but smiled.

Byrd led Keith down the path to his car and opened the back door. Keith leaned in and pulled his legs inside.

Byrd closed the back passenger door and climbed in the front, dropped into his seat, and sighed heavily, rubbing his face with his palms.

'Thank you for being honest with me,' Byrd said to him, glancing through the mirror.

Keith matched his stare. 'It was about time.'

They shared a smile together, then Byrd placed his key into the ignition, but froze when he saw something in the rear-view mirror, in the boot of his car.

Alex Richards was behind Keith, leaning over the back of the seat, the knife blade close to Keith's throat, glistening in the nearby street lights.

85

Tuesday, early evening
Willow Road, Darlington

Alex Richards sliced Keith's throat with a thick, deep horizontal cut. Blood sprayed from his throat down onto the back seats of the car. There was a look of terror in his eyes.

Byrd hadn't seen anything like it.

'You fucker!' Byrd screamed at him, turning to face the back of the car. 'You . . . you . . . you fucker. Bastard!'

Keith's head dropped forward, then his body fell to the right until he was laid across the back seat.

Byrd turned quickly and pressed the LOCK button on the car's central locking, then turned back to him. 'Now you're fucked, Alex.'

'What makes you think I want to get away?' he said. 'I'm exactly where I need to be.'

'You're going to prison,' Byrd said, matter-of-factly.

'I don't think so.'

Byrd took a deep breath. 'Why, Alex? Why all this? Mark Greenwell, Lyle Wilson, Brian Everitt. Jonny Feland. Keith Wilson. Why?'

'Because they all played a part in my daughter's death. Each one of them. Weeks ago, someone admitted what had happened. For that, I let him live. He told me what happened at the party and who was there. Mark and Lyle gave her the drugs. Brian came onto her more than once, but the fat bastard wouldn't take no for an answer and raped her. Jonny Feland was a bastard, and you know, as well as I do, I've done you and everyone in this town a favour there.' He paused for a moment. 'And Keith was responsible for the poison in the cocaine. He said it himself. If it wasn't for him, we wouldn't be in this mess.'

'How long had you planned this?'

'A little while,' he told Byrd. 'Once I found out how my daughter had died, I kept hearing Alice talking about her friend's wonderful partner, the hotshot police detective. How she claimed you had life all figured out, how driven you were. So, I thought I'd fucking show you. I registered a Jaguar I bought in your name. I'm sure you saw the letter from the DVLA?'

Byrd nodded. 'We did, but then couldn't find it.'

Alex smiled, shaking his head. 'No, Alice took it from the microwave in your kitchen when she was round. I knew the letter would come and we'd planned it perfectly. Once I told her what Jamie had said, she was happy for me to do this. She found your spare set of keys from a tin you kept in the cupboard above the microwave.' He paused a beat. 'What I hadn't planned was you turning up tonight and ruining it.'

'Well, I apologise for doing my job.'

'You're such a superstar detective aren't you, DI Max Byrd?'

'I saw the video after you dumped the body of Lyle Wilson at the Joseph Pease statue. Who was the other man? There were two of you near the library.'

'Just an old friend. He played no part in this. I paid him a hundred pound to dress in the clothes I sent him and to get out of the Jaguar so the camera would see him.'

Byrd stared, waiting for more. Then, behind Alex, through the rear windscreen, he saw blue lights flying down Willow Road towards them, sirens piercing the cold winter air.

'Your time is up, Alex.'

'Like I said, I'm not going to prison. My job here is done. It's been a pleasure, Max Byrd.'

Byrd watched Alex raise the knife to his own throat and, in one swift movement, slice across it, blood spurting as he fell backwards.

'No, you fucking coward!' Byrd screamed at him. He opened the door quickly, dashed to the back of the car, and opened the boot. Alex's dead eyes stared vacantly up at Byrd as the blood pooled around him.

Byrd sighed heavily and turned round to face the oncoming cars. To his right, he could see Tanzy in the doorway of Keith's house, obviously wondering why he wasn't on the way to the station.

He came over and saw Alex in the boot, his still eyes staring up at the stars, the knife still in his hand.

'Where's Keith?'

'In the back.'

Tanzy went to look, but Byrd grabbed his arm and shook his head.

'Alex waited in the boot for us, sliced Keith's throat. Then his own.'

'Are you hurt?' Tanzy asked.

Byrd shook his head slowly then looked down the road at the approaching blue lights.

Tanzy stepped across to the rear of the car and sat on the edge of it, next to Byrd. The backup cars came to a stop close by, followed by an ambulance.

'Well, at least we're still alive, Max,' Tanzy said, patting his shoulder.

'That's true.'

A paramedic rushed over to check if they were okay. Byrd told him they were and told a nearby PC that there was a dead body inside the house and two bodies in the car just behind him.

Tanzy and Byrd waited at the back of the car for a few moments, knowing their night wasn't over just yet, watching the frantic activity in front of them.

'How you holding up, Max?'

Their eyes met, and they shared a tired smile.

'Someone once told me to count your rainbows, not your thunderstorms,' said Byrd.

Tanzy frowned at him. 'I like it. Who said that?'

Byrd smiled sadly. 'My mam. It was the last thing she said to me before she died.'

86

Three weeks later

Byrd entered the busy Turk's Head pub just after 8 p.m. on Friday. The place was hectic, filled with indie music, waves of muffled conversations, glasses clinking behind the bar, and balls being clattered on the pool table to his right. He joined the queue at the bar and ordered two pints of lager, then looked around for a couple of seats while the barman pulled them, spotting a small, cosy table over in the corner with two empty chairs. Once served, he carried the two pints over to the table and set them down.

Tanzy texted him, saying he'd be late, something about the bus getting stuck in traffic. By the time Tanzy walked in, Byrd was halfway through his pint.

'Sorry I'm late, mate.' Tanzy settled into the chair. 'Take it this is mine.' He picked up the pint and sipped it, and gave a satisfied sigh before placing it down. 'So, what's happening?'

'It's been ages since we last went out, just you and me, and I thought tonight would be perfect. I like that shirt, by the way.'

Tanzy looked down at his tightly fitting black shirt. 'Cheers. Your grandad jumper isn't bad either.' They smiled, then he added, 'Any night is perfect for me. It's nice to get out of the house.' He gazed around the place, realising it had been years since he'd been in there. 'Busy place, eh?'

'It's changed since I was last in. Kids in bed?'

'Fast asleep by now, I imagine. Pip was reading them a story as I was leaving.'

Byrd picked up his pint. 'How she doing?'

'Six months sober tomorrow.' Tanzy beamed, taking a swig. 'I'm proud of her. She has days where I can see she struggles, but she's like a new woman.'

They clinked glasses and drank to Pip, then to his left, Tanzy noticed two men place their cues on the pool table and head to the bar. 'Fancy a game?'

'Why not?' They both stood. Byrd pulled a coin from his jeans, put it in the slot, and Tanzy set up the balls. 'Gotta warn you, Ori, I'm still a pro,' Byrd said, grabbing ones of the cues and chalking it.

Tanzy laughed. 'You've never been a pro at anything. You can break then, Max O'Sullivan.' They enjoyed several games before sitting back down at the same table as before. Tanzy ordered another two pints and brought them over.

'Here you go, boss.'

'Cheers.'

'How've you been, anyway, mate?' asked Tanzy, noticing bags under Byrd's eyes.

'To be honest, not quite myself.' Byrd smiled thinly. 'There've been a lot of changes, and it's taking me a while to adjust. My parents passing away, Claire moving in, and our hectic month at work. It doesn't seem to end or get any easier.'

'Nice to get those kids to their homes and stop that bastard Feland, though, eh?' Tanzy raised his pint. 'Cheers to that.' They clinked glasses again. 'How's Claire settling in?'

'She's already painted three rooms.'

Tanzy rocked his head back in laughter, then smiled, happy about his colleague finding love and connection. 'There'll be more, I can assure you. As a man, I think you need to accept that you're living in their home and go with the flow. It's easier.'

Byrd chucked. 'She's decorating a fourth room next week. She's struggling with the colours at the moment, though. She said she might go with creams — you know, to play it safe.'

Tanzy nodded, trying to figure out where he was going.

'That way, if it's a boy or a girl, it won't matter too much.'

Tanzy's eyes widened, and his mouth opened as if he was going to say something, but nothing came out. Byrd nodded continually at him as Tanzy put the pieces together, before he stood and put his hand out to Byrd, who found his feet and shook it, then they shared a hug.

'Congratulations,' he said, rubbing his back.

'Thanks, Ori. It's early days, so we're keeping it quiet.'

'Your secret is safe with me, Max.'

They sat back down, picked up their remaining pints, and downed them. Tanzy was over the moon finding out Byrd would become a dad and couldn't stop smiling.

'What?'

Tanzy said, 'We need to celebrate tonight! Come on, let's go somewhere else. Get some shots in.'

They both stood and made their way past the bar towards the door. Before they reached it, they heard a glass smash and a fight break out to their left. Byrd stopped and went to head over when Tanzy grabbed his wrist.

'Not tonight, Max. It isn't our fight.'

Byrd considered it, then moved as two bouncers charged in to sort it. He smiled, following Tanzy out the door. 'There's never a dull day in this town, is there?'

'Hey, that's my line, Max,' Tanzy said, as they stepped out into the cold, fresh air and headed for the next pub.

THE END

THE JOFFE BOOKS STORY

We began in 2014 when Jasper agreed to publish his mum's much-rejected romance novel and it became a bestseller.

Since then we've grown into the largest independent publisher in the UK. We're extremely proud to publish some of the very best writers in the world, including Joy Ellis, Faith Martin, Caro Ramsay, Helen Forrester, Simon Brett and Robert Goddard. Everyone at Joffe Books loves reading and we never forget that it all begins with the magic of an author telling a story.

We are proud to publish talented first-time authors, as well as established writers whose books we love introducing to a new generation of readers.

We have been shortlisted for Independent Publisher of the Year at the British Book Awards three times, in 2020, 2021 and 2022, and for the Diversity and Inclusivity Award at the Independent Publishing Awards in 2022.

We built this company with your help, and we love to hear from you, so please email us about absolutely anything bookish at feedback@joffebooks.com

If you want to receive free books every Friday and hear about all our new releases, join our mailing list: www.joffebooks. com/contact

And when you tell your friends about us, just remember: it's pronounced Joffe as in coffee or toffee!

ALSO BY C.J. GRAYSON

TANZY AND BYRD THRILLERS
Book 1: The Tees Valley Killings
Book 2: The Denes Park Killings